# THE
# ANT CHRIST
## OF KOKOMO COUNTY

THE

# ANT CHRIST

OF KOKOMO COUNTY

## by David Skinner

A Division of Samizdat Publishing Group

CONUNDRUM PRESS: A Division of Samizdat Publishing Group.
PO Box 1353, Golden, Colorado 80402

PREVIOUSLY PUBLISHED IN 2015 AS A HARDCOVER FROM CONUNDRUM PRESS.

HARDCOVER ISBN: 978-1-942280-26-2
PAPERBACK ISBN: 978-1-942280-34-7
EBOOK ISBN: 978-1-942280-28-6

LIBRARY OF CONGRESS CONTROL NUMBER: 2016939843

FIRST PAPERBACK EDTION.
For more information, email info@conundrum-press.com.

CONUNDRUM PRESS ONLINE: CONUNDRUM-PRESS.COM

*For the Wife*

*"I promise this is the last time you'll ever have to read it."*

# PART ONE

*"Take off that friggin' vest!"*
*"What the crap does it matter?"*
*"Because you're not who you're supposed to be!"*

# 1

I WAS IN A SHAKESPEARE PLAY ONCE.

To be fair, it was when I was in high school, and since I attended a smallish high school in a smallish town in the insignificant state of Indiana there's little reason to be impressed.

So don't bother.

The play was *The Taming of the Shrew* and I was Gremio, an elderly gentleman of Padua.

For those who don't remember Gremio, he was a minor character whose purpose was to be bested in his feeble attempt to woo another minor character, accept humiliation and rejection with deference and good humor, all while barely registering in the consciousness of the audience.

I tried out for the other parts, the good ones. There was Petruchio—the tamer of Katherine, strong, mercurial, quick-witted; Lucentio—young, romantic, intrepid; manservant Grumio—the fool, the comic relief. I even begged to audition for the part of the titular termagant on the grounds of staging a more authentic sixteenth-century production (something that did not go over well with the girls vying for Katherine, nor with the other prospective Petruchios). Instead, I was given the most unexceptional character—an old, befuddled sap. There I was: a brash, blustery, cocksure sixteen-year-old, being told I must—I *must!*—be the wallpaper.

When Ms. McGrath, the drama teacher, told me I was Gremio, she also said this: "Kid, you're perfect for him."


Reflecting now on the two-plus decades of life that have unfurled since, it would be dishonest of me to say my role in the cosmic drama has been altogether different from my one foray into theater.

That is, not until today, October 20, 2009, the day I, Franklin Bartholomew Horvath, will stop the end of the world.

# 2

HERE I AM:

Still in the insignificant state of Indiana—to be specific, the miniscule town of Berry which is itself but a trivial part of the irrelevant Kokomo County.

At this moment, I'm sitting in Old Tuna, a hatchback the color (and smell) of its namesake, staring at a building.

If you were to come face-to-face with me, you might be tempted to say I look like a beaten and desperate man. I can see why you might say this; I have checked the rearview mirror and caught a glimpse of my desperate, beaten-looking eyes. If this is what my eyes are saying, then it's easy to guess what the rest of me is up to.

Everything else is following suit, as everything else tends to do.


Please, don't get smug, and double please, save your sympathy for yourself. This is not the tedious, tiresome jeremiad of yet one more wrecked middle-aged melancholiac. I'm just pointing out the way things are and the way I am. Considering what's on my shoulders here—the survival of mankind—I think my beaten and desperate state is understandable, no?

I mean, does anybody think Abraham Lincoln caroled merrily through the night before delivering the Emancipation Proclamation, or that Martin Luther didn't get a little weak in the bowels at the thought of his excommunication before nailing the Ninety-Five Theses to the doors of Castle Church in Wittenberg?

Granted, neither of these men crossed their Rubicons in Berry, Indiana, something that takes a good deal of the *oomph* from it, I'll admit. Standing beaten and desperate in front of a towering German cathedral about to fire the first salvo in the war against the corruption of the pre-Reformation Catholic Church, or engulfed in the dark night of your soul during the bleakest hour of the American Civil War in a White House room that will one day be named after you—these things by definition carry a bit more *gravitas* than my present location.

And why's that? Why do I refuse to rank a milieu such as Berry, Indiana alongside more grand, majestic settings?

Well, for one, the building I'm staring at looks nothing like the White House or Castle Church. It looks like shit. For two, the same could be said about the rest of Berry, which makes the town motto all the more unfortunate:

Berry, Indiana: *Where Hope is Reborn.*

If it were up to me, it would be something along the lines of this:

Berry, Indiana: *The Gremio of Small Town America.*


A little story about Berry:

Every year some of the townspeople get together in one of their weed-infested, tire-and-no-longer-working-appliance-littered yards and have a shindig. At this shindig they eat barbequed pork ribs and hot dogs and potato salad and rice-crispy squares. They drink value-brand soda, skunky beer, and rotgut whiskey. They talk and laugh. Cavort and caper.

At some point the men go around front to look at some left-for-dead jalopy and hem and haw about whether they should fix it up or not. Or they go into the house to tinker with the plumbing, the electricity, the furnace. Every now and again they come out of the house with another addition to the no-longer-working-appliance scrapheap that functions as the host's backyard. Meanwhile, the younger boys run off and pretend to murder each other, turning the rusted-out machines and abandoned tires into makeshift fortresses and battlefields. The women smoke and gossip, oblivious as their sons play out their imaginary holocausts, whereas the little girls wander from the women to the men to the boys, trying to find somebody they can stare at without being told to go away. Mostly they meander, unhappy.

As soon as it feels to everyone present that the Moment has arrived, someone will look to someone else and say, "Is it time?" and that someone else will say, "I'd say it just about is." And then they'll ask other someones, who will pass it on to those who haven't heard, and before you know it, everybody's chattering.

"Is it time?"

"You better believe it!"

"Is it time?"

"Yes and yessir!"

"Is it time?"

"High time!"

Then, with the anticipation and excitement cresting, the men march to one of their pickup trucks for wood bought from a hardware store a town or two away and joyfully get to work sawing and sanding it into a post and a flat piece. A few of the younger boys get a chance to man the saw for a pull or two, and they do so with pride as their pint-sized peers look on in envious awe.

As soon as the men are finished sawing and sanding, they hammer nails into the post and the flat piece. At this point someone says something silly like, "Lookin' sexy!"

With the men's work complete, the women mark up the wood with a very friendly, very inviting bright green paint. Some of the more artistically inclined little girls are allowed to draw a small flower on the wood, while the rest are forced to content themselves by smearing their faces and bodies a very friendly, very inviting bright green. It should be said that all the girls are still unhappy, but to their credit they are trying hard not to be.

Once connected and painted, the wood, now a sign, says this:

*Berry, Indiana: Where Hope is Reborn.*

Carrying the sign on their shoulders like the pope on his throne, the townspeople then parade to the edge of Berry (a trek that doesn't take very long) gabbling, singing, and laughing the whole way. There, they remove the previous year's sign—now faded, cracked, and unreadable—and put the new one in its place.

"Now how about that!" they say to each other. "Isn't it gorgeous? Even better than last year's."

Sooner or later though, these townspeople, feeling proud feelings and thinking terrific thoughts, glance away one by one from the sign to take a gander at the rest of Berry—which, as already explained, doesn't look proud or terrific in the slightest.

No, it looks like shit.

And seeing how the feelings engendered by looking at one's own garbage town aren't the fun kind to feel, the citizens of Berry force themselves to look back at the brand new sign so they can smile proud smiles again and feel terrific feelings (although they still can't help but peek back at the town a time or two more, as, let's face it, people are suckers for the truth).

(And lies.)

(And train wrecks.)

And on and on it goes. Smiley face. Frowny face. Smiley face. Frowny face.

And they do it every year.


How do I know this?

Some years back, while in the throes of an unaccountable fit of do-goodery, I decided to help the people of Berry build their sign. This is what they told me:

"We do this every year."


### 3


NEVERTHELESS, THIS GODFORSAKEN DUMP IS WHERE THE FATE OF ALL MANKIND will be decided, and I am the godforsaken man who will decide it. Which means everything about and around me is significant, fraught with meaning, important.

Like this poor, misbegotten building. As said, it's shit—six stories fashioned out of cracked, crumbling red brick—and yet for the role it will play in today's events it might as well be Scaramanga's Island, or more nobly, Minas Tirith, as it is here that "the doom of our time will be decided."

Leaving aside the significance currently bestowed upon it by the circumstances (and my mere presence), the edifice seems important enough on its own to have a name: The Lawrence P. Fenwick Building.

I haven't a clue who Lawrence P. Fenwick was, but this *thing* is named after him. I'd like to think he was someone exceptional. A Petruchio or Lucentio. But then, given the context here, maybe he wasn't. Maybe Lawrence P. Fenwick was nothing more than the greatest Gremio in a town full of Gremios.

Maybe he was all Berry had to offer.

4

I AM A BUILDING OF SORTS TOO, A TEMPLE, AS THE SAYING GOES, AND IF YOU were to clap eyes on the rest of this all-too-human sanctuary, you might infer that neither evolution (if it's true), God (if He's there), my parents, nor even myself ever gave much of a damn about me. You might come to the conclusion that my drama teacher had me pegged. That if the future has proven nothing else, it has proven that I was of the appearance and presence perfect to play the part of a piddling old man at sixteen years old. Made for it, even.

But you would be wrong.

True, I am of middling height. Somewhere between five-foot-six and five-foot-eight, the sort no one ever bothers to get right—not even me. I have called myself five-foot-six, seven, eight, and even tried to get away with nine a few times before realizing all of them look about the same, aren't remarkable, and don't need to be. I am more than my somewhat stunted stature.

Besides, Poe was in the mid-fives. Same with Sinatra. Gandhi, Dali, Faulkner, Chaplin, Napoleon: all short like me.

Does height matter?

I will also admit to having slipped into a heft that settles somewhere in the nebulous in-between in this department.

Translation: I have a bit of a stomach.

Again, so what? Benjamin Franklin was fat. Same with Teddy

Roosevelt, Grover Cleveland, Taft, Hoover, Hitchcock, Jackie Gleason, and Elvis—not to mention a slew of English and French kings.

Does weight matter?

Like more than a few of the great men of history, I am of humble origins, hailing from one of the many diminutive, nondescript, carbon-copy towns here in Kokomo County: a morbidly shy, painfully modest hamlet called Little Hat.

Also like many of these same champions who have sprung from obscurity, I have worked my share of dead-end jobs, the latest and not-so-greatest being the Dagwood Corporation, whose headquarters is nearby.

The Dagwood Corporation manufactures kitchenware. Knives, spoons, spatulas, tongs, rolling pins, whisks, you name it.

My department is design. For years now, the big dogs upstairs have been hounding my colleagues and me to come up with neat new ideas for forks. My most recent brainstorm was a three-tined beauty that looked like a trident with a devil's tail. I thought it might be a neat new idea for Halloween. You know: Scary Fork.

It was rejected.

## 5

OTHER THAN THE DAY I WAS ASSIGNED THE PART OF GREMIO, THE ONLY recollection I have of *The Taming of the Shrew* is the night of the first performance. In the dressing room, we, the cast, had arrived to change into costumes that were supposed to have been laid out on tables for us ahead of the show, only to discover that the dastardly Doug Abernathy had decided to do that method acting thing where the player stays in character at all times. This meant that, immersed in the part of the puckish Grumio, Doug pulled a series of pranks.

Like shaving cream pies to the face, shoelaces tied together, and the most inspired: switching the nametags on the costumes before the show and then hiding them.

This last one turned the dressing room into a riot of frantic teenagers running hither and thither, furiously ripping through trousers and shirts and dresses and hats. Most of these items looked similar but were different sizes, making it all but impossible to determine what belonged to whom.

Not wanting Doug Abernathy to be perceived as the most dedicated among us, I did my best to stay in character as much as possible as well, meaning, as the schmucky Gremio, I was a real sweetheart about my missing costume—even though the pants I'd ended up with were far too big, the ersatz-feather cap some girl had chucked at me in a frenzied search for her dress did not fit my beautiful head, and a faded blue vest I was pretty sure was mine had settled tightly on the shoulders of Jackson Gosh, the lone varsity football player in the drama class.

Absorbed in my character as completely as I was, I knew that to order someone of such considerable size, strength, and experience with physical violence to return a vest would be something Gremio would never in a million years do, and so, remaining courageously true to my character's inherent cowardice, I opted to dig an emerald green vest out from underneath a pile of plastic prop-swords, a seemingly innocent act that nonetheless brought Kyle Trotter storming across the room wagging his finger at me.

"Get your mitts off that vest," he demanded. "It belongs to Petruchio." In other words, it was his.

Of course I knew this—Petruchio's vest had been the only one in emerald green—and if chaos and pandemonium hadn't been ascendant at that moment, I wouldn't have dreamed of touching it, let alone unbuttoning and putting it on. Other than my original vest, Petruchio's was the only other one that fit me. It also brought out the green in my eyes and made my shoulders seem almost as broad as Jackson Gosh's and I couldn't help but feel great about myself.

I also couldn't help but entertain thoughts about my rightful place in the world and what a perfectly fitting Petruchio vest heralded vis-à-vis my glorious future, where I, the greatest of all those in my graduating class, would scale such heights of success and stardom that—

"I said gimme it, Horvath!" Kyle Trotter said.

"Oh c'mon, Kyle," I said, making my voice sound as though, of the two of us, he was the petty one. "The audience won't know which vest is supposed to be whose."

"*We* will know," Kyle said. "It will mess everybody up."

"How could it do that? This stupid vest won't make me say your lines instead of mine."

"Oh, this woodcock!" Doug Abernathy piped up behind me, using his best Shakespearean voice to quote Grumio whilst surprising the poor girl cast in the life-changing part of "a widow" with a shaving cream pie to the kisser. "What an ass it is!"

In addition to that son-of-a-bitch Doug, a few of the other cast members had begun paying closer attention to my situation—or to Kyle Trotter at least, whose shaking finger had withdrawn into his hand and become part one of a five-part shaking fist. He then spoke in a thunderous, wrathful voice, as though possessed by Orson Welles or the Wizard of Oz. Basically, this meant BOOM.

"Character is everything, Horvath! Costumes, mannerisms, it's not *just* the lines. That vest is Petruchio's and I AM PETRUCHIO!"

Mouths gaped. Eyes goggled. There wasn't a soul in the room not enthralled by that voice. Even me. I kind of wanted to fall to my knees and weep. Kyle Trotter had that way about him. When he spoke, he commanded the attention of rooms. That's what a booming voice can do. It can also make everyone take your side. Every cast member and stagehand was now glowering, glaring, and snarling at me for stealing Kyle's vest, totally disregarding my broader shoulders. Not even the verdant green, now flush in my eyes, could hope to change their minds.

I should probably confess here that I fibbed a little when I said I was brash, blustery, and cocksure. The seeds were there, but they had not, as of that day, come to fruition. Back then it was the consensus opinion throughout my grade that I was something of a weenie. My voice didn't go BOOM like Orson Welles. It crackled like popcorn being stepped on, like cellophane being wadded up—yet another reason why Kyle Trotter was Petruchio and I was not. As it turns out, Kyle had also been told he was perfect for his part, and to my knowledge, he and I were the only ones who had been told such a portentous thing.

Not that any of this moved me to bend to his BOOM. In the end, it would take Ms. McGrath herself, also shaking her fist at me, before I would relinquish the vest. It would also take her raised voice, though hers was not known so much for its BOOM, but for approximating the sound of a screeching violin. For those who have heard such a thing, they know it can be as effective as BOOM, although it never garners as much respect. The screech tends to make the class run for cover.

"Take off that friggin' vest!" Ms. McGrath screeched violinily.

"What the crap does it matter?" I yelped back, cellophane-ishly, popcorn-esque-ily.

"Because you're not who you're supposed to be!"


# 6

I'm not alone here in Old Tuna today. My twelve-year-old son is with me.

Full name: Michael Jasper Horvath.

Nickname: Sparky.

Michael has been called Sparky, and only Sparky, since his first year of life, and not because he's cute and his mother and I are the dipshit sort of parents that come up with dipshit nicknames like "Sparky" for their kids. There's a reason, a crucial one, why we do this.

Or, I should say, why I do this, as his mother, my wife, is no longer around to call him Sparky.

Rest in peace, *cherie*.


A little about the boy:

He is not particularly tall for his age, neither is he particularly thin.

Standard stuff and a chip off the old block in these respects. Where we start to veer off the beaten track is with his face. No, he doesn't have exaggerated features like a Pinocchio nose or Dumbo ears or teeth arranged like Grecian ruins. Everything is in the right proportion and place. It's just that his features look more worn and windswept than they should for a kid his age. Put one way, he looks like he has spent the majority of his brief life lost at sea. Put another, he looks like a seventy-year-old man. Kokomo County's very own Benjamin Button. As though he were made to look like last year's discarded town sign. As though he was made to look beaten and desperate from the get-go.

I suppose it doesn't help matters that, since the age of four, Sparky has been going bald. Dr. Klein, the dermatologist I took him to, diagnosed the boy at first glance with *alopecia areata*—a condition where the immune system attacks the hair—but when he ran tests to confirm the diagnosis, the results came back negative.

"That was unexpected," Dr. Klein said. "But the good news is it looks like he doesn't have *alopecia areata*."

Dr. Klein ran more tests: scratch tests for skin disorders and one to see if Sparky had an overactive or underactive thyroid; but no answers would be found here either as Sparky's thyroid was determined to be even-steven and his skin to be not disorderly.

"Tip-top, tip-top," Dr. Klein said. "Everything's fine with him except he's obviously losing his hair."

Dr. Klein then quizzed me about Sparky's eating habits. He asked me if Sparky was prone to tearing out his hair. He asked me, cautiously, if I or Sparky's mother was prone to tearing out his hair. He then asked me what kind of shampoo Sparky used.

This went on for almost a year, until Dr. Klein (becoming increasingly exasperated and repeating such things as, "Whoa! I've never seen anything like this!" and, "Why, this beats the Stove Top stuffing out of me!"), after claiming to have consulted with every expert in the medical world, after months and months of appointment after appointment with me waiting in the waiting room for hour upon hour watching the same three *St. Elsewhere* episodes over and over, at long last, and with much fanfare, presented me with a piece of paper covered with his messy doctor scribbling.

*Petrilcoccus gaielocymotiosis*, the paper said. Some kind of bacterial thingy. Bugs.

"Bugs?" I said.

"Oh, yeah. Big time bugs," Dr. Klein confirmed, showing me blown-up pictures of Sparky's head and some specks that were supposed to be these bugs. "There they are," he said. "The bastards."

Dr. Klein said that with a special kind of antibiotic the bastard-bugs would die, though he did warn me it was possible Sparky would never grow his hair back and that it could continue to fall out indefinitely.

"But hey, look at the bright side. At least those little suckers will be gone," he said.


More about *petrilcoccus gaielocymotiosis*:

Curiously, Dr. Klein couldn't pronounce the name. When the time came to reveal just what in the world was afflicting my son, he pointed at the piece of paper he'd written the illness on and told me to say it because he couldn't. Without much background in medicine or the long-expired Latin language, I was not capable of pronouncing it either, so when Sparky and I went home and the wife asked what the doctor had said, I too pointed at the paper. I then told her what I will tell you now: it sounds made up.

The wife pshaw-ed. Why would a doctor make up a bacterial thingy? "Kind of against the Hippocratic Oath, don't you think, Frank?" she said.

I argued that Dr. Klein, because he didn't know what the hell Sparky had going on, decided to invent a treatable disease that would not only alleviate our concerns but, more importantly, would extricate himself from the whole mess. After all, one thing he was adamant about was that what was happening to my son was not life-threatening.

"Look at him," Dr. Klein said to me. "Is he having a seizure, gasping for breath, or going into cardiac arrest?"

"Not this instant, no," I said.

"Then he's fine."

"Other than the fact he's five years old and looks like Alan Arkin?"

"Other than that, yes."


# 7

SO. THE BOY. HE'S SHORT, FAT, AND BALDING. HE LOOKS OLD ENOUGH TO collect Social Security. But you will notice I have not called him unexceptional. Because he's not. Everything rests on him as much it does on me, if not more.

And you underestimate him at your peril.

As I peer through the fractured, filthy windshield of Old Tuna, steeling my gaze at the dilapidated Lawrence P. Fenwick Building a final time, Sparky is singing. He's singing the same song he's been singing since he was able to sing. It's the basis of every song I have ever heard him sing. It goes like this:

> *Poop and pee*
> *Poop and pee*
> *I like to poop and pee*


# 8

INSIDE THE LAWRENCE P. FENWICK BUILDING ARE MANY UNEXCEPTIONAL businesses. An unexceptional tailor, for instance, plies his trade unexceptionally on the fourth floor, while on the floor beneath him an unexceptional travel agent helps send her unexceptional clientele to unexceptional locations for what can only be unexceptional vacations.

On the sixth floor is the United Church of Satan.

Though let me say right off they do not refer to themselves as such anymore.

The reason for the change is Berry, Indiana is right on the edge of the Bible Belt, so it stands to reason that Satanists wouldn't be all that popular here. According to their receptionist, Danica, in the past they've received numerous death threats, had their cars covered in animal (they hope) excrement, and their front door egged. The last and most notorious act of vandalism was when somebody broke in—a farmer, they think—and let loose an angry pig that ran around and tore everything up. In addition to unleashing rampaging swine, the farmer copied out the entirety of the Book of Revelation with two tubes of Danica's lipstick (and her eyebrow pencils—all stolen from her desk) on the office walls.

Seems excessive to me, but perhaps the farmer couldn't make up his mind where the zing parts were and so kept going and going, hoping the sheer volume of scripture would get his point (whatever that might have been) across.

Not sure why he didn't choose something pithier, nor do I believe there's an easy explanation for the use of lipstick, but it could be he was looking to distinguish himself somehow.

I can sympathize.

The retaliation for this persecution wasn't what the townspeople feared. No evil eyes were drawn on doors. No babies were kidnapped and sacrificed. There were no wild, defiant sex rituals in the streets. The UCoS didn't even take legal action, bring in the American Civil Liberties Union, start a hubbub in the courts.

They simply changed their name.

A week after the farmer and his holy hog destroyed their office, the UCoS vacated the Lawrence P. Fenwick Building and disappeared without a trace. Then, just as untraceably, a month later (after the townspeople had finished celebrating their victory over the Devil with more ribs, rice-crispy squares, and rotgut), the Satanists reappeared and posted this sign above their office door:

# THE CHURCH OF
# EPISTEMOLOGICAL EMENDATION

The upshot?

"Everybody thinks we're Scientologists now," Danica said.

"Wouldn't that be as bad?" I asked.

"Not at all," she said. "Every month I get calls asking if we'll pitch the town to Hollywood as a location to shoot a movie. They think if one of those nutjobs out there can use it, they can turn this part of Asshat, Indiana into another famous getaway like Madison or Nashville.

"All they really care about is getting a slice of that bed-and-breakfast pie," she added.

These Epistemological Emendationists of Berry, Indiana are the reason my son and I are here today. We have an appointment with them—or, as I prefer to think of it, a showdown.

Before undertaking this journey into the heart of ultimate evil, I relied on the counsel and wisdom of a prominent biblical scholar, the spiritual perception and faith of my late wife, and my own prayers and study. You could say I have tried to be as thorough as possible with this end-of-the-world stuff. It's the skeptic in me. The perpetual doubter. The no-quit cynic.

I'll also admit to some anxiety here. I like clarification, confirmation. I want to feel good about my choices. I want to know they are right.

Hence, this appointment with destiny—with Satanists.

I know, Satanists taking appointments, difficult to believe. They even call them "appointments." Danica, the Satanist secretary, was very friendly—bubbly, even. With little in the way of prodding, she regaled me about the name change and all the misadventures that led up to it. She even wished me a pleasant day at the end.

(A Satanist wishing someone a pleasant day, imagine that.)

But if my instincts are correct, if what I believe is going to happen does, then the future of People, you and I and everyone you know—the whole schmear—will be decided today in a fight to the death with these shameless enemies of Christ.

## 9

Which brings me back to where I am. To the end of beaten and desperate. To my emergence, my becoming.

I would be remiss if I did not confess that a faceoff of this variety is not what I had in mind as a starry-eyed boy besotted with visions of future glory. Like many and most—if not everyone—I saw myself as destined for eminence of a more recognizable sort, a life blessed and defined by greatness.

It has taken a lot for me to admit a life of renown and recognition (not to mention the adoration of all humanity) does not appear to be in the cards. Thanks to all the misfortune that has befallen me, my lot seems to lie in the bitterest sort of greatness there is: the kind nobody knows of but me.

(And maybe, if He's paying attention, God.)

Still, if this is my calling, I will meet it with gusto. If this is my cup, I will drink it with relish and perform this single act of uncelebrated valor—striding forth from this lousy car into this shabby-ass building in the middle of this fucked-up town—with nothing less than *everything* in the balance.

What I've come to realize is that, metaphorically, we, the human race, have circled back to the lonely biblical mountaintop of Moriah, where once again the choice of one man will determine the course of all. But in this drama for the ages I will not take my usual place as another frivolous minor character—the background, the wallpaper, the worthless schmo nobody gives a damn about—but, rather, the most important part of the play.

Pardon my theatrics, ladies and gentlemen, but as of this moment, I am no longer Gremio. I am the second coming of the legendary patriarch Abraham, Father of Nations.

(With special guest star Sparky as Isaac.)

And as that day was for Abraham, so it will be for me, for all of us: a test. Of the most horrible sort.

The kind of test only I, the Great Horvath, can face.

# PART TWO

*Curious and more than a little frightening how so much of one's life can turn on whether one continues to smash one's face in couch cushions while someone else is talking.*

# 1

As anyone who has reached the depths of beaten and desperate will tell you, it's not something that happens overnight.

Except when it does. Like that Charles Bronson movie where gangsters shoot up his watermelon crop. One minute he has a bunch of watermelons and the high hopes of selling them at profit, then BLAM! Just useless watermelon pieces.

The story of Job in the Bible is similar, excluding the watermelons (whether he had some or not is unknown; scripture is silent on this point). So substitute his belongings, health, and children for the watermelons, and fire, murderous bandits, skin abscesses from head to foot, and a super-windy day for the film's machine-gun toting Mafia hit men. Similar to the Charles Bronson movie, Job's life got screwed up fast. Lightning quick, like a couple of verses.

For me, however, the road to beaten and desperate has been a far more drawn-out process. If we must think in watermelons though, then think *one at a time*. My watermelons have not been blasted apart by gunfire either, but have rotted and withered. One at a time. My hopes, my dreams. All the grand designs I had for myself have been spoiled by time, accident, fiasco, and tragedy to what I have now: a life nowhere near a Charles Bronson movie where all his watermelons get shot to hell.

Point being: How I got here. How it started. How I didn't become a god amongst men, or at the very least, a god amongst Horvaths.

(Yet.)

How I've failed.

(So far.)

How greatness has been stolen from me.

(Up to this point.)

And why today is my last chance to get it back.

(I think.)

# 2

LET'S BEGIN WITH THE OBVIOUS: MY PARENTS.

The blame for every thwarted life starts with the ones who thought it was such a good idea for you to be here in the first place—though for now we'll leave my mother out of this. Nobody likes it when somebody dumps on their mother.

Guess who's left.

I'll begin with the day I turned twelve. The scene: Little Hat, Indiana, the living room of the not-so-idyllic Horvath family duplex. I was seated on the couch, my father standing before me.

"Frankie, don't move," he said, and lo and behold, I didn't.

The reason for my obedience was not so much in the spirit of submission to the Judeo-Christian commandment to honor one's parents, but had more to do with the gripping episode of my favorite afternoon cartoon playing out its denouement on the television. At the time, I didn't think that much of the Fifth Commandment and was far more interested in things like boobs, cookies made of sweetened vegetable shortening in between layers of chocolate, and toy plastic soldiers, their many toy weapons, toy vehicles, and other toy accessories.

And, of course, cartoons.

For the record, I don't feel any different about that commandment today either, nor have I changed my opinion about boobs, Oreos, toys, or cartoons. My sainted mother, dead for more than twenty years now, is no longer relevant in my estimation, while the old man, as I will soon prove beyond reasonable doubt, doesn't deserve honor.

As far as the other commandments are concerned, I have done as most people: I have adhered to some and ignored others, depending on my mood, the situation, my desires, etc.

Take today: Due to conditions beyond my control and the dire straits we, the collective image of God, are in, Thou Shalt Not Kill is temporarily on hold.

For me, that is, not for you.

You just behave yourself.

## 3

"THAT'S GOOD. KEEP IT UP, FRANKIE. STAY RIGHT THERE," MY FATHER SAID, his eyes scanning the living room floor. What he was looking for I couldn't have cared less about, as the heroes of the cartoon I was watching—a community of friendly black bears living in a vast, enchanted forest—were locked in a ferocious battle with a bunch of grouchy brown bears that also lived in the vast, enchanted forest, and that was all that mattered to me at the moment: cartoon bear fighting.

The cartoon bears were fighting over stores of magic honey hidden in the trees. This honey was the highest form of sustenance in the vast, enchanted forest, and the bears found they were stronger and smarter when eating the magic honey than they were when they ate the alternatives: cottony moths, stringy plants, and blah, non-magical honey.

Now, the friendly black bears—residents of the vast, enchanted forest for centuries—had determined after careful study that there was more than enough magic honey to go around for everybody, whereas the grouchy brown bears—recently emigrated from the cold, unforgiving climate of the Mealy Mountains—had determined there was only enough honey for them. In order to make sure the honey would be forever theirs and theirs alone, the grouchy brown bears decided the friendly black bears must be destroyed, something the friendly black bears couldn't go along with, as they had been in the forest first, were nice enough to share the honey, and understandably didn't want to die.

So war broke out.

With the old man still deep in his search for that all-important whateveritwas, I was watching intently as the friendly black bears were getting their asses kicked by the grouchy brown bears, a not unusual occurrence for the first half of an episode. What was unusual this time was that the cartoon was heading into the home stretch with no sign that the friendly black bears were about to turn the tide, and I (now using the old man as a foot rest as he peered underneath the couch on his hands and knees) was starting to get a little nervous.

Ordinarily, Proust—the intrepid leader of the friendly black bears—would have brought his clan roaring back from the brink of annihilation by now, if not tipped the scales in the other direction. Proust sometimes did this with his unmatched skill in paw-to-paw combat. Sometimes he did this with wicked-looking bear knives and bear swords and such. Sometimes he used bear catapults and bear weaponry whatnot, but he always had a trick up his fur. He really inspired me. So much so that my books and backpack were covered with Proust stickers. He was a comforting, reassuring symbol whenever school became a lonesome, miserable place.

Proust's past heroics notwithstanding, just before the penultimate commercial break, the unthinkable happened. The grouchy brown bears launched a fiery rock missile that severed an enormous tree branch that hit Proust on the head, rendering him unconscious. Buoyed by this stunning development, the grouchy brown bears then stormed the magical honey stores and took off with the whole lot, leaving the friendly black bears in disarray, their leader grievously injured, and the friendly black bear community in flames.

An extended downturn like this had never happened to my beloved friendly black bears before. Proust had always come through to save the day, and I, a young, white American boy alive at the height of his country's power and influence, was used to the day being saved. It was inconceivable to imagine any other outcome.

This is not to say I had not yet witnessed or endured any of life's disappointments—I had—but these letdowns had so far been of the standard childish variety, and always seemed to have something to do with cake. As in: no second piece of cake, no cake for breakfast, no cake between meals, no cake late at night, no cake before swimming. But nothing that turned one's world upside down, made one reevaluate man's place in the universe, or provided a glimpse of Death's carnivorous leer.

Nevertheless, seeing Proust in a heap on the forest floor and the friendly black bear village in ruins made something resonate deep within my soul: a voice telling me that what I was seeing, cartoon foolishness aside, was not merely something undeniable and inexorable, but also a foretaste of what I would have to strive against for the rest of my days.

Simply put, what I heard was this: *See? Life is no picnic.*

"Gotcha!" the old man yelled, jumping to his feet. He was now staring at his hand in a way my adolescent sensibilities associated with Gargamel having at last caught the ever-slippery Papa Smurf, and indeed, my father had come into possession of an object that would turn out to have a significant impact on the events to come: a television remote.

Sadly, I could not bring myself to match his enthusiasm for this remarkable accomplishment, as I was still stunned at seeing Proust motionless beneath a large piece of tree and the grouchy brown bears hoofing it out of the friendly black bear village as fast as their grouchy brown bear legs could take them. The grouchy brown bears hadn't sniffed this much magic honey in the entire run of the show, and when one considers the effect the magic honey had on bears in general, the questions now burning in my heart were: How much more powerful would the grouchy brown bears become with all the magic honey? And what would become of the friendly black bears without it?

Nothing in this world could hope to match the importance of what was to happen next. It wasn't only the friendly black bears whose well-being was in the balance—*my* well-being was somehow tied up in all this, too.

At least it was until the old man turned the television off.


"Time for that pow-wow I've been promising you," he said with a look on his face that suggested I should be jumping up and down and/or spinning around the room at the thought that he, my father, was about to sit down and talk to me, his only son, about something important. I can only imagine what a disappointment it must have been when I offered my customary response to his requests for audience by folding my arms and scowling at him.

Why would I choose to be such a bratty little shit? Besides the obvious (who are these morons who jump and spin at the thought of their fathers talking to them?) it was my birthday. The rule on my birthday was I got to do anything I wanted, and for this one—a dozen candles in—I wanted to watch cartoons.

What I did not want was to have a talk with my father, and certainly not when said talk interfered with said cartoons. By turning off the television, my father had not just stolen from me what I wanted, but something to which I felt entitled, making this one of my first experiences with raw, naked injustice.

And I must say, it was shocking; so much so that I couldn't manage an intelligible response of outrage or even similar nonverbal expressions of fury—like a baring of teeth or a clenching of fists. This shock, so new and foreign, shot around the inside of my head uncontrolled, disoriented, unable to find the appropriate sector that would lead to a suitable manifestation of anger. Instead, lost and confused, it charged into whatever area of the brain makes me laugh and I, to my horror, heard myself do just that.

"Ha ha ha!"

The old man's chapped lips stretched into a cracked smile. He took my laugh to be a sign that I was in fact bursting at the seams to hear what he had to say, which was an immense relief to him. As I would discover with the passage of time and the assumption of maturity, my father had confidence issues. Years later, he would tell me that there were few times in his life when he hadn't been overwhelmed with paralyzing insecurity. During that confession he would reference my twelfth birthday in particular, and reveal that he had spent an extra five minutes pretending to search for the television remote when he had known where it was the whole time. Just so he could screw up the courage to talk to a twelve-year-old boy.

Which made it all the more surprising how often these discourses between us occurred. In the mornings on the way to school, in the afternoons on the way home, in the evenings at the dinner table, before bedtimes, even in the middle of the night—"Hey, Frankie, you still awake? 'Cuz I was thinking about something you ought to know..." My father was one of those intolerable people who believed everything they said should be considered the very words of God. This trait, coupled with paradoxical self-doubt, pushed him to pester me twice as much than if he'd managed a reasonable amount of faith in himself, which kept his emotions in a constant state of agitation as he vacillated between a debilitating fear and an overcompensating bravado.

As to the content of these pow-wows, allow me to sum them up by relating that my father has worked in a hardware store for the last twenty-eight years, recently peaking as assistant supervisor of the lawn and garden department. And let's not try to spruce this up by romanticizing him as the quintessential blue-collar worker: salt of the earth, heartbeat of America. He should have moved beyond L & G. Even now, at sixty-five years of age, he works under college students doing the gig for beer money.

And if you're thinking of being generous by saying that perhaps the old man is a simple but dependable fellow capable of flashes of unpretentious yet penetrating insight, pardon me as I disabuse you of that notion too. Most of the "wisdom" he's offered through the years falls under the category of Captain Obvious. Think: *Don't eat yellow snow,* or, *Get your finger out of there,* not, *Our greatness lies not so much in being able to remake the world, as in being able to remake ourselves.*


Pale and trembling, my father pulled up a beanbag and plopped down, his slightly misshapen head blocking a great deal of the now dark television set. He then lifted his hands to his head and rubbed his temples vigorously. This was a ritual known as "putting his thoughts together," and was typically accompanied by a hyperventilation similar in style to the tortured breathing of a condemned criminal in front of a firing squad.

"*Hee! Hee! Hee!*"

I, as was typical during this behavior, ignored him and craned my head to get a glimpse of the television screen in the hopes that it would, because it was my birthday, magically kick back on. When it didn't, I came to the shattering realization that magic had all but vanished from the modern world, an embittering thought that made me glare at the old man, mock his ritual via derisive pantomime, and then pretend to fall asleep. None of which stopped him.

After finishing his temple massage and hysterical gasping, the old man dove in, so I, with no other choice left to me, buried my face in the couch and made exaggerated snoring noises. With my head engulfed by the cushions and air rumbling in and out of my sinuses, what I heard from my father sounded a lot like this:

"*Murgh florfen gothig meh hestempth gofsburg wiffley.*"

## 4

A THOUGHT THAT HAS OCCURRED TO ME FROM TIME TO TIME—A HAUNTING thought, to be sure—is the possibility that everything might have turned out differently if I had managed to fake snoring noises throughout the entirety of that talk. Curious and more than a little frightening how so much of one's life can turn on whether one continues to smash one's face in couch cushions while someone else is talking.

But I couldn't keep it up; the couch was filthy. Try as I might, breathing in the noisome cushion odor of old fried chicken, stale corn chips, and a mysterious rancid smell became impossible to maintain after a minute or two, and once my gag reflex kicked in—upon my nose identifying the rancid smell as stale, sweaty crotch—I dropped the charade, flipped over, opened my eyes, and immediately found myself drowning in my father's logorrhea.

"—*gurgily-furgily—weeegtion,*" the old man was saying. Then, clear as a bell: "Frankie, name some great men for me, throughout history."

Ho boy. Despite having only just arrived at twelve, I was of the opinion that I was already pretty shrewd for that age, so here's what I, a clever, crafty lad said, and with nary a trace of irony in my voice: "I think *you're* great, Dad."

Generally speaking, such shameless flattery could be counted on to elicit a belly-laugh, perhaps a tousling of the hair, and might even result in the old man losing his train of thought, bringing whatever tedious litany he had just begun to an abrupt, happy conclusion.

Not so this time. The old man didn't smile. He did not laugh from his belly. He did not tousle my hair. Instead, he screwed up his face as one who has correctly identified a rancid smell as stale, sweaty crotch, and I knew beyond any doubt I had said something terribly wrong—and to the tune of another choked round of his wheezing.

"*Hee! Hee! Hee!*"

Then, super-choky, super-wheezy: "Don't you *ever* say anything like that to me again, Frankie—*hee*! Do you—*hee!*—understand?"

My father struggled up from the beanbag and straightened.

"I am nothing special. I am nothing great, and I never will be—*hee!*" he continued, puffing out his chest. "I will never be anything more than Robert Richard Horvath. Important, yes, but only as a cog in the Great Horvath Machine—*hee*! As a part of the Royal Horvath Bloodline. As a—*hee!*—conduit for our blood's journey, not the destination. It is what the Lord—*hee!*—has ordained."

At this, the old man un-puffed his chest, let his arms flop to his side, and fell back on the beanbag. He had been at his proudest just then, telling me how worthless he was.


Concerning what he said:

Never in my life had I heard the old man use his full name in front of me. "Cog in the Great Horvath Machine" was new, as was "Royal Horvath Bloodline." "Lord-ordained," I'm sorry to say, was fairly common stuff around the somewhat Pentecostal household my parents kept—though, as the "somewhat" should indicate, we were what our pastor Reverend Phipps referred to as lukewarm Christians.

You know, the kind that makes Jesus puke.

Which meant that we weren't as consistently gung-ho about the whole God thing as Phipps thought we should be—and he was right. Sometimes we Horvaths were into attending church and Bible studies and spending time with other church people and praying with them and singing songs and all manner of churchy activities, while at other times we were not so much into any of it. A good indicator of where the family stood was the old man's language. If liberal amounts of profanity were heard during the course of conversation, then we weren't all that into church, which in turn meant that praying, singing, and all manner of churchy activities weren't likely to be on the docket anytime soon (thank God). If rather embarrassing substitutions for swear words were popping up more—like "futzdab" and "dignibbity"—then chances were there would be mandatory grace before supper, god-awful Christian pop music looping endlessly on the stereo, and constant interrogations about what this or that Jew did in this or that book of the Bible.

You might presume by some of the salty language I employ that this hasn't much changed, but again, you would be wrong. Yes, sometimes I have doubted the Christian faith and have believed it to be lies, opting for a naturalistic agnosticism with a heavy dose of postmodern materialistic nihilism. Other times I have believed Christianity fully and with joy in my heart. But no matter which way I'm going, no matter my feelings and faith, my language remains rough. I like to swear. It's just the way I am. Naughty words are my allowance.

Other great men in history had theirs: King Solomon got away with having seven hundred concubines; Charlemagne with murdering his nephews; Napoleon with wearing that silly hat. Don't begrudge me mine.


Back to the matter at hand: the question I had answered so poorly by telling my father I thought he was great.

"Try again," my father said, and lo and behold, I did.

I proceeded to spit out any and every name I could think of that might win his approval—Ronald Reagan, Barry Goldwater, Billy Graham, Dwight D. Eisenhower, Generals MacArthur and Patton, Harry Truman, Henry Ford, John Wayne, Theodore Roosevelt. I slipped up once when I said John F. Kennedy, and again when I mentioned the all-star basketball player, Michael Jordan. In the old man's opinion, JFK had been nothing more than a womanizing, disease-ridden communist, while Michael Jordan, a fine athlete to be sure, was not to be considered as anything too extraordinary yet, as at the time of this conversation His Airness had failed to win any NBA championships. The old man furnished Larry Bird and Magic Johnson as more appropriate current selections (Jerry

West and Bill Russell were his all-time faves) told me never to mention a Kennedy in his house again, and then demanded more. By this point I had pretty much exhausted my range of athletes and historical figures, but I still knew what to do. When a pow-wow reaches a crisis point, always go biblical.

Apostles Peter, Paul, John, and James. John the Baptist. Prophets Jeremiah, Elijah, and Elisha. Not so much Jonah and certainly not Balaam (confession: I did have an affinity for this man of God—as did many of the less pious kids in church—entirely because he was famous for having chatted with his ass, heh). Kings David, Jehoshaphat, and Hezekiah. Father Abraham, Jacob, Joseph, and Noah.

I was rolling.

"Yes!" the old man said once I had paused to take a breath. "All great men. Giants among their people." He then walked over to the living room window, clasped his hands behind his back, and gazed presidentially over our tiny, dead lawn. "Now name some great Horvaths for me."

"Er...what?" I said.

My father turned from the window. "You heard me, boy. Name some great men from our family."

"Ha ha ha..." I laughed. My mind, flailing again, had once more elected for mirth.

The old man had never really talked about the Horvath family tree other than the occasional reference to dead Pappy Horvath and his farm (a farm that had been Steinbeckian in its ability to reap poverty and despair as opposed to salable crops). The only other Horvaths I knew of were Uncle Victor, who wrote the Traditional Life column for a newspaper in Nebraska, and Aunt Rosie, who had settled down in Sioux Falls, Idaho, married a bottled water salesman (a.k.a. Uncle Chuck), and had three kids. That was it. All I had.

"And?" The old man loomed over me. Despite my feeling that I was already his intellectual superior, I knew I wouldn't be able to come up with an answer that would satisfy him, disentangle me, and sweep us both off to more preferable worlds. Me: back to cartoon bears beating each other up over magic honey. Him: back to whatever it was he did when he wasn't tormenting twelve-year-old boys on their birthdays. So I gave up.

"I can't think of anyone, Dad."

"That's exactly right!" the old man shouted. "There haven't been any great Horvaths! Not anywhere in our history!"

"There's no need for the noise!" railed my mother's voice from down the hall. She was in bed with a headache. Headaches would one day kill her, but not this one. This one was humbly laying the foundation for its more successful progeny.

Oblivious to her suffering, the old man got to his feet again, rubbing his hands together and breathing desperately. This time, though, his wheezy-hees were happy, exultant.

"*Hee! Hee! Hee!* And you know what that means—*hee!*—son?"

Beats me.

"It means we're due," he said.

Laughing from his belly, the old man kicked the beanbag and tousled my hair. "Frankie, I was on my knees before the sweet Lord the other day, and He told me that He will soon raise up a Horvath in the midst of this wicked world who will go on to do great and mighty things!"

Ho boy. Though still in the waning days of my prepubesence, I was already something of a skeptic, especially when it came to the words "great" and "mighty" being used in regards to what an individual accomplished in the religious arena, the most indelible recollection being when the Reverend Mrs. Phipps had used these same words to describe the gruesome mural Mr. Huckaby of FaithWorks Services had inflicted on the church nursery the previous winter. A mural that had included a dwarf Christ with a beer belly, smeary angels with swords that looked grotesquely phallic, and crowds of people that looked like a sinister mist with eyes, all painted in a background the color of hospital scrubs.

Hearing the old man use these same terms made me wonder if this wasn't all a ruse to get me to do some volunteer work for Kokomo County Pentecostal that summer. I thought of the old man's non-gas-powered mower, the Character Developer, and its dull, rusty blades. I thought of Reverend Phipps's lawn, teeming with weeds and insects. Deeply troubled in spirit, I decided to get some clarification.

"What kinds of things?"

"I don't know!" my father said. "The Lord didn't go into details, but that's not important, son. What is important is that *our* time is coming! Our time to do something powerful! World-changing!"

What followed was predictable. Whenever the old man got the religious bug, he would do as most Pentecostals do when they get buggy, stuff like lifting his arms up high and praising Jesus at the top of his lungs, singing loudly and off-key, speaking in tongues, or hopping around the room like a bunny. And taking into account this wasn't just any old pow-wow, but one to echo through the ages, my father decided to treat me to an unholy combination of all five: He lifted his arms; he praised Jesus; he sang loudly and off-key; he hopped like a bunny; he didn't just speak in tongues, he shrieked.

"*KEEVO-REEVO-TOOMIN-LOOMIN!*"

Jarring. Not two days before, he had been cursing the Cinton brothers, the two twenty-somethings we shared a wall with who had supposedly allowed the fence separating our Lilliputian backyards to sag. My father had, at the time, referred to them as "buttfuckers."

As in: "Looks like those buttfuckers next door let the fence sag."

Now I can't say for sure, but it's doubtful the Cinton boys were buttfuckers. They seemed like the nice, normal, non-buttfucking type.

I just think the old man liked calling somebody a buttfucker.

# 5

MY FATHER'S PENTECOSTAL ARDOR—STENTORIAN, CONVULSIVE, UNFATHOM-able—jarred my mother as well and brought down another wave of reprimands along with a few violent *thwacks* on the wall for him to keep it down, prompting him to fire back with that passage of scripture where King David's first wife had rebuked him for singing to God, and God, none too pleased with her comments, had made sure the mouthy little minx had zero children to the end of her days.

"Ha, like I'd let you get close enough to try again anyway," came my mother's voice from the back bedroom. I'd like to say right now, I've always taken after her.

Remarkably, my father seemed unaffected by my mother's barbs for once and dismissed them with a wave of a hand and a chuckle as he took a seat on the couch next to me. "Frankie," he said, grinning. "I've got something to show you."

Brandishing the remote with an overwrought theatricality worthy of an out-of-work magician, he turned the television back on, and with breaking heart I saw the end credits to the bear cartoon scroll across the screen with no sign of TO BE CONTINUED to give me hope.

The bear battle was over. And if I had to go by how things stood before my father had mercilessly wrecked my birthday happiness, then there was no other conclusion to be reached but that the grouchy brown bears were the victors this time. For things to have ended differently, Proust would have had to rouse himself from beneath that tree branch, hunt down the grouchy brown bears, and get all the magic honey back in time for the credits, something that seemed unattainable in the allotted time and this made me heartsick. I hated the grouchy brown bears. They were jerks. They should never win.

Meanwhile, my father was fumbling with the remote again, anxiety once more overtaking him as he struggled to switch the TV to video mode. What he was about to show me was critical to his point, and he was terrified I would think this whole production ridiculous and that he was ridiculous for showing me. Given this added pressure, he was having trouble with the buttons. He pushed one after the other to no effect, and as sweat began to bead on his forehead and his lip quivered, my heart filled with malevolent glee.

Normally, a situation like this would have lasted quite a while—to the point where my malevolent glee would lose its luster and fade into an irritated boredom—but a quick, desperate grunt of prayer from the old man brought God—or dumb luck—to the rescue and he somehow mashed the right button, the VCR whirred to life, and the television screen abruptly filled with an enormous Pink Panther balloon floating high above New York City.

"Now watch this, Frankie. Just watch," he said, and lo and behold I did.

The Pink Panther balloon floated away, followed by a Big Bird balloon. A Snoopy balloon came next, then a Snuggle Bear, before a bloated, dyspeptic Ronald McDonald finished off the series. As each balloon passed, the old man fidgeted in his seat, patted my back, and wheezy-hee'd.

I closed my eyes. Only my dad would record the Thanksgiving Day Parade. Only my dad would make me watch it on my birthday, which does not fall anywhere near Thanksgiving. Calling in every favor I felt God owed me, I silently begged Him to make the capricious VCR eat the tape as it once had my treasured copy of *Raiders of the Lost Ark*. If nothing else, I wanted it to make those squiggly lines.

"I SAID PAY ATTENTION, FRANKIE!"

I stopped praying and opened my eyes to fresh disappointment. Neither God nor the VCR had done my bidding. On the television now were about twenty-five Asian men and women, standing on top of one another in the form of an isosceles triangle.

"Lookie there!" the old man exclaimed. Then, whispering for some reason, *"You know what that is?"*

"A human pyramid," I answered. This was now, without question, the worst birthday ever.

Clearly thinking otherwise, the old man turned off the TV again and took my hands in his. He then proceeded to share, wildly and stutteringly, the following information:

Family trees are like human pyramids. Every bloodline, with each added member, helps build a progression that eventually leads to one man, who goes on to become something special and great. For instance, there have been many Washingtons, but only one George Washington. There have been many Newtons, but only one Sir Isaac Newton. And as the human pyramid ends with one person climbing on the backs of others to reach the pinnacle, where they stand alone, so does this one great man flow through the blood of those who came before him to emerge as the best of his ancestry.

"What about the girls?" my mother interrupted from down the hall again.

My father snorted and kept going.

This is not to say, he said, that those leading up to this great man are without value. Without their blood being passed on, there can be no great man, just as there can't be an apex (my word not his) to the human pyramid if one of those Chinamen (his word not mine) in the middle decides to jump off.

This is why the Bible dumped all that ink on genealogies. Everyone, not solely the great man himself, shares in the glory, and soon, my father said, the glory due our family will shine forth like a blaze in the darkness once the Great Horvath comes into being.

The old man's voice was now crackling like popcorn being stepped on. He was squeezing my hands harder than I would have liked, and I found myself a little unnerved by what I was hearing, even more so by the tears in his eyes. Nobody wants to see their father cry. It makes you feel unsafe.

"I have sacrificed everything, all the plans I had, for you, son," my father said. "To keep our human pyramid going. I never told you this before, but I could have been a football player. I was wiry, I was mean, and I had the will and determination necessary to do harsh violence to any and all who would oppose—"

"Violence? All you did was kick the ball, Robert…"

"And why should that make any difference, huh?" my father yelled back in the direction of my mother's all-wise, all-knowing voice. "In case you didn't know, Little Miss Butkus, a field goal kicker is every bit a football player, and you need as vicious a mindset for that position as you do for any of the others!"

The old man paused here, bracing for another scathing rejoinder or perhaps Ye Olde Hurtling Shoe. When nothing came, he lowered his volume.

"Anyway, I had the talent to be pretty good, Frankie. I could kick the ball through the uprights most of the time, even make a tackle or two if everything went to heckity-heck in front of me, but the Lord pulled me aside one day and commanded me to stop with all the kicking."

"Oh, so that's what it was," my mother said. "And here I've been going around thinking you stunk and got cut from the team."

Ho boy. That did it. My father breathed in sharply but did not exhale, offered me a small but painful smile, stood, and stomped down the hall. Then, from the depths of my parents' bedroom:

"*HEE!*—that was the Holy Spirit speaking through the circumstance, working a miracle. You—*HEE!*—know that, Margaret! That's the only rational explanation for how bad I kicked—*HEE!*—during tryouts!"

"I wouldn't say that's the only *rational* explanation, Robert..."

"OH YEAH? WHAT WOULD BE, WOMAN?"

"DON'T YOU CALL ME WOMAN!"

"WOMAN WOMAN WOMAN! BIG FAT—*HEE!* WOMAN!"

Confident this was the beginning of a protracted row, I reached for the remote. The bear fight might be over, but there were other cartoons. The teen weasel rock band show maybe. That one wasn't so bad.

Alas, Mick Badger didn't get through the first verse of "Beast of Burden" before the old man reemerged, snatched the remote away from me, turned off the TV, grabbed my hands again, and resumed weeping (and wheezing).

"*Hee!*—son, despite what your unbelieving mother might think, Je—*hee!*—sus told me to stop playing football and keep my body safe for the family I would have someday. Kicking field goals was my great love and I—*hee!* gave it up for you. I didn't even realize why I was doing it other than the heavy hand of God telling me it must be so. But today He has finally told me why and He wanted me—*hee!* to share it with you, because *you,* son, are very important."

6

OKAY, I'LL ADMIT. THE OLD MAN HAD ME WITH THAT ONE. I LIKED THE IDEA of being very important. To be honest, I had been convinced of it for some time already. This is why I had such admiration for Proust the Bear. He was better than the others of his species, and I thought I was better than the others of mine.

That I had yet to demonstrate a hint of any Proust the Bear qualities was beside the point. Deep down I was something special, and now, for the first time, I realized I wasn't the only one who believed this. My father did too.

He believed it so much he was in *tears*.

I'm not ashamed to say my own eyes welled up at the thought of someone else getting so emotional over how amazing I was, but it's okay for kids to cry. It's also okay for kids to hug their fathers.

As we held each other, the old man laughing and sniffling and I laughing and sniffling along with him, neither of us said a word. The father made complete by the son and the son by the father, a beautiful thing.

I only wish I could have left it at that. At the no words said, at the beautiful thing. Let it be a silent, sacred moment we would always remember and draw strength from. Perhaps, like my face smashed in the couch cushions, my life would have gone in a different direction had I let that moment be, but a thought kept nagging me that I should get just a smidgen more reassurance, in the off chance this really was about mowing lawns all summer.

"So you really think that?" I said, pulling back from my father's embrace to gaze hopefully into his dribbling eyes, my voice raspy, my nose leaky.

"Think what?" he said.

"That I'm the Great Horvath?"

The old man let go, his face scrunching up again. He seemed frustrated, severely disappointed, and betrayed all at the same time.

"Haven't you been listening to a word I've been saying?" he said.

For once, I thought I had.

With a sigh heavy enough to indicate not only the loss of the will to stand but to live, the old man dropped back down on the beanbag, wearily looked at the ceiling, and ran his fingers through his thinning hair. "Son, come on, it should be obvious," he said.

"That I'm Him?"

"Oh lordy, Frankie, please don't do this," my father said, casting sad eyes on me, his voice full of pity. "Of course you're not."

# PART THREE

*"If that ass-fart baseball team is the reason this all goes to shit, I swear to Christ I will fucking kill you."*

# 1

WE'RE OUT OF THE CAR, SPARKY AND ME. A FEW MINUTES AGO HE WOKE FROM a short nap, and as he cleared out the cobwebs with a long stretch and a series of yawns, we listened to the radio.

It seems he doesn't suspect a thing. Why we're here. What's at stake. Or he's doing a fantastic job of pretending. You never know with kids, especially this kid.

But he can suspect things all he likes so long as he doesn't try to do anything about them, and even if he does—ruling out the use of some kind of heretofore unknown supernatural strength—I'll tie him up and throw him in the trunk.

It could be the boy is aware of this contingency, as he has started singing again, perhaps in an attempt to weaken my resolve.

> *Poop and pee*
> *Poop and pee*
> *I like to poop and pee*

"Ohmygod, did you hear that?" a pimply teenage girl asks another as they pass by my singing son on the sidewalk, laughing. "What a little creep!"

"I know!" her friend says, jeering at us over her shoulder. "I mean, seriously. How *old* is he?"

Having said those lovely things, the girls are gone, across the street and into an ice cream shop, their comments a little blindside swipe of undeserved cruelty that's knocked Sparky off course. He's hung his head and stopped singing.

I'd kinda like to go after those girls. Not because I think they're at all wrong in their observations, but so I can inform them that in addition to it being none of their damn business what my son sings, they should understand that what he sings is for their own good (and everybody else's), and might very well be one of the biggest reasons why they get to go on scarfing down waffle cones and sprouting zits for the foreseeable future.

And that isn't just something to say, either. I'm not lying. The song is absolutely necessary.

## 2

WHEN SPARKY WAS YOUNGER, HE WAS ACUTELY ANAL RETENTIVE. THIS GOES back as far as I can remember, all the way to his first Christmas.

As he grew up, the wife and I discovered that a trip to the bathroom produced in him feelings akin to a dentophobe on their way to a root canal. Why this was the case was nothing the wife and I could figure out. It was nothing we did on purpose, I assure you, but for some reason Sparky found toilets and toilet paper and all that flushing to be too horrible, and so just held everything in until he couldn't. As you might imagine, this resulted in many disgusting accidents. I was always buying him new underwear, pants. On the regular I'd find poop smears on the couch, pellet-sized poop balls going up the stairs like a trail of bread-crumbs, little gifts around every corner.

In the end, and not without much debate on the issue, the wife and I decided to do something about it, and not just for the sake of our carpets or my beleaguered gag reflex. This something we decided to do was a self-help program that Social Services provided at taxpayer cost: Dr. Decorum's Behavior Module #4.

Dr. Decorum has a whole series of these things, and they range from such indispensable topics as how to not beat the shit out of animals or people of different races, sexual orientations, and religions; how to refrain from trashing the planet; how to eat and drink without being a slob; and last but not least, how to go to the bathroom.

The secret of Dr. Decorum's modules is the songs. They are short, cheery, and chant-like. They tend to get in your head and stay there.

In regards to Module #4, there are two parts. The first is for those children who are severely anal retentive and hate to go the bathroom to the point of risking their mental and physical health. Some child psychologists believe prepubescents who are too anal retentive can express fastidious, exacting, malicious, and repressed tendencies to the point of becoming a sociopath or a schizophrenic down the road. Not to mention refusing to go to the bathroom is not good for you. That stuff is supposed to get out.

The song on the first part of the module is the one Sparky took a liking to and still sings to this day:

DR. DECORUM: Alllllllllllright kids! You know what time it is?
KIDS: What time is it, Dr. D?
DR. DECORUM: What time is it? Why, it's time for the Poop and Pee Song!
KIDS: Hooray!
DR. DECORUM: And a one and a two and a three...
EVERYBODY:

Poop and pee
Poop and pee
I like to poop and pee

The second part of the module is for those who are extremely anal expulsive: kids who have a penchant for going to the bathroom anywhere and everywhere and way too often. These children oftentimes have a fixation with fecal matter, and just as often are extra disorganized and messy. The same child psychologists from before believe that if a boy or girl becomes too anal expulsive, they are far more likely to cultivate appetites for reckless behaviors and develop attention disorders, in addition to maintaining poor hygiene throughout their adult lives.

(Also, they could still go schizo.)

To clarify, the idea is to not just get the stuff out, but at the proper time and in the proper receptacle. It's all about balance.

The second song is almost identical to the first, with one small, yet vital, change:

DR. DECORUM: *Alllllllllllright kids! You know what time it is?*
KIDS: *What time is it Dr. D?*
DR. DECORUM: *What time is it? Why, it's time for the Poop and Pee Song!*
KIDS: *Hooray!*
DR. DECORUM: *And a one and a two and a three...*
EVERYBODY:

*Poop and pee*
*Poop and pee*
*I don't like to poop and pee*

On the back of the manual that comes with the course, the following, underscored and in big block letters, is written:

## BE SURE TO KNOW WHICH DISORDER YOUR CHILD HAS, AND NEVER, EVER PLAY THE WRONG SONG.

Unfortunately, as most people tend to do when they acquire a sense of purpose, the wife and I pushed things a tad far. Hence, Sparky still sings the anal retentive song to this day, even though he's long since kicked that problem, now making his home at the other extreme. He's untidy, doesn't focus all that well, and loves sitting on the "pot," making "doo-doo stew" (as he calls it).

Occasionally, he still shits his pants.

The difference between how he shits his pants now compared to how he shit them before is that before, he would take off his pants, fling them away in loathing, and bawl his head off. These days, he likes to sit in the shit and cackle.

That's right, my son is twelve years old, looks like Winston Churchill, and likes to sit in his own shitted pants. For reasons that will be revealed, I am okay with that. Not thrilled, not ecstatic, but okay. Over time I have learned to accept Sparky's refusal to adopt traditional toileting methods, falling back on the motto the wife and I have clung to whenever there is a question about our parenting ethics:

Better Safe than Sorry.

Hitler was anal retentive. So was Stalin, Mobutu, Pol Pot, Ho Chi Minh, Ahmadinejad. The list goes on and on.

Which isn't to say that the list of evil men on the anal expulsive side isn't long as well. It is, with big names like Genghis Khan, Benito Mussolini, Jean-Bedel Bokassa, Idi Amin, Muammar Qaddafi, and Hugo Chavez, but for whatever reason, those names aren't as scary sounding as the others. Like many of the big decisions in life, it comes down to this:

Pick Your Poison.


# 3

NOW THAT THOSE NASTY, PUSTULE-RAVAGED GIRLS HAVE RECEDED FROM mind and view, the boy and I can finally begin to make our way to the Lawrence P. Fenwick Building and to all the horrors that await us within.

Yes, it's time to stop stalling. High time. I don't think even Satanists from Kokomo County take too well to those who show up late for appointments.

The following is one of the Eight Emendationist Laws of Existence (pulled from their website), No. 4:

If a traveler on your property aggravates you, rip him limb from limb!

Here's another, No. 8:

When traveling on common ground, keep to yourself. If someone inflicts himself upon you, tell him to mind his business. If he refuses, bash his brains in!

Natch.

What we are wearing:

For me, it's white Reebok tennis shoes, my most comfortable pair of Levis, and a roomy blank-blue T-shirt made by the fine folks at Fruit of the Loom. The T-shirt hides my bit of stomach, making me feel more slender than usual and thus more confident.

Sometimes I worry about my weight, sometimes I don't. Sometimes when I see my bit of stomach I want to stick my head in the oven. Sometimes when I see my bit of stomach I think about a chicken in the oven, because I'm hungry. Why this is the case I couldn't begin to tell you.

Another reason for the roomy, blank-blue t-shirt: to hide the 9mm pistol stuffed down the front of my jeans.

Talk about a confidence boost.


Sparky, meanwhile, is clad in brown loafers, khaki pants, and a smart-looking Polo shirt. He looks ready to play golf.

On the Senior Tour.

To hide his balding pate, which has been known to freak people out, I make him wear hats. The hat he is wearing today—the only thing in the world I know for sure he loves—is blue and has a big red "C" in the middle. Like most over-cherished possessions, it is worn out and faded—and in Sparky's case even stained—but beware, this is no ordinary hat. Its shabby appearance notwithstanding, it is the hat that nearly wrecked us all not too long ago, a hat that nearly shattered the world.

The "C" on the hat stands for "Chicago."

It also stands for "Cubs."


## 4

A LITTLE MORE THAN SIX YEARS AGO, SPARKY TOOK AN INTEREST IN BASEBALL. By this I mean he found a baseball in our backyard—presumably left there after an errant throw or hit by other boys in our neighborhood—and being curious, brought it into the house.

Just so there's no mistaking things here, the wife and I would never have given him something like a baseball to play with. You never can tell where things like baseballs might lead, especially in this day and age when the really good players have more money than entire nations. Also, people have a troubling inclination to worship the really good ones, so no baseball for the boy.

Better Safe Than Sorry.

Anyhow. Sparky rolled the ball around on the living room floor a minute or two before looking up at me, mystified.

"Wut zis?" he asked, holding it up like a street urchin with his begging cup.

And as I would do so many times when he would ask me questions, I stroked my chin, furrowed my brow, hemmed and hawed for a moment or so before taking a deep breath, shrugging my shoulders, and saying, "Aw hell, son. I don't know."


The following is one of the rules we lived by in regards to raising this son of ours:

*The response to any question, query, or curiosity put to us by Sparky shall be "I don't know."*

*I don't know* is the answer always, even if the answer is known, unless the answer in some way helps to achieve the primary objective.

For instance:

Wut zis?

*I don't know.*

Wer' zis?

*I don't know.*

Why zis?

*I don't know.*


With the baseball still in his chubby fist and *I don't know* still lingering in the air like the smell of doo-doo stew, Sparky, frustrated with my lack of answers, took it upon himself to make sense of the stitched little sphere. Limited in intuitiveness as he was though, the only thing he could come up with in the way of further analysis was to roll it back and forth across the carpet a few more times before his eyes glazed over.

Confident that *I don't know* had once again closed an avenue of potential disaster, I went in for the kill and turned on the television, knowing whatever inquisitiveness was gasping for breath inside my son's head would almost certainly be smothered via the glorious, imagination-asphyxiating power of the boob tube.

Which brings me to another of our rules:

*If at any point should Sparky begin to take it upon himself to ascertain the nature of something, or to acquire knowledge of any kind at cross-purposes to the primary objective, all manner of distraction, disruption, disturbance, and/or commotion may be used in order to obstruct him.*

And although there are many, many ways to distract, disrupt, disturb, and obstruct a child, none are as effective as the idiot box. It's my ace in the hole. Like napalm, wipes out everything.

That being said, no matter how smart you think you are, there are times when the reach of your cleverness exceeds its grasp—like Icarus's ill-advised hubris toward the sun—and you end up with melted wax-wings.

Apropos, when I went in for the kill and flicked on the TV, what came on was a baseball game.

As it turns out, I had already left for the kitchen, eager to finish a crossword puzzle and comfortable with the assumption that whatever was on the television would serve as more than adequate distraction and disruption—a foolish mistake. Because while I was figuring out the five-letter first name for the clue "Peace Nobleist Root" ("Elihu" for those keeping score), Sparky was watching a baseball game featuring the New York Yankees, which was something of a double-whammy.

For those not in possession of even a rudimentary knowledge of America's pastime, the New York Yankees are pretty good at the game of baseball. In fact, they are the most successful organization in the history of North American professional sports. This means that not only was Sparky being shown what the ball on the floor was for, he was being shown how to play with that ball by the best—i.e., he was being introduced to excellence.

If the wife had walked into the room at that moment she would have screamed bloody murder.

Luckily, only a few minutes elapsed before I realized what I'd done, changed the channel, and engaged in another of our tactics by enticing Sparky with eight cups of ultra-refined sugar-imbued chocolate-flavored puffed-rice cereal (159 calories per cup) soaked with ten servings of half-and-half (400 calories total). The former ingredient was good for making him toss the couch cushions about the living room, cackling like a loon, while the latter's lung-and-artery-clogging soporific effect kicked in shortly thereafter, bringing all mental and physical functions to a crashing halt. Little more than an hour later, Sparky was curled up fetal on the floor, blinking listlessly at muted Japanese cartoons flashing across the TV screen like a strobe light—something that is deadening to the senses even if you aren't susceptible to seizures.

The baseball now lay forgotten near the sofa, and later on, in the midst of a brisk evening constitutional, I threw it long and far into the twilight nothingness beyond the outskirts of our neighborhood.

Close call.

# 5

As Sparky and I traverse this treacherous Berry, Indiana sidewalk, my phone starts blaring that unparalleled masterpiece of modern music, "Eye of the Tiger."

Like most people who experience this tune, it has been known to really rev me up, make me want to do some hard exercise, like go berserk on a punching bag or run real fast around the block. So you would think hearing this song now would be a nice lift for my morale, and considering the magnitude of this day, a much welcomed one at that.

Too bad it's not. Not anymore, anyway.

Now my gut reaction to "Eye of the Tiger" is not to monkey-climb a gym rope or bounce the hell out of a medicine ball, but to sit down and put my head in my hands, all because of who is waiting for me on the other end of the line, one of three people who will more than do their part in making the time we spend conversing the metaphorical equivalent of having one's nose shoved up another human being's fundament.

The first of these people: my father, who loves to call up to a dozen times per week to crow and rave and brag and swank over my eight-year-old half-brother.

I hate that little twerp, and I really hate hearing about him from the old man. Why this is I'll get to later, but for now, take my word for it. Younger brother is a piece of work.


The second person: Little Eddie Reddingham.

Despite the wife's and my largely successful campaign to keep Sparky isolated and buddy-free, he has recently acquired a playmate—Little Eddie—who likes to call my phone about as often as my dad and leave long, disturbing messages for my son.

But for this one, I have nobody to blame but myself. I've been somewhat careless and less watchful over Sparky's activities of late, no doubt about it. In the past, the wife would have made sure we stayed on target and wouldn't have allowed things to fall apart like I have, which is why, up until the last year or so, Sparky never had a friend.

On my own I've proved unequal to the task. The wife's death has been quite a blow and my efforts have not been enough to make up for her loss.

It also doesn't help that, since his mother's departure from life, Sparky has become sneakier. And rebellious.


A bit more about Little Eddie Reddingham: On the surface, he would appear to be nothing more than your harmless, everyday, garden-variety dork. He wears glasses. He's skinny. He's small.

The one thing that makes him worth mentioning (and fearing): his favorite movie is *The Producers*.

Quite taken with the comedy's breezy, cavalier tone toward Nazis, Little Eddie Reddingham likes to go around town belting out the songs from the film. Wouldn't be such a big deal if he concentrated primarily on some of the more innocuous numbers, such as "Prisoners of Love" or even "Der Guten Tag Hop-Clop," but since I've had the pleasure of knowing the lad, it's only been "Springtime for Hitler" and at a volume and clarity that's impossible to ignore.

This may or may not come as a surprise, but ripped from the playfully irreverent confines of its own context, the song tends not to elicit great peals of laughter from those that hear it, but rather confused, concerned looks, or, in one case—Diane Crunk, a neighbor who claims to actually know someone Jewish—outraged phone calls to yours truly.

Why, pray tell, would she dial me? Because Sparky has willingly joined Eddie in his one-boy attempt to unsettle as many Kokomo County-ites as possible, turning what was once an ill-advised solo act into a less-than-dynamic duet, ensuring that "Springtime for Hitler" would not be a brief, thankfully forgotten phase during the tender years of one little small-town idiot, but something that could possibly have dire, far-reaching consequences for the rest of the world.

Naturally, I've complained to Eddie's parents, Ozzie and Belinda, about their son's behavior, but they seem to think it's all in good fun.

"It's just a silly movie for crying out loud," Belinda said to me. "It's not supposed to be taken seriously. It's ironic."

"You familiar with the term 'satire,' Horvath?" Ozzie added. "And hey, Mel Brooks is Jewish. You think he didn't know what he was doing?"

Being the good—no, *great*—person that I am, I have tried my best to inform Ozzie and Belinda how reckless it is to approve of Little Eddie singing songs extolling Nazi virtues around such a dangerous boy as my son (though I don't describe him as such, opting for words such as "pure" and "innocent"). Sparky, I've told them, has no idea what satire and irony are and so might get to thinking the Third Reich was a magical, musical place, which, for about 13.3 million reasons, would not be a good thing. But these arguments have proven ineffectual, as have been my endeavors to keep Sparky and Eddie apart, to the point where my repeated wishes that the boys not be allowed to see each other have been deliberately flouted by the Reddinghams themselves.

"Lighten up, Horvath!" Ozzie has said to me.

"Kids need friends!" Belinda has said to me.

"Your wife would have been thrilled that they've gotten closer since she passed," they both have said to me, betraying the truth that neither of them had the slightest clue what would have thrilled my wife.

If they had mentioned the old man they would have been dead on. He had been elated at the news that another flesh-and-blood human being would want to spend time with his grandson.

"It's about time he started having a normal childhood," he'd said.

The third person I dread hearing from: Joyce. My stepmother. I owe her five grand.

Full disclosure: I've gotten a little spendy the last year or so with my limited income and have not been prompt in paying off a loan she extended (unbeknownst to my father) to help me get by. But with her call, I do not plunge into despair. It does not make my heart rage as it would if it were the old man, neither does it throw a spotlight on my failures as a father like Little Nazi Eddie Reddingham. Mostly I feel guilty and entirely because of how nice she is about it. And although she does call roughly once a month to see how that first payment is coming along, she has yet to act like she's all that concerned about it.

I only wish I could say her patience and long-suffering will pay off, but I can't. Because if today goes like I think it will, then all of that compounding guilt and debt will be rendered utterly moot.

Besides, many great men were bad with money. Mozart, Van Gogh, Dumas, Ghandi. That's damn good company.

So. We're almost to the entrance of the Lawrence P. Fenwick Building where the Church of Epistemological Emendation resides, my phone is still blaring "Eye of the Tiger," my confidence is in the tank, while the rest of me is overcome with the irresistible need to sit and put my head in my hands. But seeing how there's nowhere to sit on the sidewalk, and because no matter how tough things get we've just *got* to keep going, I sigh wearily and smack at the phone in my pocket until the song dies.

In the meantime, I will keep my eyes peeled for somewhere to sit and put my head in my hands. In the meantime, I will try to think about something else.

# 6

A LITTLE WHILE AFTER THE AFFAIR WITH SPARKY AND THE BASEBALL, LONG after I thought the crisis averted, he returned from school one afternoon with a baseball mitt.

I was already home from work for the day as there hadn't been a whole lot to do in silverware design other than wait with bated breath for the judgment on my latest and greatest brainchild: a large, ten-tined dinner fork (target demographic: dudes of any age who want to take really big bites).

You know, Girthy Fork.

(It was rejected.)

The wife, thank God, was out grocery shopping. If she had been home and had seen such contraband as a baseball glove anywhere near Sparky, she would have screamed bloody murder. She didn't handle those kinds of situations well, so it was a good thing they mostly occurred on my watch.

"Uh, where didya get that...doo-hickey, son?" I asked him, calmly, friendly, not bloody murderly.

"Hanzy," Sparky mumbled.

"Hanzy, huh?" I said, trepidation suddenly clawing at my throat. "W-would you like an Oreo or two?"

In addition to the scores of sacchariferous cereals and copious amounts of half-and-half available, the wife and I were also meticulous enough to make sure we were stocked floor to ceiling with additional brain-addling junk-foody stuffs, such as cookies and donuts and potato chips and jelly beans and chocolate bars—the boy can't resist them. So when I waved the package of Oreos in his face, Sparky's eyes popped, his lips smacked, and before I could even say, "One at a time there, pal," he had dropped the mitt and was double-fisting those wonderful shortening-packed chocolate cookie sandwiches (approximately 53 calories per), and chasing them with crazed, delirious gulpfuls of deliciously thick, waistband-exploding, mind-clabbering half-and-half (40 calories *per tablespoon!*) right out of the carton.

Offering the boy a smile as close as I can make to a fatherly one, I once more played my ace in the hole. Oh, and what do you know? A Japanese cartoon marathon. Hypnotic. Anesthetizing. Perfect.

Eat your heart out, Ivan Pavlov (and your little dogs' too).

In record time Sparky was splayed out on the sofa, the half and half, cookies, and TV coagulating his mind and body. Now free to begin the next phase of my mission, I snuck out to the garage and hid the mitt underneath a stack of Christmas sweaters before returning to the kitchen, where, via the astonishing invention of the telephone I would, with extreme prejudice, confront and destroy his second grade teacher, Mr. Hanzy.


A little about the man: Put charitably, he's an enthusiastic, conscientious, knowledgeable, and extremely effective teacher, renowned and celebrated amongst other educators and parents for knowing how to get the best out of any student. Put less charitably, he's a meddlesome, annoying putz who does his job way too well for an elementary school teacher in a shithole like Kokomo County.

If I'd had a kid other than Sparky, I'd have been ecstatic that Elmo Lincoln Elementary* had a teacher of his quality and energy, but since I didn't, Mr. Hanzy was an annoying putz. And dangerous.

"WHY DID YOU GIVE MY SON A BASEBALL MITT?" I barked at him through the phone. My voice, thanks to the conclusion of puberty almost twenty years earlier, no longer crackled like popcorn being stepped on. There even may have been some BOOM in there. At least, I'd like to think there was, like distant thunder.

"Michael asked me to tell him about baseball, Mr. Horvath," Hanzy said. "You're not gonna get upset over this, are you?"

Allow me to take a moment to point out that Mr. Hanzy—and all the teachers of Elmo Lincoln for that matter—believed the wife and me to be a couple of paranoid nutcases. This was somewhat intentional on our part, to keep them at arm's length, but also one of the unavoidable consequences of having to obsess over every aspect of our son's life.

We demanded copies of syllabi and lesson plans for every class and subject well ahead of time, as well as lunch menus, recess activities, and field trips. We wanted to know what Sparky was going to be taught and how he was going to be taught, what his homework would be like, what kind of exercise he would be getting, what sort of meals he would be eating, etc., all to ensure he would be one of the worst students every year.

We worked tirelessly to make sure he had no idea about Ben Franklin and that kite and the lightning storm. No clue about the difference between igneous and sedimentary rock.

Where's the United States on a map of the world? *Gurgle...*

What's five times five? *Jabba!*

For a while, we did our job a little too well, as at the time of my confab with Hanzy, Sparky was in the midst of his second go-around through the second grade, meaning more individual attention from his teacher.

---

\*    Named after the silent film star known for his Tarzan pictures. Born in Rochester (which, strangely enough, is not a part of Kokomo County), Indiana, in 1889.

Seeing how the last thing the wife and I wanted was for Sparky to have extra attention paid to him (the perfect scenario is and always will be for him to be the quintessential forgotten child), this held-back-a-year stuff constituted a sizable mistake on our part, especially when you consider the teacher vowing to save Sparky's scholastic soul was one of the most competent practitioners in the field. Truth be told, I had begun to worry Hanzy might be on to us, or at minimum that he believed we were responsible to a degree for how stupid our son was. Thankfully, the thing he would never figure out was that we were doing it on purpose, which gave the wife and me the upper hand.

And that we knew how to play. We played it paranoid and crazy. We screamed and shouted and made outrageous accusations. We threatened legal action at the drop of a hat. We were so smart back then. Brilliant. What a shame we couldn't keep it up.


Since Hanzy had added a touch of indignation to his voice, implying he didn't think he had done anything to deserve my barky, slightly boomy voice, I knew it was incumbent upon me to steamroll him before he wrested control of the conversation.

"And how did TELLING him about baseball end up with you GIVING him a mitt, Hanzy?"

"Let's try to stay calm, Mr. Horvath," Hanzy said. "Your son asked what a baseball is for. I told him I could show him if he had a mitt. He said he didn't know what a mitt was, and so I let him borrow an old one of mine, that's all. He's not *allergic* to it is he?"

Heh. One of the ploys we've used in the past to prevent Sparky from participating in anything was to lie about his health. I know, Christians and honesty are supposed to go hand in hand, but like the abolitionist heroes of the Underground Railroad lying to Confederate soldiers about hidden slaves, we felt we had no other option here, as, despite his awful diet and *petril-kaka* whatever-the-whatchamacallit, Sparky has remained remarkably disease-free and of a more durable constitution than we would have preferred. Given that, the wife and I felt we had no choice but to pore through the *American Medical Association Family Medical Guide* and assign various illnesses, allergies, and afflictions (like chronic fatigue syndrome, *fibromyalgia*, IBS) to Sparky so as to force his teachers to exclude him from almost every school activity you could think of, but in particular those that could help him develop intelligence, friendships, cardiovascular health, even basic hand-eye coordination.

All bad. Trust me.

"No, he's not allergic, Hanzy," I said, "but I don't understand why you would think to give him a baseball glove. To be honest, I wonder what your intentions are."

"My intentions? That he learn about a game he has shown some interest in!"

"Well, it seems on the inappropriate side to me," I said. "I assume you didn't give mitts to all the students in my son's class, which puts this into the category of special treatment, and *that* makes me suspicious."

"How in the world could you possibly—"

"I don't think I need to remind you there are a lot of sickos out there, Hanzy. Remember Mr. Quimby and all those bicycles and—"

"NOW YOU WATCH IT THERE, SIR!"

Heh. Mr. Quimby was a high school biology teacher in nearby Punchy Hills who had been caught sniffing boys' sweaty bicycle seats for reasons other than scientific inquiry. The subsequent wave of disgust and outrage that swept through Kokomo County gave birth to a new era of distrust between parents and teachers (it also made things easier for the wife and me).

"All I'm saying is that everybody trusted Mr. Quimby," I said to Hanzy. "He was a pillar of the community, and look what he turned out to be. One can't be too careful these days."

"Okay, you know what? I'm sorry for the glove," Hanzy said. "I shouldn't have given it to him without consulting you first—but can I tell you something, Mr. Horvath?"

"I'm listening."

"The only reason I gave Michael the mitt was because he was dying to know about baseball. I've never seen him like that before. It was like the lights had finally come on. And I figured if I got him playing baseball, then maybe I could figure out how to tie it to his schoolwork and get him moving forward for once.

"I mean, I can't *teach* him anything, Mr. Horvath. He has the worst retention skills I've ever seen. Anything he learns one day he forgets the next. His test scores are terrible. His homework hardly better. Arts and crafts time he has to put his head down because he's allergic to everything we use. I've gone out of my mind trying to figure out an activity that won't make him itchy or swell his head up or fracture something!"

None of those things would likely happen if Sparky were to come into contact with art supplies or experience light to moderate exercise. It's surprising how no teacher has ever really tried to sneak past our rules. Amazing the fear lawsuits and a Republican governor inspire amongst educators. I, for one, am pleased they don't make much money. Keeps them in line.

"But I still have hope for him," Hanzy said, "and I have to believe the pieces are there for him to be an average student at least."

"Maybe all he needs is more time," I said. "Some of mankind's brightest minds got off to a slow start in school, you know."

"Be that as it may, this can't go on for much longer. Some of my colleagues think I should recommend your son for Special Needs, and I'm starting to believe that might be the best place for him."

Ho boy. Special Needs. Even more attention. We had gotten sloppy. Instead of making sure Sparky understood rudimentary aspects of his subjects in order to guarantee barely passing grades, the wife and I had been skipping that part and simply doing his homework as poorly as possible for him while he was socked out on the couch.

"Not that any of this should come as a surprise to you, Mr. Horvath. You and your wife monitor your son's grades closer than any other parents in the school," Hanzy said.

"That's only because we care," I said.

"What do you propose I do, then? Help me out here."

I hated the thought of it, but I was going to have to give in a little here. Otherwise, our intentions might be exposed, increasing the odds Sparky would one day be taken from us, and if that happened, well, might as well bend over and kiss your ass goodbye.

"Try the baseball thing," I said after a huge sigh. "Maybe that will help."

"*Thank you*, Mr. Horvath. Thank you so much. I know this will work. And I know how to teach it to him so his math, writing, spelling—all of those skills will improve dramatically."

"Let's hope so," I said. *Or not*, I thought. *Really, really not.*

"We'll play catch. I'll teach him the basics of the game, and maybe he can get into a league somewhere."

Good God, what the hell had happened here? Somehow we'd gone from me barking and booming and hinting at pederasty to Sparky playing catch, playing games, and joining leagues to boot. Soon he might learn gamesmanship, working and playing well with others; soon his mind might be freed, his imagination unshackled. Perhaps the most terrible of qualities—ambition, leadership—would begin to manifest, and all because of that stupid baseball and this fucking putz.

"A league like T-Ball?" I asked, my voice, like my nerve, crinkling like cellophane.

"He's probably a little too old for that, but there are a number of beginner leagues out there. No pressure. All about learning and having fun."

"Sounds nice, but let's take it one step at a time. I don't know if Sparky's knees will hold up for all of this."

"I agree one hundred percent, Mr. Horvath. One hundred and *ten* percent!"

Phoo. This had gotten ugly. Hanzy was now pretty much slobbering everything he said, so worked up over the prospect of rescuing Sparky I could have sworn I heard "Eye of the Tiger" in the background. One more hopeless child rescued by the unparalleled genius of the Kokomo County public school system's superstar second-grade teacher.

"We'll go slow and steady, Mr. Horvath," Hanzy said. "Baby steps. Good enough?"

# 7

IN CASE YOU'RE CURIOUS WHAT WE'RE UP TO NOW, SPARKY AND I ARE, without dispute, inside the Lawrence P. Fenwick Building.

That's right. We made it.

Where we are precisely in the Lawrence P. Fenwick Building is in the Lois Esther Fenwick Foyer waiting for the elevator. I decided against the Jonathan Frederick Fenwick Stairway as stairs are good exercise, one of the last things Sparky needs.

Parenting: it's all in the details.


Speak of the devil, the boy had something to say to me as we walked inside. This is what it was:

"I want to go home."

Here's how I responded:

"No."


In other good news, I am no longer looking for somewhere to sit and put my head in my hands. Like most feelings, it has passed. The bad news is it has been replaced by sullenness, which makes me want to frown, trudge around with my hands shoved in my pockets, and squeeze my eyes in irritation. All in all, not much of an improvement.

Why sullen? My phone. It has news for me. A message from the old man. One I have no desire to hear, as messages from him tend to go something like this:

*Hee-ay, Frankie! How ya doing? Things are going sooper-rooper here. Your brother scored not one, not two, not three or four or five, but SIX goals in his soccer game yesterday. Some kind of record they say. Did I tell you he's in that league he's three years too young for? Well, he is, and they're saying he's going to play in some kind of statewide all-star tournament next spring. Hee! Only eight years old. Anyhoo-ee! He doesn't seem to think it's that big of a deal. He says soccer, and I* quote, "'Tis but a childish trifle and only useful to the extent it will be a foundation for future endeavors." Hee-hee! Can you believe the way he talks? So refined and intelligent. And only eight years old. So how's my grandson? Are they still talking about putting him in with the dummies? Boy, I sure hope that's not true anymore. I mean, after all, he's just off to a slow start, kind of like you. That reminds me. Your brother said that he's more than willing to tutor Michael if it will do any good, and I think it would, you know? This kid of mine tells me things in ways I never thought of before, and sheesh, he couldn't get a bad grade if he tried. Only eight years old. So yeah. Give me a call. Oh, and Joyce says hi. She wants to ask you about something but she says she'll call you later.

And they're all like that. Younger brother is a god. Is your son still a moron? Ain't life grand? Yaddity-bladdity. So I believe I'm being fairly gracious by cloaking myself in sullenness. I should be beside myself at the thought of another message from the old man. I should be maniacally plotting his demise along with that of my show-offy, smartass brother. Instead, I suffer. Instead, I endure. Instead, I *sullen*.

And wait for the elevator.

# 8

AFTER HANGING UP ON HANZY AND COMING TO A FULL APPRECIATION OF THE jeopardy the human race was now in, I realized there was nothing left to do but pray. Pray that Mr. Hanzy's meddling would come to naught, and that something as seemingly unimportant as baseball wouldn't undo everything the wife and I had been working so hard to prevent.

Speaking of, when she came home that night and heard my confession of what had happened (yes, she screamed bloody murder), she came to the same conclusion:

"All we can do now is pray."

And lo and behold, we did. We prayed to God that our son would remain an uncoordinated, overweight, friendless imbecile. That the Lord would have mercy on us and cover for our screw-up.

I said before I can be a skeptic, and some days I am that and then some, but one thing I do know is that when your back's against the wall you can always kick it Upstairs, and that is a big advantage even we wishy-washy religious people have over all of you godless nitwits.

You never feel something is ever lost.


In addition to praying, the wife and I danced around in a Pentecostal sort of way. Like most people of our special strain of Christianity, we saw it as prayer in motion meant to move the Hand of God.

Hoppity-hop. *Please God, make it so our son won't catch the ball.* Shuffle-step! *That he won't get coordinated.* Turn and kick! *That he won't improve his math.* Spin, clickety-step, clickety-step! *Or read better.* Arms up and shimmy! *Or have friends, dear Jesus...*

Superstitious? Absolutely. Batshit? Based on the rules of rational thought you could make a convincing argument. But in our defense, the wife was frantic and terrified, I wasn't feeling too great either, and compared to all the unspeakable things human beings are capable of, I think we can agree praying and jumping around is rather tame. So while you could make the argument that the above craziness may not do any perceivable good, it sure as hell doesn't hurt anybody—at least not in a way that can be proven in a court of law. Scoff and mock all you like, but the dancing and praying stuff, goofy though it was and is, was and is harmless. No more unsafe than a boisterous game of Twister without a mat or a spin board.

I assume you've played the game before, yes? Probably not one of your finer moments, and it got you absolutely nowhere in life, so back off. Because what we did worked.

I think.

★

A miracle! A coincidence!

Maybe our prayers moved God to action, or maybe what happened was inevitable regardless of what we did beforehand. I could give a shit, really. What matters is we got what we wanted.

Sparky got nowhere near a baseball league of any kind. He did not learn gamesmanship, the thrill of victory, ambition, or leadership. He made no friends. Truth be told, he got no further than one session of playing catch.

At recess the day after Hanzy and I spoke, he and Sparky went to the field behind Elmo Lincoln with two mitts and a baseball. Starting just a few feet from one another, they began to throw back and forth.

Hanzy said it took Sparky only a few minutes to get the proper form down, and after a dozen tosses or so, he was able to throw and catch the thing with surprising consistency.

"By the way, are you sure he's never played before?" he asked me.

Sparky hadn't, but I couldn't allow anyone to think there might be more to my son than met the eye, so I lied.

"Here and there when he was younger," I said. "He didn't seem to like it back then, so we quit."

"Oh. He told me he'd never been allowed."

"He probably just doesn't remember. His memory isn't the greatest, you know."

"Right."

Next, Hanzy said he had Sparky run around and catch longer throws. He promised me he did this only after Sparky had assured him I had granted him permission to run (I hadn't).

"ALL RIGHT!" Sparky yelled, according to Mr. Hanzy, before taking off after a popup.

*Great,* I thought. *Enthusiasm. Excitement. Running. So it begins.*

"Your son's got raw talent," Hanzy said. Thank God he only said that to me. The wife would have screamed bloody murder.

Finally, the recess bell rang. Time to pack it in. "I told Michael we'd throw some more tomorrow," Hanzy said.

64

"One more," Sparky pleaded. "Just one more."

"Okay, Michael, but this is it," Hanzy said, again marveling at the ebullience bursting from my son, something he had never seen from him before. And being something of a sucker for the *joie de vivre* of children anyway, he let this previously half-comatose numbskull-cum-effervescent youngster trump his better judgment. He proceeded to throw the ball a lot harder and farther than he had before, with the idea there would be no way Sparky would catch it, giving him something to shoot for—egads, a *goal*.

And Sparky tried his damnedest to catch the ball. He hauled ass after it, I was told, and much faster than Hanzy would have thought a pudgy old man-child would have been capable of. As Hanzy told it, Sparky got close enough to leap up after the ball, barely miss it, and come down hard in a divot in the field.

A marvelous, magnificent, miraculous divot that just so happened to blow out Sparky's left knee. ACL. MCL. To smithereens.

As my father would say: Puh-raaaze Jee-*hee*-zus!

"I'm so sorry, Mr. Horvath, I'm so sorry," Hanzy said. "I'll pay whatever it takes to make sure his leg gets fixed. It's all my fault. This was so careless of me." Babbling on and on.

At last, I had the son of a bitch by the balls. I could do anything to him. Scream anything, threaten anything, and he would shrivel, collapse, beg.

What a wonderful power to have!

I knew with the wife and me at our most paranoid, our most nutcasey, we could have Hanzy fired, sued to the last dime, and probably even beaten up. A few of the parents had caught wind of what had happened and were furious. Knowing how fragile our son was, they said it was reckless and irresponsible. George Crunk, the husband of Diane and a fellow parent of an Elmo Lincoln child, dropped by and told me he'd always had a funny feeling about Mr. Hanzy, and if I wanted to know, well, he knew where he lived.

That was all he was going to say. He knew where he lived. Then George Crunk punched his hand. "The putz!" he said.

Which is all the more proof of my greatness that I did the Christian thing. It was one of those days when I felt compelled to be what I professed. It was one of those days where it felt like it was true.

By the way, for you snarky anti-religious types out there, this does not mean I had Hanzy burned at the stake, put on the rack or through Strappado, fitted with Spanish Boots, hung from a locust tree, or shut in an Iron Maiden. I did not have him cast down in the village square and stoned by the masses. I did not tell George Crunk to "take care of it."

What I did was tell Hanzy not to sweat it. No joke. I let him off the hook. I said stuff like Sparky's knee blowing out happens. It's life. No biggie. He'll be fine. We'll have to be more careful in the future but live and learn, yaddity-bladdity.

Hanzy, his voice already fragile, let out a girlish sob of relief. The school board had launched an investigation into his conduct, and he knew if I didn't say otherwise, he was going to get cashiered. He would never be allowed to teach anywhere else in Kokomo County, and being a teacher in Kokomo County meant everything in the world to him.

I know, what a putz. An adorable putz, but still.

That said, I still had his balls. Forgiveness had somehow made my grip stronger. Hanzy now felt obligated to continue pestering me for mercy after I'd already bestowed it, and beyond that compelled to follow whatever I said he must do for further expiation to the letter—and entirely because I had shown him Christian mercy to such an admirable degree.

Perhaps Jesus was on to something with this.

And so, with such power and might over another human being, I made sure there would be no other activities involving Sparky and baseball. I also hinted that it would be nice if Sparky would be allowed to continue on to the third grade in light of his improving homework scores (the wife and I had answered a handful more questions right than wrong on the last few assignments, boosting Sparky to the edge of the passing line in a couple of subjects), and Hanzy eagerly responded he would count homework for more than tests (Sparky had failed every one so far, which is about what you would expect when your parents do all your homework for you while you're mainlining chocolate syrup and running full speed into walls), and that that should get it done.

And it did. Sparky's report card came back that May with straight Satisfactory minuses across the board. Just good enough to move on, but not anything that would be remembered or celebrated.

Mediocrity. Anonymity. Insignificance.

Perfect.

## 9

CHALK UP ANOTHER ONE FOR THE GREAT HORVATH: I'M IN THE ELEVATOR and with the boy. All the way inside and waiting for the doors to close. This feels good. Almost as if something of import has been accomplished.

Maybe it has.

Like everything else around here, the elevator is named after one of the many branches from the apparently quite fructiferous Fenwick family tree. It is posted on a plaque to the right of the buttons.

*The Gladys Marie Fenwick Memorial Elevator.*

I'm not sure what Gladys Marie Fenwick did to deserve an elevator other than stop breathing, but she's got one.

Wait, I do know why. There's a plaque underneath the other plaque. It reads:

*This elevator is dedicated to the memory of*
*Gladys Marie Fenwick*
*daughter of Lawrence P. and Lois Esther Fenwick, in honor of*
*her courageous battle with renal cancer.*

*May every passenger in this elevator remember the soul's blissful flight back to its Creator with every ascension made, and with every descent, the painful separation from their loved ones on earth.*

*God Bless.*

What would an elevator be without music, right? And considering this is a memorial elevator and not your run-of-the-mill sort, you would think the music would lean toward the transcendent. Mozart's *Requiem*. Brahms's *Requiem*. Anybody's requiem. Something solemn and majestic to accompany one's thoughts as they alight on the concept of the soul's flight to Eternity. A fairly obvious thing to do, I would think, but that's not what's playing here.

No, we're getting, "Joy to the World."

Still fitting you say? Still works because, from a Christian point of view, the celebration of the birth of Christ ultimately results in the redemption of humanity, thereby creating the possibility for Gladys Marie Fenwick's soul to take its blessed flight to Paradise instead of consignment to the fiery depths of Hell? Perhaps in a roundabout way you'd be correct, except what is playing is not the Christmas hymn. It's the classic pop song by Three Dog Night. You know, the one with the chorus that ends like this:

> *Joy to the fishes in the deep blue sea*
> *Joy to you and me.*

## 10

BACK TO THE PAST. BACK TO SPARKY AND BASEBALL.

Despite his crippling injury, the boy's interest in the sport did not wane. From time to time, I would catch him changing the channel from stupefying Japanese cartoons to Yankees games when he thought nobody was looking. Whenever I went out to rent a movie, Sparky begged that I bring back *The Natural*, while at dinnertime he would entertain us with reenactments from great moments in Yankees history via greasy tater tots and mozzarella sticks.

The wife's untouched salad and hateful gaze in my direction said it all: this was my fault, and I had better do something to fix it and damn soon.

But what could I do? I dwelled on the problem for days and did not like what I saw. A shredded knee and the usual distractive devices had not killed the boy's passion. Then there was the most worrying aspect: his affinity for the best team in the history of the world.

And it hit me. He'd only just started to like baseball, and the Yankees were the only team he'd seen so far. If I could somehow turn this affection, so early in its inception, to another team, a perennially unsuccessful, inept one, then wouldn't that neutralize the situation at worst, and at best, turn it to our advantage?

Giddy with my sensational idea, I ran to the wife, who, as the situation had turned more grim, had responded by hiding for whole days in soapy baths.

"This is what you came up with?" she asked from within a puff of suds. "Make him like a bad team? Even if that somehow worked, he'd still like baseball."

"It's the only way, honey," I said.

"Why can't we figure out a way to get him back on those stupid cartoons, or . . . or playing with mud?"

"Because his world has opened up and he has evolved," I explained. "The rules have changed."

"Well, you'd better be right or it's your ass," she said.

"Hon, if I'm wrong," I said, "it'll be all our asses."


Now, there are a number of organizations throughout Major League Baseball that can fit comfortably under the wide umbrella of "unsuccessful" and "inept."

The Milwaukee Brewers for one. A god-awful organization defined by horrendous players, dipshit management, a history replete with failure, and a future that holds little in the way of change.

So, good choice, yes?

Actually, no.

While everything above is true, I could tell you from my own experience of watching the Brewers play that they weren't what I was looking for. Sure, they played bad baseball and lost a ton of games: 106 out of 162 possible the year I studied them, good for last place in their division and one of the worst records in baseball.

But, again, isn't that good stuff?

Again, no.

See, the problem was, even with all the useful traits their organization exhibited, they were missing something. Something that would keep a fan coming back to watch, hope, pray, no matter how dreadful the team was. All the home games I watched the Brewers play that summer were to a mostly empty park. Summed up, they were not just bad, they were boring.

I found the same issue with a number of other god-awful teams with almost no hope for the future and a past their meager fan base would just as soon forget (and many times had): the Tampa Bay Devil Rays, the San Diego Padres, the Detroit Tigers. All bad, but all missing that special something.

Looking back now, the choice should have been clear from the beginning. I certainly took the long way to the right answer, but that has been something of my M.O. in regards to almost everything. The good news is I get there eventually.

After eliminating the aforementioned teams in addition to those that consistently met with success, I finally came across two organizations that didn't just enjoy massive, rabid fan bases, but were also, at the time (2002), renowned for the kind of pervasive failure that can rip a person's guts out. Two teams infamous for fans that see their passion as unbearable, like an affliction, a disease, an addiction, and for whatever irrational reason, their own meaningless lives as irrevocably entwined.

Who am I talking about? Even if you're not much of a baseball fan, you should already know.

The Boston Red Sox and the Chicago Cubs.

# 11

AT THE TIME OF MY RESEARCH, BOTH TEAMS WERE STILL MIRED IN THE LONGEST droughts of futility any sport had ever heard of.

The Red Sox—who have since won two World Series championships (2004, 2007)—had at the time gone eighty-four years since their last title. Do the math and you'll find that's right around the last year of the First World War.

The Chicago Cubs, not to be outdone, had gone since 1908 since their last taste of glory, taking us back to the days when Roosevelt was president—TR, not FDR.

I could go through all the advances in technology, all the seismic historical events that occurred, even tell you how many billions of people have come and gone along the way, but I won't.

I'll give you a hint, though: a lot of stuff has happened.

Both the Cubs and Red Sox have fans that live and die with the fortunes of their teams, fortunes that, at the time of my analysis, had reliably ended in agony for generations.

Up until everything changed for them, Red Sox fans were morbidly fatalistic. One of their ex-pitchers called them the most manic-depressive of fan bases, and you would have noticed when speaking to these fine, fine people that, before the miracle season of 2004, most had developed a substantial amount of loathing for their team. At times it even seemed they hated the Red Sox as much, if not more, than they loved them.

Much has been said and written to this effect, from semi-literate fans to opportunistic sportswriters looking to cash in on the suffering of a tribe obsessed with a team they have no control over, whose exploits, win or lose, don't have any real effect on their lives and in the big picture mean *absolutely nothing.*

These people all portray things along the same lines: tragedy. Greek tragedy. Shakespearean tragedy. *Romeo and Juliet, Rigoletto, Madame Bovary, Death of a Salesman,* the Oedipus Cycle. Or pick recent or ancient history that went sideways. In the course of my study, I came across one

Red Sox fan who compared the team's fortunes to the quagmire that was the Vietnam War. Another compared it to the Palestinian effort to win independence. Another to the volcano that took out Pompeii.

Direct quote from this perspective-free individual: "Only with us it's worse, because the volcano happens again every year, and we get burned all over again every year."

The Cubs too, like the Red Sox, have had an avalanche of stories, articles, and books written about their cursed history—but don't think tragedy here. Think farce.

Chaplin's *The Little Tramp*. Buster Keaton. The Three Stooges. Or maybe something more literary, like *Candide*; and much like the titular character of Voltaire's seminal work, Cubs fans maintain their ridiculous hope in a better tomorrow against an Everest of evidence that screams at them to do otherwise. Change *Best of all Possible Worlds* to *Wait 'Til Next Year* in the slogan department and the transfer is nearly seamless.

Not that this means Cubs fans are nothing more than cockeyed Liebnizian optimists, taking every fresh loss in unflappable stride. They can bitch up a storm with the best of them, just not with the same terrifying rage as Red Sox fans.

For whatever reason, Cubs fans' bellyaching can't help but come across as frivolous, and no matter how hard those around them may want to genuinely sympathize, the best a whiny Cubs fan can ever do is arouse amused pity.

So it must have been simple for me, right? Pick the team with the fans that have fused their identities with the fortunes of their team but without all the spleen, without all the determination that, come hell or high water, they would get it right someday.

Pick the team with the fans who accept their fate, who take unceasing disappointment without a fight, who perceive defeat as immovable a part of life as death.

Pick the team that has as its celebrity attendants, lesser actors and entertainers. Like James Belushi (who is and will always be the Lesser

Belushi). Like Joe Mantegna, a recognizable presence maybe, but not the kind of actor you go to a movie to see. Even the pinnacle of Cubs fan celebrities, John Cusack and Bill Murray, portray characters many would call loveable losers, which just so happens to be the best-known nickname for these same Cubs.

Pinnacle Red Sox celebrity fans? Steven Tyler, Robert Redford, Stephen King. All royalty in their chosen professions.

Around town, I saw Cubs hats on people's heads more than any other team—and who were these people? Blockheads, Gremios. People whose needs and wants are simple, who expect little out of life and of themselves, and get precisely that.

Don't get me wrong here, I'm not saying one's headwear has everything to do with it (you see a lot of Yankees hats on janitors, too), but it's a question of attitude and outlook, and after seeing all these ordinary schmucks and their insane devotion to what these blue hats with the big red C's stood for, I knew that if there was a baseball team out there that would be a boon to the wife's and my determination to ensure our son's mediocrity—lest civilization crumble and evil reign—that baseball team had to be the Chicago Cubs.

So yes, as a matter of fact, the decision was, in retrospect, a very easy one.

## 12

MY METICULOUS RESEARCH AT AN END, THE MOMENTOUS DECISION MADE, the baseball season of 2003, I saturated my son in all things Cubs.

I made sure he was in front of the television for every game. No cookies, no chips, no half-and-half, no mind-numbing Japanese cartoons. I wanted him to have whatever ability to concentrate he possessed to be focused solely on Incompetence Incarnate.

Sparky didn't take to it right away. After a few innings of his first Cubs game he asked if the Yankees were on. He also refused to wear the Cubs hat I bought him, neither did he wear the Cubs jersey I gave him—the uniform of a player I will call Particularly Undistinguished Bench Guy. The plan behind this was that if Sparky found a player on the Cubs he could really like, he would then start to really like the team.

Cast-iron logic on my part.

However, it proved difficult to convince my son to emotionally invest in a bad player, as, strange as it may sound, even my boy loves a winner. Resisting my best effort (which consisted of me pointing out the Particularly Undistinguished Bench Guy on television during those fleeting seconds when the camera panned across the dugout and saying, "Look Sparky, there he is! He's not playing! Isn't that great?"), Sparky refused to glom onto said player and thus to the idea of an equally undistinguished future.

But take heart. I kept at it. I am unyielding.

I tried other undistinguished players. I bought Sparky a jersey for the Cubs' Terrible Third Baseman (who would, incidentally, become a strong contributor to the Red Sox's drought-ending championship a year later), and when that didn't work, I gave Disappointing Nondescript Backup Catcher a try. I tried one player after another until finally, closing my eyes and aimlessly pointing at names on the roster, my fickle, fateful finger landed on Six-Fingered Second Rate Middle Reliever.

And he, I'm proud to say, worked. True, the extra finger made him stand out, something that would have been a bad thing in normal circumstances, but when you factor in how it didn't improve his pitching in the slightest, the superfluous digit, with the help of a fib on my part, became the big reason why Sparky finally glommed onto the Cubs.

"Hey hey, there's Six-Fingered Second Rate Middle Reliever, Sparks!" I said one day.

Sparks, as it were, said nothing. He was plopped on the couch in front of the television, glowering, probably because he wanted to watch the Yankees game. He also might have been jonesin' for some Oreos.

All the same, I continued. No quit here.

"Do you know what they call Six-Fingered Second Rate Middle Reliever?" I asked.

Still nothing from the boy. If he were of cleverer, more precocious stock, he might have come up with the idea of thwarting me by smashing his face in the couch cushions while making exaggerated snoring noises. As things stood, not clever, not precocious, he just sat there and kept glaring.

Nevertheless, I forged ahead. I am tenacious. I am implacable.

"They call him, Ol' Six Fingers," I said. "Wanna know why?"

*No*, said the boy's glare, now searing through my skull.

"Because he has six fingers on his right hand. Isn't that cool?"

I then thrust Six-Fingered Second Rate Middle Reliever's jersey into Sparky's face.

Sloppy, I admit, and it probably should have failed like all the other attempts, but I caught a break this time. The same game I bequeathed his replica uniform to Sparky, Six-Fingered Second Rate pitched, and Ol' Six Fingers, at the peak of his powers, gave up four runs without recording a single out before exiting the game to thunderous boos.

Boos that just so happened to pique my son's interest.

"Why are they being so mean?" he asked me.

"Because he's different than they are, and that scares them," I replied hastily, forgetting the *I Don't Know* rule. (Also, I didn't want Sparky to realize the obvious, that Six-Fingered Second Rate's bad pitching had everything to do with the outpouring of abuse.)

"Just 'cuz he has an extra finger?" Sparky said.

"You got it," I said.

The boy smiled. You could say it was a chilling smile due to the circumstances, but the way he cocked his head, it was chilling in just how not chilling it was. It was the kind of warm, delighted smile you might give upon bumping into an old friend you haven't seen in years.

Sparky then said this in regards to all those Cubs fans he thought were hating on Six-Fingered Second Rate for his sixth finger—and cheerfully too I might add:

"Good."


And there's a clue. A sign. A portent. An augury. The first one for you, one of many for me.

Just so there's no confusion on the issue, the wife and I did not raise Sparky to hate people with deformities. Never would we teach him such a thing. We were Christians after all, and not the kind that weasel out of the scriptural admonitions to love all people regardless of whatever reason they might have to be unlovable, in this case extra body parts.

And while we're on the subject of clues, here's a second:

The elevator has stopped. As in, between floors. As in, we're stuck. It would seem this reenactment of Gladys Marie Fenwick's ascension is experiencing technical difficulties.

That is my first thought anyway. The second is that perhaps someone I know is behind it.

I look at Sparky sitting cross-legged on the floor of the elevator, like Marlon Brando circa *Dr. Moreau* channeling the Buddha.

"Did you do this, Sparks?" I ask.

No answer.

"Come on, son." I say, my voice rising. "Pay attention."

"Joy to the fishes in the deep blue sea, I like to poop and pee!" Sparky sings.

"No, no singing," I say. "Answer me. Did you make the elevator stop going?"

Sparky smiles. The smile is chilling. "I dunnooooo," he says.

Now how do you like that? Taste of my own medicine.

# 13

AFTER WATCHING OL' SIX FINGERS GET BOOED OFF THE FIELD FOR WHAT I had said was his polydactylism, Sparky became a Cubs fan.

He never wore the jersey. I found it cut into pieces a week or two later, and when I asked Sparky why he had done this, he said it was because Six-Fingered Second Rate had six fingers.

"He's a freak!" he happily explained.

I tried to make it clear, one more time, how having an extra finger in no way made you a freak, only different, but Sparky wouldn't hear of it.

"He's a monster!" he said with a laugh. Then, good-naturedly, "I hope he gets hurt."

And that's where this starts to get a little scary. Sparky would get his wish. Six-Fingered Second Rate Middle Reliever would hurt his arm in late July and not return until early August.

I know, only a week, and certainly, pitchers get hurt all the time. Still, when it happened it made me nervous.

Had I unwittingly made a grievous mistake? Was this another mess of my own making that I would now have to clean up? Was it useless to even try? Was I like Creon with baby Oedipus, or Astyages with baby Cyrus, or Pharaoh with baby Moses, or Herod with baby Jesus, or any ancient Mediterranean potentate, fictional or no, who lost his mind over what some oracle or prophet said about the futures of babies? Was I, like them, helping to bring about the exact thing I was trying so hard to prevent? Could it be? *Must* it be?

In my calmer moments—which tended to occur after a string of Cubs losses—I found myself pretty pleased with everything and on the whole impressed with my ability to mold a small human to my whims. Because of me, Sparky had forgotten the Yankees entirely and had become obsessed with the Cubs. Without my prodding, he now parked himself in front of the television every afternoon to watch their games, and with that Cubs hat practically glued to his head. So while the prejudice and intolerance were regrettable, I still couldn't help but be thrilled with how this whole baseball business was looking more and more like one of my greatest triumphs. I firmly believed that once the culture of losing that epitomized Chicago Cubs baseball fully permeated my son's consciousness, it wouldn't matter what he thought of people with extra fingers or anything else. He'd end up as another average, narrow-minded bigot, of little value or consequence in the grand scheme of things, and that's a fine compromise.

I could handle a bigot of little consequence. There are tons of those out there.

But then, wouldn't you know it, the worst happened. And the upside to that hateful horseshit turned out not to be that up of a side at all, as the Cubs, who had been wonderfully below average through the first part of August, as always, suddenly won a bunch of ballgames, thrusting themselves into the middle of the pennant race.

No longer looking bush league and bumbling, the Cubs played good baseball now. They had shutdown pitching and, after acquiring some better hitters via a couple of shrewd trades, they began scoring enough most days to win.

As before, Sparky was being shown excellence, but this time it was excellence of the absolute worst sort. He was being taught that a human being could be worthless, a nobody, good for little other than the condescending amusement of their betters, and yet, through hard work and tenacity rise up to become the antithesis of worthless, a big-time somebody, and that it could happen in the least likely of cases.

Can you imagine a more catastrophic scenario? I couldn't, and neither could the wife.

And oh, was she ever pissed at me. As the season rolled into September and the chances of the Cubs making the playoffs got closer to reality, in the midst of a feverish prayer-and-dance session, she stopped, turned to me, and said:

"If that ass-fart baseball team is the reason this all goes to shit, I swear to Christ I will fucking kill you."

Then she went right back to praying and dancing.


## 14


HOPING REALITY WOULD REASSERT ITSELF IN TIME FOR EVERYTHING TO still turn out as it should, I let Sparky watch the Cubs until the end of the season and I watched right along with him. Together, we saw them clinch the division title on the second-to-last day of the season, and I stared at the TV in disbelief as the team celebrated at Wrigley Field with their fans, Sparky next to me, jumping on the couch, waving his hat in the air.

"Cubs win!" Sparky exclaimed, happy.

"Oh boy," I said, not happy.

Next, we watched the Cubs upset the World Series-favored Atlanta Braves in a harrowing five games to advance to the National League Championship Series.

"Cubs win!" Sparky yelled, running circles in the yard.

"Oh boy," I said, not yelling, not running.

Then we watched as these same Cubs crushed their next opponent, the Florida Marlins, through three of the first four games of the National League Championship Series, bringing them within one win of their first World Series appearance since 1945.

One win.

As some hipster Chicago sports-radio host put it: "One more dubya, and all bets are off, Daddy-O."

A plague of excitement and anticipation spread from Chicago through the state of Indiana, infecting even us backwoods bumpkins in Kokomo County. Cubs jerseys and hats and signs and flags were everywhere, and everyone was aflame with World Series fever. In school and around town, Sparky basked in the glow of the moment, high-fiving and cheering with all the other schlubs in Cubs gear that were now, more than ever, legion.

I, on the other hand, went slouching around Little Hat with a palpable sense of doom, viewing these keyed up, jackbooted fans and the sea of adorable blue bears and big red C's they created with a fear that in times past would have been reserved for the hammer-and-sickle or the swastika.

The wife, not one to take things lying down, embarked on a series of twenty-four hour prayer vigils. All hours, day and night, I could hear the pitter-pat of dancing feet, croaky, off-key singing, and periodic shouts of hope ("YES, LORD! CUBS LOSE, LORD!") or anguish ("LORD, PLEASE...PLEASE...OH GOD...PLEASE SMITE THE CUBS IN YOUR RIGHTEOUS ANGER!"). There were also more than a few times where she yelled at the devil, in case he happened to be within earshot ("GET THEE BEHIND ME, SATAN! YOU HAVE NO PLACE

IN THIS HOUSE OR AT WRIGLEY FIELD! I BANISH YOU FROM THE PLAYOFFS IN THE NAME OF JESUS!").

She refused to eat or sleep and would only drink blessed Diet Coke (with lime).

She performed the Pentecostal ritual of the laying on of hands with Sparky, who giggled through it. ("Please—quiet, Sparky!—oh, Father! Let this cup pass from him—STOP LAUGHING, I MEAN IT!—oh, Jesus—STOP IT!")

She anointed Sparky with holy (canola) oil, something he has never liked ("GREASY HEAD!"). Telling, perhaps.

She prayed over Sparky's Cubs hat and anointed it with oil too, a move that also brought out no small amount of consternation from the boy ("GREASY HAT!").

She even tried stitching Six-Fingered Second Rate Middle Reliever's jersey back together ("Ever since Sparky tore this up they've been winning...").

Granted, in the merciless view of hindsight it is easy to say all this hubbub over a baseball team's fortunes and what it portended for a young child's future was much ado about nothing, and yet more proof that that child's parents were out of their minds, but the screwy things in life have so much to do with momentum, with getting caught up in the current. At the time, it made sense to take leave of one's senses. Because you never know what matters and what doesn't, what has cosmic significance and what doesn't, what matters to God and what doesn't. Better Safe Than Sorry, right?

So go ahead, ridicule us all the more, but all that dancing, praying, shouting, anointing, and kicking the devil out of the wide world of sports, well, it worked.

I think.


Another miracle! Another coincidence!

Game five rolled around and the Cubs got stomped. The opposing pitcher threw a complete game shutout, and the Marlins won 4-0.

The wife, her confidence soaring as the game progressed, prayed, danced, and made whatever she could find in the house greasy with holy (canola) oil while I quietly gave her updates and offered encouraging thumbs-ups between innings.

With Sparky I had to pretend I was as let down as he was that the Cubs had failed in their first attempt to put the Marlins away, as I wasn't sure what he was capable of if he decided I was partly to blame for the loss.

There I was, doing Smiley Face-Frowny Face from the wife to the boy and back again. I was busy, busy, busy.

"Booyah! Cubs *lose!*" I said to the wife in the kitchen, thrusting a fist of solidarity in her direction that she reciprocated by punching her own into a loaf of bread.

"SUCK ON THAT, LUCIFER, SON OF THE MORNING!" she yelled at the now-pummeled Roman Meal before turning to karate kick in the general direction of nothing. "GOD ROCKS THE CASBAH! PRAISE YOU AND GO FISH!"

"Don't worry, son," I said to Sparky in the living room with as false a Frowny Face as there's ever been. "They've got two more shots at it, and the chances of the other team coming back are still really small."

"Yeah, I know," said my son, not nearly as concerned, in retrospect, as he should have been.

## 15

WHICH BRINGS ME TO THE IMMORTAL GAME SIX.

The wife took up her position in the spare bedroom, a place she had dubbed her "war closet." Sparky set up camp three feet from the television.

It goes without saying that when two people living under the same roof are determined to see outcomes diametrically opposed to one another, a natural antagonism develops. This would explain why, before taking his post in the living room, Sparky took to the offensive by standing outside the wife's war closet, scowling and whispering through the door.

The wife, either hearing the whispers herself or informed by some heavenly entity of infernal doings nearby, yelled at Sparky to leave, which, naturally, only succeeded in getting him to kick it up another notch.

To this day, I have no idea what he was saying as I had no intention of getting in his way. From the bottom of the stairs it sounded like tongues, but I would bet everything short of everything that it wasn't tongues of the church-approved variety. I bet it was something else.

The wife, obviously thinking along the same lines, began shouting in tongues to defend herself against whatever it was he was whispering, and thus was the Horvath household turned into a spiritual battleground between two indecipherable gibberers fifteen minutes before game time.

"*Cheeka-peeka-seeka-feeka!*" the wife said.

"*Creepy whisper, creepy whisper,*" Sparky shot back.

"*So-la-la-la-cheeka-so-lo-lo-lo-lo-peeka!*"

A chortle from the boy, then a growl.

This went on through the National Anthem, and although I couldn't say for sure—maybe it was the growl—it sure seemed like Sparky was winning.

That, and the wife finally called out, "Frankie, will you get *your* son away from the door?"

*My* son. Like this was my fault.


"Yo, Sparks? Buddy?" I called from the living room. "The pregame's on. I got Oreos and Pringles and Mountain Dew ready."

A minute went by, no more than two, and Sparky came down the stairs, a smug little smile on his face. "Go Cubbies!" he said.

"Yep. Go Cubbies," I said.

It didn't occur to me to check on the wife.


Game six was a cuticle-masher from the start. The Cubs snuck out to a 1-0 lead early and held it as the Marlins mustered nothing the first few innings against the Cubs' starting pitcher. The Cubs then tacked on another run in their portion of the sixth, before eking out another in the seventh to take a 3-0 lead.

As the game advanced and the odds of victory increased, the crowd at Wrigley grew more rapturous. A prominent black comedian even had the chutzpah to prematurely crown the Cubs "the champs" as he led the seventh inning stretch and, instead of gasping in fright at this ill-advised taunting of the baseball gods, everybody cheered their brains out, Sparky along with them.

For my part, I did not cheer or sing along. I was more concerned with trying not to stick my head in the oven.

It then occurred to me that not a peep had been heard from the wife's war closet since the game had started. No shouts to the Lord, no bursts of song to the Lord, no pitter-pat of dancing feet to the Lord, nothing to the Lord. Nothing, period.

Then I remembered Sparky's smile when he entered the room, how calm he had seemed when he had sat down, the way he had kept his composure during the game itself (while I had found myself rather gassy with stress).

Fearing the worst, I jumped from the couch and ran up the stairs.

"Babe?" I yelled, banging on the door.

As these things tend to go, I received no answer.


"WHAT DID YOU DO TO HER?"

I had found my beloved on the floor, not moving.

After a brief and unsuccessful attempt to rouse her, I had rushed back to the living room, where I was now shaking Sparky, demanding an explanation.

Sparky, to his credit, was trying to answer, but, thanks to me, all he was able to get out were intermittent squeals and sobs. Which brings me to another drawback to having a small child who looks like an old man: when he cries, it scares the shit out of you. And once you have the shit scared out of you, it's possible to lose focus on what you're doing and experience a kind of shock where you keep performing the same action over and over.

For example, when I first found out my mother's headaches might be something that could soon kill her, I was in the kitchen cutting up some cheese for a sandwich. As she was laying out her schedule of endless doctor appointments and tests, I became unaware of what I was doing, and just hacked and hacked at the block until it was nothing but a pile of haphazard chunks, like I had been to the planet Cheddar and had returned with some of its rocks for analysis.

In these kinds of situations I think the brain gets caught in a repetitive pattern impossible to control, and here with Sparky, scared shitless, I kept shaking him and Sparky, being shaken, bawled and screamed, which only scared me further and made me shake him all the more, until:

"STOP IT! STOP IT! LEAVE HIM ALONE!"

The wife, resurrected, was standing next to me, shaking off the last vestiges of what looked a lot like Sleepy Face. Turns out she had not been stricken dead by creepy whispers after all, but had been taking a nap. Later on, she would claim she had been in deep communion with God and it had only looked like she was asleep, something I did not for a second believe.

I knew Sleepy Face when I saw it. I also knew Harpy Face, which was what Sleepy Face had become. Typically speaking, this ill-boding transformation would reduce me to dust, but this time it had no effect on me or my shaking of the boy. Not even the wife's shrill, harpy voice could make me stop. It took the game returning from commercial to break the pattern.

At which point the wife took Sparky by the hand, sat him on the couch, and shot one helluva nasty look at me before catching sight of the score on the screen.

"Oh, for Chrissake!" she said, and took off up the stairs.

Within seconds I heard this: *"Beeka-reeka-heeka-peeka!"*

I heard out-and-out stomps and singing that sounded like the tortured screams of the Gulag put to melody. Worried all over again, I ventured back upstairs to the war closet to check on her, if for no other reason than to make sure she hadn't stepped on a nail.

When I arrived, I found the door was open and the wife was not, as I had pictured, hopping around on one foot with the other gushing blood, but totally naked.

Evidently, she felt that if she were to rend her clothes as Old Testament believers had done (though she was not so much into the sackcloth and ashes) and dance around with her breasts flapping and her ass wiggling, Jesus would do whatever she wanted.

After all, it had worked with every other man she'd known, especially me.

And considering how the wife cavorting about in the altogether was not a common occurrence these days, I would have stayed and enjoyed the show, but with mankind's future at so much risk, I reluctantly decided to leave her to her luscious nudity and return to the game.

It was now the top of the eighth inning. The Marlins were at bat. There was one out and nobody on base. Sparky had his trademark chilling smile going again and was clapping and laughing. For a moment, I wondered if he had somehow sustained some kind of irreparable head trauma from being shaken, but this proved to be wishful thinking.

"Sorry about the shakes there, son." I said. I did feel bad about what I had done despite the small hope that he had become a little bit brain damaged.

"Eh," Sparky said, demonstrating full control over his faculties with a wave of his hand. "We're gonna win," he said. "She can't stop 'em."

He was right. The Chicago Cubs were about to win their first pennant since 1945 and move on to the World Series. Everything I had hoped to accomplish by forcing this execrable baseball team down my son's throat was swirling around the drain.

In a flash I saw the future. Perhaps it was a vision from the Lord; perhaps it was merely my own febrile imagination. Whatever its genesis, I saw a flash, and it was of the future.

I saw Sparky defeat all our attempts to ruin him. I saw him thriving at school: beefy, athletic, excellent grades, starting on the varsity baseball team, thundering away in a debate meet. Yeah, he still looked like an old man, but he looked like a brash, blustery, cocksure, *muscular* old man. Like Ernest Borgnine. Or Sean Connery.

I saw him accepted to Harvard. Yale. I saw him playing lacrosse, wearing preppy sweaters, dating leggy cheerleaders.

I heard his teachers marvel at the genius, cunning, and leadership that were in such preternatural supply in him. How he was destined for great things, to lead, to govern.

"Politics," they said to me. "He was born to run."

To rule.

The fact that he was barely twenty-one yet looked like Nixon at his resignation? Meaningless.

"That face has character," they said to me.

I saw him delivering his class commencement speech from a podium. I saw the eye and ear of every student, parent, and professor enraptured, dazzled by every felicitous inflection, every exquisite turn of phrase.

I saw him surrounded afterwards. Those same students, parents, and professors. Not friends or mentors, but admirers. Worshipers.

I saw his eyes rise above the throng pressing in around him, begging to be healed, and find me, his father. I saw him lift his thumb and forefinger at me. I heard myself call out for him to stop all this, to come down and spend the rest of his life under his old man designing silverware. "Knives, Sparky!" I pleaded. "We're going to start inventing new, neat kinds of knives!"

But my cries were in vain. Sparky smirked and peered through the space between his thumb and forefinger like you would through the sight of a gun.

"Thanks for all the help, Dad," he said.

Then he pinched his fingers together and everybody's head exploded.


The vision at an end, I duly panicked and ran back upstairs to join the wife in her war closet. Shamefully, I admit to rending my own garments—destroying a favorite shirt in the process—and dancing around very un-clothed with her. Jerking, spazzing around, I became aware of my own ass fat and the bit of stomach I had reacquired within the last couple of years, as well as my weenie slapping up and down like a wild garden hose and my testicles colliding with the inside of my legs, sending tendrils of white-hot pain through the rest of my body.

Quickly ascertaining the need to take my mind off my increasing discomfort, I looked back to the wife, and, for the first time it seemed, I became fully aware of just how incredibly naked she was (she was now prostrate on the floor, kissing the ground, her hindquarters in the air). Fully aware and fully appreciative.

And yet, somehow, I managed to pray with all my might that the Chicago Cubs would not win the pennant, even though it was pointless. Had I learned nothing from the Creons and the Herods? All the wife and I could do was help Sparky along the path we were trying to keep him from. All we could do was help pave the way to the end of the world. The fervency of our prayers notwithstanding, I knew this was all a token gesture, the proverbial "here goes nothing,"— and yet I prayed so hard anyway.

How brave I can be sometimes!


Despite the loss of all dignity and decency when it comes to spiritual warfare (I have yet to find anything in Pentecostal theology that approves of lusting over a woman's nakedness—even if it is your wife's—while you yourself are doing battle, naked, in the heavenly realm), despite the wife and I giving up after a few more minutes to collapse in each other's arms and engage in tragic, All-Is-Lost Despair Sex, in our earnestness, the Almighty looked down at our revolting manner of appeal, took pity on us, and once more gave us what we wanted.

Another miracle! Another coincidence!

As the wife and I were making love, crying, grieving, the Cubs were adding quite possibly the most humiliating chapter yet to their long, wretched history.

Here's how it went down:

With the score still 3-0 in favor of the Cubs in the eighth inning—a mere five outs away from the World Series—the Marlins center fielder doubled.

Then, right at the moment my wife's body united with mine (or so I

87

would like to think), the Marlins second baseman hit a catchable foul ball that a fan got in the way of, knocking it out of reach of the Cubs left fielder.

Ask any Cubs fan worth their salt about that moment, and they will tell you, right then, they knew it was over.

After the second baseman drew a walk, the Marlins catcher rapped a single to left ("Aaaaaahhhhh!" went the wife, but gloomily—don't forget this is still Despair Sex; "Ooogh!" went me). The Marlins center fielder scored. The Cubs lead was cut by a third.

The Marlins right fielder came to bat and hit what should have been an inning-ending double play grounder to the Cubs shortstop—but he biffed it ("Ohyahohyahohyah!" went the wife, weeping; "Ooogh!" went me). Everybody was safe. Every Cubs fan in the world groaned in anguish. The wife groaned with mournful pleasure. Bases loaded.

The first baseman then knocked a fat pitch down the left field line. ("Mmmmmm!" went the wife, bleakly; "Ooogh!" went me). Two Marlins scored. Tie game.

Desperate to stop the bleeding, the Cubs brought in a new pitcher. No, not Six-Fingered Second Rate Middle Reliever, but a regular chap. Ten fingers and toes. This new pitcher intentionally walked the Marlins third baseman to set up another double play ("Eeeeheeeeheee!" went the wife, desolately; "Ooogh!" went me), but the next batter spoiled it by hitting a sacrifice fly ("Uhhhhuhhuhhuhhuh!" went the wife, forlornly, "Ooogh!" went me), giving the Marlins a one run lead. Add another intentional walk to this, and then, with two outs, the bases full of Fish, and the hearts of every Cubs fan at the point of bursting, the floodgates opened.

Launching another meatball high into the night, the Marlins short-stop doubled ("YOOOOEEEEAAAAH!" went the wife, inconsolably; "OOOOGH!" went me), clearing the bases. The Marlins were now up by four. Ballgame.

A few minutes later, the wife and I emerged from the war/sex closet, haphazardly clothed, arms wrapped around each other. Yes, we still believed we had failed in pretty spectacular fashion, but we'd also just had some pretty spectacular sex, and that can make whatever it is you think you've messed up seem like no big thing.

I was even of a mind that there was something that could be done down the road to counteract all this. I mean, this couldn't be *that* important, right? With the expulsion of seed came a modicum of perspective and a realization of how illogical this all was to begin with. That dumb vision, with Sparky squishing his fingers together and heads popping, would that *really* happen?

I felt the cobwebs, the clouds, the haze, lift. So what if the Cubs won? There were plenty of other ways to hamstring Sparky's progress down the road, and so long as I could have spectacular sex now and again, I knew I'd be able to find one.


Having made our peace with everything, the wife and I entered the living room.

Sparky was less than a foot from the television. His little old man fists were clenched and shaking. He was hissing.

On the television the announcer was gushing about how incredible the game had been, how heartbreaking for the Cubs and their fans, about the poor sap who had knocked away the foul ball, how this had been one of the greatest playoff games in baseball history, yaddity-bladdity and...*holy shit!*

The wife and I looked at each other and screamed. We resumed our dancing: a dosey-doe one beat, Happy Feet Snoopy the next. Suddenly, my plan was a masterwork. Suddenly, I had succeeded beyond my wildest dreams. In my own smallish way, I felt like Hannibal after the Battle of Cannae, King Charles after the Battle of Vienna, Churchill after the Battle of Britain (translation: I was pretty happy), and this feeling was heightened further by the look on my son's face as he struggled to come to grips with the worst kind of failure: defeat snatched from the jaws of victory. He must have felt like Xerxes after Thermopylae. Napoleon after Waterloo. Hitler after Stalingrad.

I wanted to stick my tongue out at him—you know: *nyah nyah nyah*—but decided to let him stew in it alone. As well I knew, this brand of loss soaked in best without anyone to help it along.

So I wisely let it soak.

Life sucks, little old man.


Of course, there was still one more game to go.

Sparky sat down for game seven with Smiley Face much like he had for game six; he said "Go Cubbies" like always, but the strain had begun to show. Fear was etched around the borders of his smile. His voice trembled. He looked (and sounded and smelled) gassy with stress.

In contrast, the wife and I didn't even bother with long prayers, fasting, dancing, or even All-Is-Lost-Despair Sex. The clarity we achieved in afterglow from the previous game carried over, and we opted for a quick and simple, "We trust you, Lord," before the first pitch instead. Call it overconfidence, call it foolhardy, but we knew this was a done deal.

The game was a see-saw affair early on, with both teams trading leads, but the shock of having blown the previous game in the manner in which they had was too much for the Cubs to bear (no pun intended), they wilted by the fifth inning and ended up losing big.

The second the final out was made, Sparky asked me to change the channel to Japanese cartoons. He then went into the kitchen and emerged a minute later with a big bag of chips, a box of Oreos, a large glass of half-and-half, and a can of Coke.

An hour later, he shit his pants and sat in it.


## 16

WE'RE HERE. ON THE SIXTH FLOOR. WE MADE IT OUT OF THE ELEVATOR.

How did we get out?

The elevator started up again, that's how.

A shade on the anticlimactic side, I agree, but that's the way most stopped elevator stories end. What's important is that we're here. On the sixth floor.

Not that it should come as a surprise at this point, but this floor is as unexceptional as the rest of the Lawrence P. Fenwick Building. I'm guessing the architect saw no need to spruce this level up and I can't say I blame him. Why start here?

I have yet to see the other floors, so maybe they look better. I sincerely hope they aren't all this dismal gray.

As though Sherwin-Williams gave the interior designer a super deal on the color Inner-City Trash Can.


Besides the Church of Epistemological Emendation there are other offices here on the sixth floor.

One appears to be home to some sort of mail-order service for quilts, as I can see, through a sliver of window, stacks and stacks of what look like quilts.

There's a sign on the front of the door that looks like whoever designed it thought they could do calligraphy while fleeing on horseback. The sign says something to the effect that quilts are behind this door, but considering the illegibility of the writing, the view of actual quilts is necessary for corroboration.

I suppose it might not be a mail-order service, but if it isn't, then whoever is in charge of this quilt shop hasn't bothered to awaken whatever beast lurks in the subconscious that has an insatiable desire for quilts. It certainly does not awaken the quilt-loving beast within me.


The next office on the floor is empty. Just a number on the door: 647. At the end of the hall is the last door and office. I'm betting you were expecting a number of a certain satanic significance, yes? So was I, but it is not to be. Instead: 687.

On a sign next to the door, written neatly, is this:

## THE CHURCH OF
## EPISTEMOLOGICAL EMENDATION

What I fear beyond this door:

A big mess, for starters. Empty pizza boxes everywhere. A couple of grimy couches littered with crumbs and crushed beer cans. A large, blinking, inverted, red neon cross (as in, *Take that Jesus, your cross is so lame we turned it upside down!*). A strung-out, long-haired, leather-clad couple fondling each other on one of the grimy couches. One of these two people will be Danica. She'll have nose rings and lip rings and tongue rings and cheek rings and nipple rings.

Yeah, she'll be topless.

On the other grimy couch littered with potato chip crumbs and empty vodka bottles I expect someone prepping a heroin needle, maybe taking a bong hit.

Music? Something grunty, shrieky. Lots of clashing guitars and pissy screams.

Finally, foosball. I expect a foosball table. And nobody playing foosball.

(Why? Because nobody ever plays foosball.)

But keeping in mind Danica's excellent phone etiquette, the neat, clean sign, and how I'm not hearing anything pissy through the door at all, but what sounds like opera, the unappealing picture I have in my head can't be true.

Still, I hold on to it for good luck. I don't want to jinx things. Shooting a bunch of grungy, flipped-out, half-naked crankjobs crowing about the Prince of Darkness ("Satan rocks, man!") before they take a hit, screw, and pass out isn't what I'm here for. If that's what I'm dealing with, the boy and I are going home. But if what I'm hearing is right, then what's waiting for me beyond this door—I reckon, I yearn, I ache—will be the great crucible of my life, the aforementioned fight to the death against the real deal Other Side in a spiritual war that has been raging since before the foundations of the world.


So here we go.

I take a deep breath, put my hand to the doorknob, and flash a smile at Sparky (a smile he does not reciprocate).

This is it! Surely, truly. My becoming. My moment. Greatness.

You're invited to join us if you like. Or you can be a big bummer and wait out here. Go buy a quilt or something.

Either way, we're going in.

# PART FOUR

*Which reminds me of a line from one of Rev. Phipps's sermons:*
*His Judgment Cometh and That Right Soon.*
*Take that, Billy Slider.*

# 1

AFTER MY PRIDE HAD RECOVERED FROM THE BLOW OF THAT IGNOMINIOUS Thanksgiving Day Parade birthday, I vowed to spend the remaining years under my old man's roof proving the bastard wrong.

I studied. I stopped blowing off homework. I paid attention.

I retired from my esteemed position as class cutup (a position I had held without dispute since the first grade), breaking my schoolmates' hearts. With my hijinks and tomfoolery no longer around to regale them, they had to look elsewhere for their amusement, and since the classes were so small and the pool of replacements so shallow (Doug Abernathy was a year behind us), they had to settle for whatever anemic daydreams their sterile imaginations could produce, or the inescapable tedium learning so often is.

To make matters worse, I went so far as to try to become one of the achievers, the brainiacs, the suck-ups. I, previously so rascally, so mischievous, so devil-may-care, unexpectedly morphed into another of those insufferable, ultra-competitive go-getters that drive everybody else up the wall.

I don't think I can fully relate here how much of a betrayal this was to my contemporaries: the ranks of middling irrelevancies, who, though at the height of their oh-so-thrilling teenage years, were already dismayed over how mundane and empty their lives were; who only wanted something or someone to add a dash of zest to all of the present and coming blah before death; who saw me, yes, as one of them, but special in that I could put up a fight against the suck-ups and our nemesis teachers. For so long they had been able to rely on me to be a provider of that zest—the loveable rapscallion with a talent for disruptive hilarity—that when I abruptly and irreversibly changed into what they despised the most, it proved a bit much for them to take.

Some turned on me right away and deemed me a weenie. Others, in denial, held out hope that the old funny Frankie Horvath they knew and loved would return after these ridiculous experiments with exertion and ambition, and once again comically mess up Spanish verb conjugations on the blackboard, glue a teacher's coffee mug to her desk, and/or make funny fart noises and blame them on the girl with the bloated face that nobody liked, Delia Nordsbury.

But that Frankie Horvath was gone forever.


## 2


THE NEW AND IMPROVED ME, REBORN IN THE FIRE OF MY FATHER'S CHAL-lenge, had decided my jokester/prankster side, such a relief and joy to my coevals, if resurrected—even temporarily—might destroy my chance at a greatness still in its wet, stinking infancy. But beyond my transformation into model student, I wanted more: to do more and be more than most people. After a few weeks of the new experience of completing minimum requirements, I learned it wasn't enough to merely pay attention, finish my homework, try hard on tests, and smile toothily at teachers. I wanted to get ahead, not just reach what was expected of me. I wanted to be gifted, a prodigy, a genius, and I wanted everybody else beneath me.

As Gore Vidal once stole from some French writer nobody's ever heard of (and whose name I cannot pronounce):

*It is not enough that I succeed. Others must fail.*


I went beyond the books and worked ahead, managing to get a hold of lessons from months down the road and familiarizing myself with them in advance. I got into word power exercises, the idea for this coming from a book recommended by a clerk named Chip in the only bookstore in Kokomo County who guaranteed it would help me dazzle the world with such big, important words that everybody would have to go scurrying for a dictionary just to be able to understand me.

The following summer, I saved up the money I earned mowing Reverend Phipps's lawn with the Character Developer, not for a dirt bike or a long-coveted Sega Genesis video game system, but for an infomercial cassette set and workbook that promised to turn me into a human calculator, capable of computing impossible sums in the twinkling of an eye. I liked the idea of being able to compute impossible sums in the twinkling of an eye and fantasized wildly about situations arising in the Horvath household where the old man would be faced with, say, a life-or-death multiplication problem and I would reel off the answer so eye-twinklingly quick he would tumble right out of a chair and onto the floor.

"Why, Frankie," he would sputter in disbelief, grabbing at an end table to hoist himself up, "you did it!"

"That is affirmative, Father," I would reply, folding my arms, not stooping to help him. "My unparalleled computative proficiency integrated with my insuperable analytical capability has denaturized this jeopardous mathematical imbroglio into an abecedarian bagatelle."

And then the bastard would go scurrying for a dictionary.

That Christmas, I bought myself the next product offered by the miracle workers behind the human calculator creation, one that promised the same shrewd soul who had invested with them before that if he or she would but send them whatever was left of their summer work savings (as well as a healthy chunk of their winter snow-shoveling earnings), they would in turn bestow upon them another tape set that would teach them to never forget anything ever again.

I, feeling at least as shrewd as before, sent in the funds and they, true to their word, sent me the tapes that promised to teach me to never forget anything ever again.

And I listened to those tapes. And I learned how to not forget stuff.


I composed intricate, sophisticated study guides in thick spooly notebooks; I made flash cards in a variety of bright, memory-enhancing colors. I had my mother use these flash cards to test me frequently. I, unlike other students who made study guides, actually used mine.

When exam time came, my essays were always two to four pages beyond the allotted space given and written in tiny, fastidious handwriting. (I had read somewhere that prodigies and geniuses wrote in such a way.) On these same exams, I always attempted the extra credit question, and in case there was a chance that finishing before anyone else would influence the teacher to look more favorably at my work, I was almost always the first one done.

Yes, throughout my years at Red Skelton Middle School* and Strother Martin High,[†] I was, as many of the IndyCar-loving citizens of Kokomo County would say, "revvin' in the red."

I joined the debate team. I ran for Student Council. I signed up for drug awareness programs and wore drug awareness t-shirts. I entered the spelling bee every year until I was too old to compete. When the class drama came around, I auditioned for every part. In band, I played the clarinet and I practiced two hours every day. For sports, I did the holy trinity: football, basketball, baseball. I even made myself available to fill in for track if needed.

What about the soul and the spirit? The content of my character? I had that covered, too. In addition to academic and athletic magnificence, I wanted to be a notable man of faith, the consummate moral example. Like St. Augustine, Thomas Aquinas—hell, even Reverend Phipps.

So you'd better believe I was in the front row at church every Sunday morning, doing everything Reverend Phipps told the congregation to do. When he told everyone to sing songs for Jesus and jump on the sanctuary trampoline, there I was, singing songs for Jesus and jumping

---

* Named after the beloved 1950s comedian who was born in Vincennes, a town that is not a part of Kokomo County.

† Named after the American actor from the actual town of Kokomo (which again, and weirdest of all, is not a part of Kokomo County) best known for his role as the prison captain in *Cool Hand Luke*.

on the trampoline. When Reverend Phipps reminded everyone to pray to God on their own, I made sure to pray to God on my own—and I even remembered to include others in this prayer time when Reverend Phipps told us to include others and started a devotional meeting before the first bell. When nobody showed up to pray with me, I offered free donuts. When a couple of students showed up, I prayed with them and ate donuts.

I began caring about the Ten Commandments—and not just the movie either.

I even spoke in tongues between classes.

A sample tongues-sentence from me back then: "*Gorzy-morzy rolio-chee-andelio gorzy-morzy-worzy.*"

Like any other Christian giving tongues a go, I had no idea what the hell I was saying, but I thought God knew and wanted me to do it a lot. So I did it a lot.

"*Gorzy-morzy-worzy-gorzy-morzy!*" I said in the hallways, convinced that God was happy with me for talking like this so often and that He would, when an opportunity presented itself, tip the scales in my favor.

What a shame He never did.

Remember the old saw, "God helps those who help themselves"?

Thieves caught mid-burglary would disagree. Fat children whose hands are slapped at the dinner table for digging into the mashed potatoes too early would disagree. I would disagree.

## 3

LIKE I SAID, I STUDIED. THAT DIDN'T WORK. I STILL GOT THE SAME UNDER-whelming grades as before. Those much ballyhooed study guides of mine ended up being a complete waste of time. Somehow—and I'm still not sure how I managed it—the guides focused too heavily on the wrong details while glossing over what was important, and I tended to miss the proverbial forest for the trees.

Also, incredibly, I forgot stuff.

It was uncanny, astonishing, miraculous. Every single test this happened, I swear. It nearly drove me to madness a time or two, but I kept making study guides all the same. My only explanation for continuing to do something that seemed to hinder far more than help is that someday I expected my luck to even out and one of my study guides to finally aid me in nailing every single question on a test (or on many tests, if luck and I were to get square). And although that never happened, if you want my honest opinion, I still recommend study guides. They just didn't do it for me.

My flash cards weren't anything to write home about either.


Moving on to my test essays, they were never marked up for the amount of work put into them. There was no such thing as getting an "A" for effort at Strother Martin. This school, despite its inability to foster excellence from the majority of its students, nevertheless remained one of the last bulwarks against contemporary educational standards, meaning they only gave exemplary grades for exemplary results.

Hence, my essays, which were many times long on composition but generally found wanting in clarity, were panned as "muddled" and "rambling." Mr. Roark, my eleventh grade American History teacher, once wrote the following in the margin of what I had thought to be an insightful critique of *Uncle Tom's Cabin* (but had also gone on well past the six-inch space provided and had required four pieces of paper from my notebook):

"Zzzzzzzzzzzzzzzz..."

I did get the extra credit question right most of the time, though, as most students who do them know, they never substantially raise your grade. This is because doing extra work has and always will be for chumps.

What about word power? The human calculator? Never forgetting anything ever again? What about all the time, energy, and precious capital spent in pursuit of those skills?

To answer these questions I will leave you to find two time-honored quotes: one attributed to P.T. Barnum (but was actually said by a rival), and the other a classic English proverb.

C'mon, you know what they are. One is about the birth frequency of suckers. The other tells of how easily and quickly these same suckers and their wealth can be divorced; and as I will say until Judgment Day or Oblivion: Kids are idiots and suckers and fools, and I, tragically, was no different.


# 4

IN PLACE OF ACADEMIC ACHIEVEMENT IN THE TRADITIONAL SENSE, I WAS forced to look elsewhere for some measure of success, eventually setting my sights on the progenitor to all modern methods of student evaluation in twenty-first century schooling: the Perfect Attendance Award.

Perfect Attendance Awards are typically given to students of unusually sturdy constitutions either too naive to realize school need not be attended every day or too stupid to figure out how to play hooky.

Up until I realized my avenues for distinction were not as numerous as I'd thought, I considered the Perfect Attendance Award a joke, similar to being commended for making it through the year without eating earwax or hoarding used sanitary napkins. However, the permanence of my struggles forced me to rethink this stance, to where I was not only able to ignore how absurd it was to receive accolades for doing nothing more than appearing at the same location five days a week for nine months, but to where I could also delude myself into believing such an award was something I had to have at any cost.

Thus, with the type of anticipation normally reserved for the likes of Christmas Eve, I excitedly started going to bed every school night, with the following morning finding me shot out of the sack like a sprinter off the blocks, and dressing and eating my breakfast with a deranged intensity most would not associate with such mundane activities like putting on pants and eating Fruit Loops.

Every morning I was the first kid at the bus stop, the first kid in the classroom, the first kid in a desk. I longed for the call of the first bell like a jihadi longs for the muezzin's call to prayer, and when the teacher took roll I barked, "PRESENT!" with the passion of a rabid SS officer *jawohl*-ing to every order from his *Hauptsturmführer*.

Every day successfully attended was marked with a big smiley face on the Proust the Bear calendar above the desk in my room. If I reached a perfect month, I would allow myself a package of strawberry licorice. If I reached a perfect semester, I would get a whole supreme pizza. And if I made it the entire year: gallon of Neapolitan ice cream on one knee, bottle of chocolate syrup on the other, huge spoon.

If you would have been around for all of this, you wouldn't have been able to help but admire my resolve to show up to school every day come rain or shine. You might have even given me a compliment on my clever rewards system. You would not have admired, though, my ability to see this plan through. Somehow, despite my doggedness and desire, despite all the smiley faces and payoffs to come, I always ended up missing at least a day's worth of classes every year.

This was in part because I don't have an unusually sturdy constitution. For whatever reason, it seems, every now and then I get sick.

Freshman year my appendix burst. I had to have surgery. I missed two weeks.

I sought a reprieve upon my return, showed the teachers my scar, and assured them I really wanted to be there and that my exploded organ had been an extraordinary circumstance no kid could have attended class through. But alas, my pleas fell on deaf ears, as Ms. Munt, who was known around Strother Martin as a perfect attendance hardliner (and for her insidious ways of swaying the vote to the negative on borderline cases), said she didn't care about the reason I had missed class.

"You weren't here every day," Ms. Munt said. "Therefore, Mr. Horvath, you are disqualified by the very first rule of perfect attendance: The student must be in class every school day."

(Note: The very first rule is also the only rule.)

The following year, my mother, the old man, and I flew out to Idaho for the holidays to see my Aunt Rosie and the bottled water salesman she'd married (still Uncle Chuck). We were to fly home the night before school started, but a vicious snowstorm blew in from out of nowhere and prevented the plane from departing; so instead of being in my desk at the sound of the first bell of the spring semester, ready to take on the scholastic world anew, I was in a folding chair at gate 1A in the Sioux Falls Regional Airport, shaking my fists at a rotted portion of the ceiling and cursing the day I was born.

When I did return the following day, I begged for mercy again, complained about the injustice of snow in wintertime, the cowardice of airlines, and how it was all out of my hands, but Ms. Munt was unbending.

"You didn't *have* to go to Idaho in the first place, Mr. *Hor*-vath," she said. "I guess you just didn't want that Perfect Attendance Award badly enough."

And my junior year of high school, what would turn out to be the last and best chance I would ever have for the Perfect Attendance Award, the diabolical Billy Slider tricked me into thinking classes would be canceled on Arbor Day.

Arbor Day, for those who don't know, is a holiday for trees. It falls on the last Friday in April.

Up until then, I had run the gauntlet. Not a single runny nose, vomit fit, or failed kidney the entire year. I had stayed in Little Hat for every holiday and had made it to class, on time, each and every day.

This was it. The beginning of everything. Perfect attendance, which had evaded me for so long, would not escape this time. This time, the son of a bitch was in the bag. So in the bag—and specifically, my bag—that on the Tuesday before Arbor Day, I was strutting down the hall between classes whistling a cheerful tune.

Soon my study guides and flash cards would come through for me, I would stop second-guessing everything, my grades would spike, and my crackly popcorn voice would mature and deepen with BOOM. I would be the Petruchio in the next school play. No more Gremios for me. Not ever again.

All I had to do was get through the next week without missing a day, a foregone conclusion, since there were no trips to exotic Idaho on the horizon, while the chances of another rupture of a vestigial structure were miniscule.

Yep, there could be no doubting it: I was in the home stretch. I was cruising. And so I was whistling a cheerful tune as I strolled down the hall, cruised, until—

*Bump!* went Billy Slider's shoulder into mine. *Bumped!* went my shoulder into his.

"Hey, weenie! Did you hear?" Billy Slider said.

"No," I said.

"They just announced it. No school on Arbor Day."

"No way!" I said.

"Way," Billy Slider said.

This was a lie from the pit of Hell. There would be school on Arbor Day. Billy Slider was lying.

To make sure it stuck, Billy Slider had a bunch of other students and none other than Mr. Roark himself in on the conspiracy (the students, because they still hadn't forgiven me for no longer making funny fart noises and blaming them on Delia Nordsbury, and Mr. Roark, I suspect, for pissing him off with my Tolstoyan-length test essays), so when I asked them about it—you know, for confirmation—they told me with straight faces that, yes, there would be no school on Arbor Day.

This would directly contradict what Ms. Munt would say at the end of class Thursday; that being, that she would see all of us tomorrow.

"Tomorrow" being Friday, Arbor Day.

Catastrophically for me, at the time this was said, I happened to be going over a study guide I hoped would make me invulnerable on the upcoming test on the Eisenhower presidency. As it would turn out, my reward for this extra studying would be a C plus. Most of what was in my study guide ended up being worthless (such as Ike's enthusiasm for golf and his favorite dessert being prune whip), and only served to bog me down with unnecessary information (also, incredibly, I forgot stuff). And since Ms. Munt did not exactly have my undivided attention, I only half-heard what she said, which is roughly the same as saying I didn't hear anything at all (although I would remember her words with regret and fury later), so when Arbor Day finally arrived in all its tree-loving glory the following morning, I happily slept in and *did not go to school.*

What else did I do with that glorious day off that really wasn't? For the first time in years: bear cartoons. And they were terrific, even more so than I remembered.

In one sense, it felt like redemption for that twelfth birthday of mine, where bear cartoons had been ripped from me and my self-esteem had been laid so low, while in another sense, I was experiencing my first feelings of longing for those much simpler times. Before all talk of the Great Horvath. Before choosing memory boosters over video games. Before I sacrificed my affable buffoonery for my much less admired suckuppery.

It was quite the day. Far better than school. At one point, after finally getting to see the end of that episode the human pyramid had preempted so long ago, I even got a little misty with nostalgic joy.

To my delight, I learned the grouchy brown bears hadn't run off with the magical honey stores at all, but had been tricked by the friendly black bears into only thinking they had. So in conjunction with the grouchy brown bears' celebration (a somber, goose-stepping parade) what they thought to be their finest hour, the friendly black bears, led by the unbeatable Proust (the tree branch had only momentarily stunned him), were high-fiving each other over their latest victory and laughing over the honey the grouchy brown bears had, which was not only non-magic, run-of-the-mill blah, but mixed with something that would make them fart uncontrollably.

Just where were my parents to put a stop to this all-too-wonderful day?

Well, the old man was at the hardware store, making his co-workers miserable no doubt, and my mother was in bed with a crushing head-ache. Consequently, nobody answered the three phone calls from school wondering where the hell I was, which meant none of us had any idea I had been duped until I saw Billy Slider through the Horvath living room window at 3:15 that afternoon, laughing, dancing, *and wearing a backpack*.

"Ha ha-ha ha-ha haaa!" Billy Slider laughed and danced.

# 5

Now, sometimes, when people get really angry, they like to commu-nicate the extent of their rage through idioms such as, "I got so pissed," and, "I saw red," when in truth bladders were not emptied nor did any seeing of primary colors occur.

But not with me. No kidding, I became so angry over the sight of Billy Slider wearing a backpack that I honest to goodness pissed myself. I also literally saw red.

What was red? Billy Slider's backpack...and tongue, which was now french kissing the Horvath living room window. As this sickening display unfolded, my mind was reeling with two cataclysmic thoughts: *Billy Slider only wore backpacks when he was going to and from school! Billy Slider only went to and from school when there was school!*

At that moment, peeing, seeing red, I vowed to hate Billy Slider until he died. But Billy, unaware of my dark pledge, kept tonguing the window and laughing all the same. In his mind, see, he had just won.

★

What happened was this: Billy Slider tricked me because *he* wanted the Perfect Attendance Award.

What Billy Slider didn't understand was that more than one student can win. He had not been paying attention when previous winners had been granted the award, nor had he counted the number of students who had won. If he had, he probably would have left me alone. But Billy Slider hadn't paid attention to much of anything his entire life—something his grades accurately reflected—to where the teachers debated often over whether to cut their losses and pack him off to Special Needs.

Billy Slider, aware of the forces striving against him, knew he would have to do something about this before it was too late—and something other than being a better student. Much like me, Billy Slider came to believe perfect attendance would make those bad grades go away, or at least give him something to fight back with. He figured showing up every day had to be worth something as all the teachers made such a big deal out of it.

Hadn't he been told how perfect attendance had its own special feature during the school awards banquet and even its own theme song played by the Strother Martin High School Fipple Flute Orchestra? Hadn't that perfect attendance plaque he'd once seen in the hands of Delia Nordsbury the year she'd won been so shiny? Hadn't he figured that was why Ms. Munt had a massive banner above her blackboard with a quote from that goofy-looking Woody Allen guy: "Ninety percent of life is just showing up"?

This could be the ticket, he thought, and with a bit of luck, if he got it, it might be good enough to keep him out of Special Needs. Forever.

After all, ninety percent of anything is an A minus. And since A minuses were far better than the grades he usually got, Billy Slider swore to win a Perfect Attendance Award, even if it meant his very soul.

Where it got tricky for Billy Slider was when he followed his squirrelly logic to the dismaying possibility of more than one student making it through the whole year with perfect attendance. His long ignored mental faculties straining to their breaking point (and perhaps beyond),

Billy inferred that the students who didn't miss time would have to keep attending school—through summer vacation if necessary—until all but one of them gave up and took a day off.

Since Billy Slider hated the idea of going to school all summer, he hatched the Arbor Day Plot, and with me, the only other student in the running, now out of the way, Billy Slider thought he was a shoo-in, as he only had to last another three days.


How do I know all this?

Little Ozzie Reddingham, the future father of Little Nazi Eddie. He told me all about it afterwards, the whole scheme.

Naturally, at one point, I asked him, "Why are you telling me this?"

"Because Billy Slider sticks my head in the toilet," Ozzie said.

"Why didn't you tell me before all this happened then?" I said.

"Because you're no fun anymore, Horvath."


Yet, for all of his nefarious intrigues, Billy Slider ultimately failed to get the Perfect Attendance Award. This would be because on the second-to-last-day of school, Billy, perhaps soaring with a feeling of invincibility over having vanquished me, attempted to summit the Little Hat water tower, failed, and tumbled headfirst to the pavement. Subsequently, he missed the last day of school. In fact, he never went back to school again (this was because he was dead).

Which reminds me of a line from one of Rev. Phipps's sermons: *His Judgment Cometh and That Right Soon.*

Take that, Billy Slider.

# 6

ON WITH MY HUMILIATING HIGH SCHOOL YEARS!

I never won Best Speaker in a debate meet. I sucked at sports. I finished in the middle of the pack every student council election. My best performance in the spelling bee was eleventh place. The pinnacle of my career as a thespian came as the dull, pathetic Gremio, the aging suitor of Bianca in *The Taming of the Shrew.* In band, I was fourth chair clarinet, third part, which meant I spent most of my time counting rests and playing notes that nobody noticed if they were played or not. My daily prayer meetings survived a mere three weeks before being cancelled by the administration, largely due to an incident with Penny Turney, the class tramp who had asked me to pray for her to stop putting penises in her mouth.

Just so nobody gets the wrong idea, here's what happened:

Penny attended one of my early morning prayer meetings and asked for help with the crushing guilt. She was the only one who showed up that morning. Me and her. And the donuts.

"Yeah, you really shouldn't do that," I told her, munching on a Long John. I was politely referring to, of course, putting penises in her mouth.

"I know," she said, barely touching her plain cake donut. "I've been told I'm not even very good at it."

"Plus, it's dirty," I said, moving on to an apple fritter.

"I dunno. Sometimes it can be kinda fun," Penny said.

"No, it can't," I said, as sternly as a cellophane-ish voice thickened by sugary apple chunks can be. "Not fun at all."

"Okay," said Penny. "It's not fun."

I imagine she would have agreed to anything I said. She desperately wanted help. Guidance. Salvation.

"Pray for me," she said, and lo and behold, I did.

This is what I prayed in my head: *Please God, save Penny's soul and help her to not put penises in her mouth.* Wanting a little extra spiritual power though, this is how I prayed it out loud:

*"GORZY-MORZY-WORZY-GORZY-MORZY!"*

Not healed as I was hoping, but freaked out for some weird reason by the presence of God (and the awesome power of my tongues), Penny

Turney backed out of the room and raced to the principal's office.

Her attempt to get her life turned around having failed, she went back to putting penises in her mouth.

And from what I heard, over time, she got better at it.


So for all the innumerable pains taken in athletics and extracurricular everything, I never received any recognition or acknowledgement. I never lettered in any sports. I never won an award at the school banquet. I never got a trophy or medal. I didn't even get a pat on the back or a *Keep at it!* from a coach, a teacher, or my parents.

What I did get was a shitload of Participation Certificates, and an even shittier load of frustration, as I fervently prayed every year for the opportunity to be the big hero in something when the going got tough—like playing in a basketball game in the final minute with the score tied; or speaking with the outcome of a debate in the balance; or being offered a word like "zwischenspiel" to win a spelling bee; or performing a killer clarinet solo that would set hearts on fire (and win the band a contest); or having the opportunity in prayer meetings to save a Penny Turney from putting a final, fatal penis in her mouth.

If situations like the above were to present themselves, I was certain I would make good in a way that would cast off my mediocrity forever. All I needed was a chance with everything on the line, whatever that everything was.

Twenty years later and here I am.

# PART FIVE

*And speaking of points, what's the point of having a 9mm stuffed down the front of your pants if, when it seems high time you used it, you forget it's there in the first place?*

# 1

WE'RE IN. THE CHURCH OF EPISTEMOLOGICAL EMENDATION. I SAID WE WERE going in and now we're in. It's good to be in. Much better than being outside preparing mind, body, and soul to go in. This time there's no question whether something of import has been accomplished.

Something has. We are in.

As we were in the process of going in, Sparky tugged on my arm. "I still want to go home," he said.

And I said: "Still no."

The office: Pretty ordinary. No pizza boxes. No upside-down crosses. No grunty music. No drugs, no guns, no foosball table. Nobody passed out. Nobody with their shirt off. Nobody anywhere, really. So far so good.

There is a couch near the far right wall, but it isn't grimy nor, as far as I can tell, rife with crumbs. It is an eye-pleasing champagne color and looks like a nice, clean, comfy couch anybody would be thrilled to sit on. The floor, covered in a nice, clean, almond-colored carpet, is free of debris as well and looks like the kind of comfy carpet anybody would be thrilled to walk on.

For the record, I'd like to take my shoes off and walk on the carpet in just my socks. I also wouldn't mind trying out that couch.

The walls are a tranquil, neutral, cream color and there are no pictures, signs, or decorations anywhere to be found. Not one depiction of the Prince of Darkness feasting on the souls of mankind, blood dripping from his jowls. No propagandistic sloganeering poster about how stupid other religions are and how cool and smart Satanism is. There's not even an Ansel Adams, something I think would work well in this décor (or lack thereof)—over by the coffee station, which is, like everything else, immaculate.

Then again, what do I know about interior design? Maybe they'd tried an Ansel Adams and it hadn't looked right.

"Until we figure something out," they might have said to one another, "we will leave the walls the way they are."

And so they did. And so they are.

I mentioned before there's music playing, and it's still going, shimmering, glistening, as it falls on our ears from speakers perched at the four corners of the room, connected to hair-thin black wires that run down the corners, across the baseboards, and down a hallway. So unless my eyes are deceiving me, the music's source is not the Malebolgian Symphony Orchestra, piping in through the floors via black magic from the eighth circle of Hell, but the much more banal, though no less infernal, invention of Muzak.

Right now it's the beginning of Maurice Ravel's "Bolero": gentle, tapping drums.

*Tap taptaptap tap tap tap taptaptap tap*
*tap tap taptaptap tap tap tap...*

Then, a flute: mirthful, mischievous, but gentle. Like Pan at play in a quiet wood.

*Doooooooo doodoodoodoodoodoo doo doodoo-*
*doooooo doodoodoodoodoodoodoooooo...*

I also said there are no shirtless people here, so scratch shirtless Danicas. There is, however, a Danica, singular, wearing a smart-looking green blouse and black slacks, just arrived from down the hall and now seated at a desk.

How do I know this is Danica?

She's wearing a nametag that reads *Danica*.

I know, a Satanist with a nametag. The mind boggles.


Right off the bat there's something problematic about this Danica though, that being she looks a lot like a young Jane Fonda—and not the batshit pinko Hanoi version either.

Think *Cat Ballou*. Think *Barbarella*.

Which makes her—if a young Jane Fonda is your thing (and it is very much mine)—beautiful. You may recall me saying earlier that if upon entering this office I were to catch sight of a topless Danica, the boy and I would be going home.

Feel free to disregard that.


"Welcome to the Church of E," Danica says as I reach her desk. "You must be Mr. Horvath." Good lord, she even *sounds* like a young Jane Fonda.

"Uh...yeah, that's I—me," I answer, and way too bashfully for someone packing heat.

Unable to endure the sight of this gorgeous creature, I look down at Sparky to see if he's seeing and hearing what I'm seeing and hearing. Perhaps I'll throw a wink at him as if to say, *You seeing and hearing what I'm seeing and hearing, pal? Yowza.*

But this look down not only tells me that Sparky does not see nor hear what I do, it also tells me not to waste my time throwing any *Yowza* winks at him either.

This is because he's gone.


# 2


ALTHOUGH MY LIFE THROUGHOUT HIGH SCHOOL HAD BEEN NOTHING MORE than one disaster after another, the good news is, shortly after I turned seventeen, my mother died.

To repeat: for most of my adolescence she had been suffering from crippling headaches and had been to doctor after doctor about them. Tragically, none of these doctors could figure out what the problem was, mostly because doctors in general are not the gods society makes them out to be, but flawed, limited human beings who, faced with so many people who expect the impossible from them, have no choice but to guess and lie.

I can't really say I blame them for any of that. The human body—as any doctor will tell you when you get him inebriated to the point of honesty—is still too much of a mystery and for every symptom bodies do or do not exhibit, there are oftentimes limitless possibilities as to what could be wrong with them.

Doctors know this. It drives them crazy. It's why a lot of them are closet drunks and sex maniacs and have wives and children who despise them.

Unsurprisingly, all the doctors to whom my mother went were these sorts of doctors. They also didn't guess or lie very well about what was causing her headaches.

Dr. Wiley, Mom's general practitioner, said it was probably an issue with stress and lack of sleep. He guessed this because a few patients he'd had with headaches had mentioned stress problems in addition to not sleeping very well, but after he had told them to get more sleep and find ways to relieve stress, they hadn't come back right away.

A patient not coming back right away was, to Dr. Wiley, the best measure of success.

Dr. Cobb, the first neurologist my mother saw, said—after scanning her head and finding nothing—that her headaches might be due to a lack of sexual activity. He guessed this because he too had been having a headache here and there of late and had found that after expelling his seminal vesicles he felt better. *What's good for the goose is good for the gander,* Dr. Cobb thought. But then, Dr. Cobb thought the answer to everything was sex because he was a sex maniac.

The second neurologist my mother went to see, Dr. Cogswell said—after scanning her head—it was due to not getting enough vitamin C in her diet. This supposition of his was the result of a kickback deal he'd worked out with a local vitamin company that was hoping to get more sales for its supplements.

"Promote our vitamins and you'll never have to pay for a round of golf again," they'd told him.

"No problem-o," Dr. Cogswell had replied.

To justify this to his conscience, Dr. Cogswell thought about all the good things vitamin C does for the body, and he figured that even if the extra vitamin C didn't do any good, it wasn't going to hurt anything. He thought this even though one of the side effects of excess vitamin C is headaches.

Also: kidney stones.


These three doctors had specific tasks they wanted my mother to do and specific medicines they wanted her to take. Doctors' guesses are almost always accompanied by such things. Doctors know human beings feel more confident about convalescence if they have something to do or take, even if whatever they tell people to do or take doesn't make much of a difference one way or another.

In conjunction with more rest, Dr. Wiley prescribed my mother a miniature squishy soccer ball and told her to mash it in her hands when she felt stressed. He also prescribed loads of aspirin.

On top of loads of aspirin, Dr. Cobb also prescribed loads of sexual activity. He then prescribed a night of drinking and dancing and sex—maybe with him?

Dr. Cogswell said three oranges a day, tons of strawberries, carrots with every meal, vitamin C supplements from a certain vitamin company—"No, no, Mrs. Horvath, it has to be Life-a-Holic Vitamin C!"—and don't forget the aspirin.

★

How do I know all this?

A handful of years ago, in the midst of a rough emotional stretch, I decided to spend the better part of the winter holiday season tracking down all of my mother's former doctors and getting them blitzed out of their minds. I then got them to confess about all the ways they had failed to save her life.

The merriest of Christmases it was.

All three of them remembered her, which would have been unbelievable if not for this little tidbit about Mom that I have been loath to relate and leave to the words of Dr. Cobb after his fourth double vodka soda:

"Your mother had the most fantastic bazoombas any doctor could hope to lay a stethoscope on."

Upon receiving her instructions and prescriptions from these worthless dirtbags, my mother decided her best course of action was to follow everything they told her to do to the letter. This was, in her words, "throwing everything at the wall to see what would stick." She figured something out of this mess of advice would have to get the job done.

She mashed a squishy ball in her hands when she felt nervous or upset, took a mid-afternoon nap every day, started surprising my father in the nude in the hopes that her most fantastic bazoombas would bring about more intimate moments with him, and when he wasn't around, she rubbed up against the dishwasher as it was running.

She made fruit salads with lots of oranges and strawberries; she put oranges and carrots on chicken; she drank orange juice, carrot juice, took fistfuls of Life-a-Holic Vitamin C supplements, and ingested gobs of aspirin (which upset her stomach and gave her heartburn).

How do I know all this?

Amongst my mother's effects after she passed was an explicit and detailed diary chronicling her long war with headaches. The intent here being, I think, that someday a memoir about her life would be published, something along the lines of: "Irreverent but warm-hearted Midwestern housewife overcomes debilitating headaches and all the stupid people in her life without losing her mind." And yes, to answer the obvious, it was very uncomfortable and sad reading about how she used to get off on the dishwasher.

There are just some things a son should never know about his mother. Amorous encounters with vigorous "Pots and Pans" cycles is one of those things. That would be the very uncomfortable part. The very sad part is that, even after all this effort, she still had the headaches.

Don't ever let anyone tell you hard work always pays off. Sometimes it doesn't. Sometimes it does you no good whatsoever.

## 3

In lieu of relief of any sort, and becoming increasingly concerned that her war with headaches wasn't going to end in a best-selling book and movie of the week, my mother decided to use a considerable chunk of the meager savings she and my father had cobbled together over the years to venture to northern Indiana to see yet one more brain specialist: Dr. Ragan, allegedly the best in the state.

What did he do? According to my mother's diary, he dumped all over the other doctors she had gone to see and then chided her for not coming to him before anyone else.

"Why didn't you come to me first?" he said.

"How would I have known to do that?" my mother replied, her hopes already sinking that this "arrogant butthead" (her diary words verbatim) would be able to help her.

"Because I'm the best," Dr. Ragan said.

"Says who?"

"Says the best damned neurologist in the state of Indiana, Mrs. Horvath."

"And who would that be?"

Dr. Ragan grinned, took the two thumbs God had blessed him with and pointed them at himself.

"Ah, I see," my mother said.

With that cleared up, Dr. Ragan began talking about migraines. "That's what it's gotta be, Mrs. H. That's what it always is."

"The other doctors didn't seem to think so."

"And they're dumbasses."

"Says who?"

"Says the best damned neurologist in the state of Indiana."

"Who's that again?"

Dr. Ragan guffawed at my mother's needle-sharp wit and asked her about the squishy ball, the aspirin, the dishwasher, and the vitamin C.

"None of this helps?" he said.

"Seeing as I'm here, I guess not," my mother said.

"Migraines migraines migraines!" Dr. Ragan said.

"But that doesn't fit with some of my symptoms."

"Do you want it to be something else, Mrs. H? Something worse?" Dr. Ragan asked.

"Of course not, but some women friends I have with migraines—"

"—say you've got migraines?"

"No, they don't say that at all."

"I suggest finding some better friends with migraines then," Dr. Ragan said, scribbling on a pad. "All right. Here's what we're gonna do. Sometimes I find it useful to have patients read their ailment out loud. Helps them find the courage to accept it."

Ragan held up the pad. "Now what does this say?"

"I have no idea," my mother said.

"I'd say you've got problems far worse than headaches if you've never learned to read."

"I read fine, doc."

"Then what's the problem here?"

"I can't see."

"Literally or...not literally?"

"Literally!"

"Since when?"

"Since about ten seconds ago. My vision's blurry all of a sudden and my head hurts."

"Well then, we'll say it together. You ready?"

(I believe at this point my mother might have been crying.)

"I'll take that as a 'Heck, yeah, Dr. R!'" Ragan said. "Now, repeat after me…"


Even with the abrupt and terrifying onset of vision loss during her appointment, Dr. Ragan did nothing more than scan my mother's brain.

In answer to her exasperation over another repeat of the same old test, he assured her it was just to be on the safe side and that if it did so happen to be something other than migraines—"Extremely impossible," he said—then he would be able to make a much better guess than Drs. Cogswell, Wiley, and Cobb.

"I don't know if I told you this already, but they're dumbasses. Pardon my French," he said.

"That's not French," my mother said.

"My, aren't you feisty for somebody with a serious migraine issue," Dr. Ragan said. "Must not hurt that bad."

Once the scan was finished, Dr. Ragan did as the other doctors had done before him. He took the floppy plastic sheets that had images of the inside of my mother's head and analyzed them for anything that might give him a clue as to what to guess. What he was looking for was something like a smear. If he saw such a thing, then his guesses could be narrowed, and if the smear was in the right place, Dr. Ragan could refer her to a neurosurgeon, who would then cut her head open and possibly get the smear out of there. Like Drs. Cogswell and Cobb though, no smear did he see, so Dr. Ragan sent her home and told her to keep doing what the others had told her to do ("They're not really dumbasses, you know," he had said. "Just some healthy competitiveness coming out.") and added damp cloths to the forehead, dark rooms, and silence whenever flare-ups occurred, along with various migraine medications.

"The best thing about migraines is that you can take migraine medicines for them," he said.

"But I don't have migraines!" my mother pleaded.

"Stubbornness is a piss-poor cure, Mrs. H," Dr. Ragan said, sweeping her out of his office.

And so, my mother, without proper medical training herself and therefore no better ideas than Dr. Ragan, went home and implemented her newly tweaked regimen.

Big shock: she still had headaches.

This was because there did so happen to be a smear on the floppy sheet, but it had been too small to be seen by the human eye. Over the next few months though, the smear, also known as a cancerous brain tumor, began to stretch its legs at an exponential rate, gifting my mother with intermittent seizures as well as the occasional blackout.

Livid, Mom went back to Dr. Ragan and demanded better guesses, to which Dr. Ragan refused, electing to go the easier route and rebuke her for her lack of courage instead.

"You gotta suck it up with these migraines, Mrs. H."

"Why don't you go suck up your own dick, Dr. R.?" Mom snapped.

"Margie!" my father interjected from behind a three-year-old *Sports Illustrated*. The bleeding of the modest Horvath savings account had forced him off the sidelines. "He's the best neurologist in the state of Indiana," he said.

Dr. Ragan thumbed himself again.

"Okay, Robert," my mother said, gathering herself. "You suck up his dick then. And while you're at it have him stick those fucking thumbs up your ass, too!"

Dr. Ragan hid his hands, thumbs and all, behind his back.

"We're Bible-believing Pentecostals, sir," the old man said to Dr. Ragan. "And we don't talk like that. At least I don't."

"Buttfucking Cintons! Buttfucking Cintons! Who says that every other day?" my mother screamed at him.

In case you're wondering, this exchange could not be found in the diary. But then, it didn't need to be. I was there for this one.

"Still no smear!" Dr. Ragan said as he handed the floppy sheets to my mother after doing yet another scan. "Do we need to go over a certain word on a certain piece of paper again?"

"What about this?" my mother asked, pointing at what looked like a blotch the size of a key lime on the floppy sheet.

"What about it?"

"What is that?"

"That, Mrs. Horvath, is your brain."

"And it looks like a smear on my brain. A big one."

"For God's sake, Margie! Do you think you can read one of those things better than he can?" my father shouted.

But my mother would not be denied this time. She got, as the youths like to say, right up in Dr. Ragan's grill.

"This is a smear!" my mother said.

"Ridiculous! There's just something goofy going on with the...you know, the scanner thingamajig," Dr. Ragan said, scribbling on his pad again. "It's been doing that all day."

"Enough!" my mother said, taking me by the hand. "Frankie, we're going."


And off we went. To Ohio this time, the world-famous Cleveland Clinic. The old man, kicking and screaming, with us.

Once there, my mother showed the floppy sheets she had refused to return to Dr. Ragan to a Dr. Scanlan, considered throughout the medical world as the best damned neurologist in the history of damned neurology, and apparently that's what it took for us to get the correct guess, as he shot one look at the floppies and said this:

"Looks like a big smear to me."

"Ha! I told you," my mother said to my father.

"A smear like that is not good news, by the way," Dr. Scanlan pointed out.

Worse yet, the smear was now too big to be operated on and Dr. Scanlan knew from past mishaps of other surgeons who had operated on such big smears that if this smear was operated on, there was a high probability my mother would die during the procedure.

"What about chemo?" she asked him.

"An excellent idea if you wish to die feeling even worse than you already do."

"What do I do then, doctor?"

Dr. Scanlan paused, then informed her there was nothing she nor he nor anybody could do.

"The only thing to do is hope the smear will go away on its own," he said finally.

"Why would it go away now?" my mother said.

Dr. Scanlan stroked his beard and kept his eyes down. He had no idea what to tell her. He knew that smears don't up and disappear, but what else could he say? Beg a higher power? Maybe that would work?

"There are no higher powers, goddammit," the old man moaned, wringing an issue of *Popular Mechanics* from the Carter administration in his hands.

At the demand of my now panic-stricken father (he had believed my mother had been making the headaches out to be more than they were), Dr. Scanlan offered a guess as to how much time she had left. This is another piece of information that patients expect doctors to be able to give to them despite its rank unfairness, as doctors are not the sorts of beings who exist out of time and therefore have the gift of second sight. They have a hard enough time finding smears on floppy sheets.

Nevertheless, Dr. Scanlan offered my father a super specific period of time (two to eighteen months) in which he could expect the love of his life to die and told him (and her and me) to go home and wait for it.

"Is it possible I could make it to Frankie's seventeenth birthday?" my mother asked, patting the head of my father as he wept into his hat. (I had taken to standing in a corner and pressing my face as hard as I could into the wall.)

"Sure. Maybe. I don't know," said Dr. Scanlan. It was one of the few times he could get away without having the answer, and the good doctor felt his skin tingle. "I really don't know."

How do I know how Dr. Scanlan had felt?

He was the last leg of that happy little holiday doctor tour way back when. I drove to Cleveland, found him at his favorite watering hole, and he told me, well into his sixth gin and tonic.

Or as he called it, "Gee-and-tee."

"Other than a nice, stiff 'gee-and-tee,' nothing makes my skin tingle more than when I can tell somebody I don't know what the hell is going to happen and there's nothing I can do to help them anymore," Dr. Scanlan had said.

He'd slurred that, by the way, as six stiff "gee-and-tees" tend to send one's "bee-ae-see" skyrocketing to dangerous levels, but I have cleaned his words up for clarity's sake. As to how he  remembered my mother so vividly, Dr. Scanlan, even bombed out of his gourd, had managed a lascivious smile and familiar-looking wink; and just so there wasn't any confusion as to what that wink meant, he added this: "*Yowza.*"

# 4

I'VE RETURNED TO THE GLADYS MARIE FENWICK MEMORIAL ELEVATOR. Triumphantly too, if I do say so myself, after conducting an exhaustive search for Sparky in the sixth floor hallway and restroom.

I realize that most good parents, in pursuit of their missing child, would have streaked down the stairs as fast as their legs could carry them, taking great care to look as harried and distraught and terrified as possible. Like anybody else, I thought about doing those things too, but I'm of the opinion that the elevator, even with its recent stoppage (which I'm still convinced was the boy's doing), is the safer bet.

The unassailability of my logic aside, I can't help but wonder if I'm being too rational given the circumstances, and that for appearances' sake it would be better for me to stick to what's expected of me and keep my look as harried, distraught, and terrified as I can—something that's tough to do while standing still, humming along to elevator music—even at the risk of falling down the stairs. If necessary, when I reach the lobby, I'll run like hell out of the elevator to reassure any lookers-on that while I'm trying to be smart and safe by using the technological advances available to me in order to maximize the chances of my search's success, I'm also just as harried, distraught, and terrified as any good parent with a missing kid would be.

Besides, Danica's already got the Jonathan Frederick Fenwick Stairway covered. That's right, she's helping me.

I know, a Satanist helping a parent find their missing child. The mind reels.

Though it has occurred to me she's figured out who Sparky is and, through the guise of assisting me, is trying to get to him first so she can snatch him away. Perhaps what's going on here is a race: a race between both sides of that endless spiritual war I blathered on about earlier.

I must say I like the sound of that, of being in a race. Especially when the outcome doesn't depend on whether or not I'm in superior physical condition.

Gonna be tons of fun to see who makes it to the bottom first: me or her. The future of the human race may depend on it. Stay tuned.


# 5


DURING THE LAST FEW WEEKS OF HER LIFE, AND AT THE REQUEST OF THE OLD man (his erratic Christian faith having been recovered now that he no longer had any other options), my mother begrudgingly allowed him to procure the services of a healer in the hopes that he would in turn procure the services of the Almighty Himself, who would then, properly procured, reach down from the heavens and rub out that cancer smear.

This would explain why, for a series of afternoons and evenings before my mother succumbed, the ubiquitous Reverend Phipps sat at her bedside, reading passages from the Bible out loud, making the sign of the cross on her forehead with holy (canola) oil, and peppering his language with short, sharp jabs of his own peculiar dialect of Church-sanctioned gibberish.

*"Yee-ya-yee!"* Reverend Phipps said, poking my mother's forehead with an unctuous finger. *"Yagga-yagga-yo!"*

*"Gunky-stunky-funky-munky!"* my mom responded, but only after Reverend Phipps had insisted she do so (she wasn't too keen on the idea of prayer languages). *Gunky-stunky* was her half-hearted way of agreeing with the *yee-ya* stuff.

Who knows what God thought of it. Not much, I would say, as her headaches continued.

Undaunted, Reverend Phipps's next play was to accuse my mother of having done something wrong to bring the smear upon herself.

"Many times disease has its origin in a sin we have not acknowledged," Reverend Phipps said. "It's God's way of getting our attention."

"Couldn't He have just used a burning bush?"

"No, Sister Margie, He couldn't. Otherwise He would have used a burning bush."

Reverend Phipps then grilled Mom over secret sins she might not have confessed that were making cancer in her brain. From what her diary said, a significant amount of time was wasted on this, but outside of her trysts with the Maytag (these were frowned upon, but were ultimately deemed not a cause as she hadn't started doing that until well after her headaches had become chronic), they could not come up with anything else.

"Gotta be the Devil then, Mrs. Horvath," Reverend Phipps said. "He's putting on a full court press here, and he wants to score a touchdown in your end zone."

"I thought it was God trying to get my attention."

"Obviously you thought wrong. It's Satan."

Deftly switching gears, Reverend Phipps started casting out demons of brain cancer, spending the better part of the next two hours kicking his legs around the room and bleating hymns, ostensibly so that the cancer demons, dislodged from the warm, witty comfort of my mother's brain, couldn't whiz around the room, bide their time until he was gone, and then simply jump back into her.

Phipps also lit a tiki torch.

"Fire of God! Fire of God!" Reverend Phipps screamed, swinging the torch in the air in what I assumed was an attempt to singe the demons' butts as they flew around the room. Can't say the torch had any effect on her condition, but it did make Phipps's paroxysmal dancing much more dazzling to the eye.

Even more so when it set the bedspread on fire.

This went on for days, with the only progress my mother saw being the addition of a couple of nosebleeds along with the loss of movement in her left leg, and so Reverend Phipps, becoming frustrated, took to pointing accusatory fingers at the ceiling and making pissy-sounding demands of God in non-gibberish.

"Your word says You heal our diseases, Lord," he said, "and we know You're not a liar, so do it already. I, as your anointed one, command this woman's deliverance in Your Name! You will heal her now, Jesus! Now, I say, now! Enough already! Now!"

Then, with a loud war whoop, Phipps picked up a bucket near the bed and began water-boarding my mother.

*Splash!* went the water. *Splashed!* went my mother's face.

"SISTER MARGIE, YOU ARE BAPTIZED AND YOU ARE HEALED!"

"Hooray," my mother sputtered.

"God and I have done our part; now it's on you. You've got to accept your healing or you're not gonna get it. SO ACCEPT!"

*SPLASH!*

"Ick. That water smells awful."

"ACCEPT, SISTER MARGIE!"

"Bleck. You didn't fill that bucket up in the laundry room, did you? Those pipes are rusted out—"

"—NEVER MIND...THAT! YOU HAVE TO YELL IT, YELL IT TO GOD! YELL IT TO THE DEVIL! ACCEPT YOUR HEALING! SAY IT!"

*SPLASH!*

"I (sputter) accept (gasp) my healing."

*SPLASH!*

"My eyes are burning—"

*SPLASH!*

"SAY IT LIKE THIS, MARGIE: I ACCEPT, LORD!"

*SPLASH!*

"SAY YOU ACCEPT!"

*SPLASH!*

"ACCEPT, CHILD OF GOD! ACCEPT, SISTER!"

My mother, now soaked to the bone, raised her left hand.

"Yes!" Reverend Phipps shouted. "Raise that arm to God! An arm of victory to a God of victory!"

"This isn't an arm of victory. I just want a favor."

"I know, Margie. The water. I'm sorry about that—"

"Forget about the water, Reverend."

"What's the problem then?" Phipps said. "Am I going too fast? I know I can be like a kid cramming all his coins in a candy machine at once, but what can I say? God moves fast; I move fast, and you gotta keep up! The quicker I get the words out, the quicker you can accept them and God will do what we want."

"No, I think you're going at a fine speed, Pastor, but what I would like is for you to take a timeout here and ask the Lord to help me with something."

"Like what? Wait, don't tell me. Those pesky medical bills. You want God to pay them. Now that's faith, sister Margie, and I love it! Think ahead and think big. Health *and* money. Why shouldn't you have both?"

"That's not what I want either."

"What else is there? Peace like a river? Joy like a fountain? What is it that you want me to do?"

My mother cleared her throat and wiped water out of her eyes.

"Just let me go."


Where was I during all of this? Front row, center stage, in the Horvath family beanbag at the foot of the bed.

I got to watch as Reverend Phipps jumped and danced and screamed and gibbered and accused and bitched and whooped and splashed water. I even got to help some—though I should probably say right off that my desire to be of assistance ended as most of my endeavors do.

What did I do wrong? Well, if Phipps hadn't been such a stupendous asshole, then nothing that should have been that big of a deal.

For starters, I offered my own tongues phrases in the hopes of lending some extra power to Phipps's *yee-yas* and my mother's *funky-munkys,* only to find myself shushed as my *gorzy-morzys* were said to be "interrupting the flow of the Spirit." (I was also told my tongues phrases were nonsense: "*Gorzy-morzy* is baby babbling, Frankie; this isn't a game," Reverend Phipps said.) Next, I filled up Phipps's baptismal bucket with rusty, orange water from the laundry sink (only because I was pissed over the rejection of my *gorzy-morzys*; I had no idea he was going to dump the water all over my dying mother's head). Third, while it's true I was the one who set the bed on fire (sending my mother into hellish shrieks of terror and the old man charging into the bedroom to dive on top of her) when the tiki torch I was ordered to hold, as Reverend Phipps relit it, slipped from my sweaty hands, I think this can be, at most, only half my fault as clearly our roles should have been reversed in that situation. Anyway, for the grand finale, I bawled upon hearing my mother's wish for the end, and then, for an encore, threw up on Phipps's shoes.

This prompted him to broach the possibility that I myself might be possessed with a demon and that the above incidents were this demon's attempts to sabotage my mother's healing, but Mom set him straight.

"Oh, there's no demon, you can trust me on that one," she said. "That's one hundred and ten percent Horvath right there."


In the end, Reverend Phipps, at my mother's behest, agreed to scale his grand design down to a simple prayer that she do nothing more than survive to my seventeenth birthday, and lo and behold, she did. She even made it two days beyond, and passed a large kidney stone along the way.

Miracles! Coincidences!

"I *told* you I am his anointed one," Reverend Phipps said to my mother, holding her hand on the morning of my birthday. "I even prayed for a couple extra days for you in case you might want them."

"I don't, but thanks anyway," my mother said, pulling her hand away.

This was true. She didn't want any extra time. What she did want was to say "Happy Birthday" to me and then float away to Eternity. But after checking into hospice later that day and ingesting a bunch of morphine, she could only manage to croak, "Happig berfik, Froggie," before losing the power of speech and laying there pointlessly for another forty-five hours.

And boy, did her head hurt.

# 6

I'M OUT OF THE ELEVATOR AND STANDING BY THE STAIRWAY DOOR. DANICA has not arrived, but I think I can hear her coming. Given the speed of her steps, either she's not aware this is a race or she's quite a bit out of shape.

Regardless, I win, and man does that ever feel good. Maybe it's a sign, a portent, an augury. The beginning of big changes. Sometimes that's all it takes: winning a little something here and there. Then the dam breaks, then lots of winning.

It would be nice if this could be the beginning of big changes. I am sick and tired of waiting for big changes, and I'm more than ready for lots of winning.

I've already given the lobby a good once-over. No sign of Sparky. I'm thinking he's gotta be out by the car. It's not like I wasn't listening when he said he wanted to go home.

The reason I'm still in the lobby as opposed to outside grabbing him by the scruff of the neck is because I want to wait for Danica so I can keep an eye on her.

I also want her to know she lost the race.

"Well, he's not on the stairs!" Danica pants, racing out of the stairway door. "How did you get down here so fast?"

"The elevator is quicker," I say, my chest swelling up with pride.

"Not if there are a bunch of stops along the way," she says. "You got lucky."

"And about time, too," I say.

"So is he here?"

"Nope. Not in the lobby either."

"Oh no!" Danica says, taking off for the front door. "He could be anywhere then!"

"Yeah, he could be," I say before starting slowly after her.

I'd like to stick behind a moment or two longer and enjoy my win and all the delectable future possibilities it might be hinting at, but I guess that's not the sort of thing Greatness does. Greatness also probably doesn't, when searching for missing children, linger behind Jane Fonda lookalikes so as to stare at their hindquarters.

# 7

WHILE IT'S TRUE THE DEATH OF MY MOTHER WAS INITIALLY DEVASTATING, what eventually brought me through was the realization that her passing qualified as a considerable hardship for me, and that this adversity could prove to be the impetus I needed to propel me to heights I never could have reached had she remained alive.

I now had inspiration, a driving force. I could perform great deeds in honor of my dead mother. It all made sense: her death was necessary for my transformation into the Great Horvath.

How many stories of great men had I read where they had suffered the death of a loved one, in particular their mother, at a young age? Lincoln lost his at nine. Beethoven at sixteen. Toss Michelangelo's hat into the ring, and don't forget Da Vinci's beloved stepmother bought it when he was but a boy as well.

Then there's Proust the Bear. His mama bear had been killed by grouchy brown bear spies when he, Proust, was but a cub (and Darius, his papa bear, died of a broken heart soon after). I know we're talking cartoons again, but at this sorrowful time of my life I didn't make the distinction between reality and make-believe, and, when seen in terms of what these great men (and bear) had become, it was obvious that they never would have done much of anything had their mothers remained among the living—a hard truth I now had to face. Whether I liked it or not, my mother's death was a necessary sacrifice for the greater good, which was (and is) me, and although it took me some time, weeks even, I finally learned to accept and embrace it.

Thanks, Mom.

## 8

HERE'S A SURPRISE: SPARKY IS NOT OUT BY THE CAR. AND ANOTHER: HE'S nowhere in sight. I thought for sure he would be sitting on the hood, arms folded, pouting.

For the first time, I'm a little concerned about this. Maybe I shouldn't have stood around waiting for Danica and relishing the outcome of the race (and her ass), but I honestly didn't think there was anything to worry about. Sparky doesn't know Berry, Indiana all that well, and although my campaign to keep him sluggish in mind and thick in body has been a smashing success in so many ways, he can't be dumb enough to think home is right around the corner. He has to have some awareness of geography, time, and distance, right?

The good news is it doesn't take us long to pick up his trail.

"Mr. Horvath. This gentleman says he saw a kid run down here," says Danica, standing next to some guy who is nodding and pointing down an alley.

And it is here that a thought occurs to me: this might not be a race or a search at all, but a trap. Perhaps Sparky never slipped out of the upstairs office at all. I never saw him leave. Because he hadn't made it past me and wasn't behind me when I looked for him, I assumed he had snuck out and gone downstairs to the car, but it could be he didn't take off at all. Maybe there are trap doors and false walls or something, and one of the other Epistemological Emendationists leapt out from someplace hidden as I was lusting over Danica and snatched Sparky away before vanishing back through the floor or the wall or wherever. Maybe this alley search is the setting for the kind of trap where I get bonked on the head, shoved into a waiting car, and whisked away to the middle of nowhere, left behind with only a note that goes like this:

*We have the boy. You will never see him again. Do not go to the police. Do not come looking for him. We will be watching.*

In fact, you know what? This is *precisely* what's happening. Gotta be. What else would you expect Satanists to do? Not kidnap kids when they get the chance? Not bonk someone on the head and leave them in the middle of nowhere? What's the point of being a Satanist if you don't do these things every now and then?

And speaking of points, what's the point of having a 9mm stuffed down the front of your pants if, when it seems high time you used it, you forget it's there in the first place?


Once we're far enough down the alley to where nobody can see us, I draw my nine, and oh, do I ever draw it. Waves and waves of excellent feelings flood through me as I point the gun at Danica, who is leading the way.

"Get down on the ground!" I say.

Danica turns around. Her eyes go wide. "You can't be serious," she says.

"Sure I can," I say. "And I am. Very." To underscore this, I wave the gun around very seriously. "Now where the hell is my son?"


You might think that an Epistemological Emendationist, being of similar mind and attitude as the original rebel Lucifer, would become rather spunky and insolent if a gun were put to her head. You know, swearing and hissing and daring me to shoot her while calling all manner of demonic entities to come to her aid.

Not so with Danica. She's on her knees, weeping quietly as I have promised her that if she screams for help or cries too loudly, I will blow her pretty little brains all over the alley walls.

If things are what they seem here, then it sure seems like she believes me, which is nice. It's also nice to be pleaded with between sobs and whines and sniffs.

"The sooner you start talking, the sooner I don't shoot you in the face. Now where is he, devil-whore?" I say, with as much simmering menace as I can muster. I figure this will be more effective than going in a bombastic direction. Simmering menace is a sign you're one cool customer, and one hundred and ten percent capable of blowing pretty little brains all over alley walls.

And I am. I swear to Christ I am.

"How (*sob*) could (*shiver*) I know that?" Danica says, then hiccups, which is a problem.

Sobs, shivers, shakes, whines, and sniffs are one thing; a hiccup is something else. One, it's adorable. Two, it's sort of sexy. I know it's stupid, but I sorta want to put my gun away and ask her to dinner. Pretty girl hiccups slay me.

"Don't play games," I say, my voice becoming considerably less menacing. "I know how you people operate. You kidnapped my boy."

"Why would we do something like that?"

"Because that's what Satanists do," I explain. "Rape virgins and kidnap kids and sacrifice them and drink their blood and all that crazy shit."

Danica sighs, and though I'm no expert in interpreting such things, if pressed to guess, I'd have to say it's of the *not again* variety. "Nothing could be further from the truth," she says. "We don't hurt people outside of self-defense and we would never harm children. They are the purest magic and the most precious and exalted form of life there is."

"Oh, get real. Children, virgins, the infirm, old ladies and their pets. You harm everybody."

It dawns on me that I really don't know this for sure. I am retreating back into stereotype, what I was told in Sunday School, the occasional mass market horror novel, and that Tom Hanks movie where he blows up his neighbor's house. To be honest, I wasn't expecting what I just heard.

"No. All our rituals and practices conform to every conceivable law. If you would just put the gun away and accompany me upstairs I could show you some literature that would disabuse you of these fabrications that have been forced upon you by the mainstream media and intolerant Christian culture."

"Not until you tell me where my son is."

"I already told you, I don't know where he is. In case you haven't noticed, I have been trying to help you find him."

"Or maybe you've been leading me down an alley so you can bonk me on the head and leave me for dead in the middle of nowhere while you take my son and do God knows what to him!"

"That makes absolutely no sense," Danica says. "We don't do things like that."

"You lie!" I say, my confidence finally beginning to rally. Maybe the power of her hiccups are wearing off. Maybe I am about to overcome them. "Gimme back my son!" I scream, reaching back into my past to channel the violin screech of my old drama teacher.

In answer to this, Danica goes back to the well for another hiccup, but it's much more like a burp this time, which is neither adorable nor sexy and therefore ineffective. Yes, it's beginning to feel like I've got the wind at my back again, and, to this much more gastric singultus, I smile.

"Not even your hiccups can save you, bitch-demon!" I snarl.

But then I am interrupted.


By music. From my phone. Which is ringing.

Oh, man. Not now.

"Eye of the Tiger" intruding on your day when you're in line at the grocery store, out for a Sunday drive, or raking leaves is fine. "Eye of the Tiger" when you're trying to keep your wits about you as you hold a pistol to a young Jane Fonda lookalike's head while you fend off her gorgeous eyes and hiccups—well, it can shift whatever wind you'd been thinking was at your back to something approaching gale-force right in your face.

Suddenly, I feel like a dork, and dorks don't do anything with guns.

Danica, hearing the song as well, is rising to her feet, and from the look on her face she also seems of the opinion I'm now a dork who won't do anything with a gun.

"Hey now," I say, backing up a step. "W-watch it."

I do my best to right the ship by keeping the gun on her with one hand while slapping at the phone in my pocket with the other, hoping against hope that I'll hit the button that shuts the phone off—but of course my smacks only succeed in turning up the volume.

The control, the menace, the power I'd felt coursing through me seconds ago has all but vanished thanks to this unjust turn of events. If I were to call Danica a "devil-whore" or "bitch-demon" now, I'd probably sound like a wuss.

"Okay," Danica says. "Is this a joke? Did the Rev put you up to this?"

"Who's the Rev?" I say, shrinking back further.

"That gun's not even real, is it?" Danica says.

"It sure as crap is!" I say, cocking and un-cocking the hammer. "See?"

"Uh, don't take this the wrong way, but I think I'm gonna go now," Danica says, turning. "And if this isn't one of the Rev's pranks, you've got about two seconds before I call the—"

But then she is interrupted.


By more music: a single voice singing from the far end of the alley. I know that voice. You know that voice. It's the same little boy voice we've been listening to all day.


Peering into the shadows at the end of the alley, I can just make out Sparky standing on his tiptoes as he sings softly in front of a small window.

To be honest, I can't decide whether I'm relieved to find him or over-whelmed once more with a yoke I hadn't noticed was so heavy until I'd thought it taken from me. Part of me wishes Sparky hadn't turned up, but the other part of me, the talking part, says this: "Oh, thank God."

Danica, still with me for some reason, arches an eyebrow. As much as I might like to, I'll probably never be able scare her with a gun again unless I do go ahead and shoot her a little. Nobody arches an eyebrow at somebody with a gun unless they aren't scared of them anymore.

Neither do they attempt to correct the verbiage of the gunman.

"Hail Satan," she says.

I'm gonna be the bigger person this time and let that one slide, though, like most people, I don't like being corrected.

Also, "Hail Satan" sounds ridiculous.


Taking care to mask the sound of our footsteps, we creep up on Sparky as he sings, as though approaching Pan at play in a quiet wood.

Why we are sneaking I have no idea. Maybe there's some instinct in adults that causes them to advance with caution so as not to disturb children when they are singing alone. Why Danica is following suit and not tearing down the other end of the alley to alert the police is either yet another testament to the spellbinding power of singing children, or she's going above and beyond to show just how different Epistemological Emendationists are from other religious peoples.

*You can make me get on my knees and put a gun to my head and I'll still help you find your stupid kid. You think one of those Presbyterian dickheads would do that?*

Or it could very well be that this is still part of an elaborate Satanist scheme that I am not working out fast enough, that will end with a bonk to my head and my body dumped in the middle of nowhere.


We're close enough now to hear that Sparky is singing along with a Doris Day recording playing through an open window a level above the alley floor. Here's the song:

*Que sera, sera*
*Whatever will be, will be*

And here's Sparky:

*I like to go POOOOP and PEEEE*
*Que sera, se—*

And then *he* is interrupted.

By me, by Danica…and by a forty-something-year-old Asian lady perched on a toilet, screaming, very much aware that she is being ogled by the three of us standing outside what has turned out to be a bathroom window.

Which means it's probably time to get going.

# 9

THE THREE OF US TEAR OUT OF THE ALLEY AND STOP AT THE MOUTH. MY BIT of stomach heaves in and out, Danica is holding a stitch in her side, and Sparky is coughing like, well, a little old man.

As we catch our breath, we look at each other. What to say? Kind of uncomfortable here.

I consider apologizing for the gun business, but I'm sort of hoping Danica's forgotten about it in all the excitement that followed. One thing that might help would be to figure out a way to tuck the gun back into my waistband without her seeing.

Feigning additional fatigue (not really all that feigned), I back up against the doleful red brick of the Lawrence P. Fenwick Building and angle my body away from Danica, sliding the gun down the small of my back and—

"No way, Mr. Horvath!" Danica says. "You drop that right this instant or I'll scream bloody murder!"

Sigh. Bloody murder. Just like my beloved wife used to scream.

Defeated, I drop the gun. Danica runs over and kicks it down the alley. Then, with her hands on her hips, she shakes her head in disbelief before looking at two bald, skeletal men who have just appeared next to her.

The men are dressed in all black, like roadies, but I've got a sneaking suspicion that's about the last thing they are.

"All right, boys. What are you waiting for?" Danica says to the men. "Get them!"

# PART SIX

*There I was, twenty-five years old, and like so many fathers before me, my life was over.*

# 1

WE'RE BACK IN. SPARKY, ME, AND DANICA MAKES THREE. WELL, FIVE, IF YOU count the two goons from the alley, but I'd rather not. They just got here.

I must say, getting back in the offices of the Church of Epistemological Emendation feels like an even greater accomplishment than getting in the first time. This is because of all the crafty manipulation (begging) I had to employ in order to convince Danica to ignore the criminality of the incidents in the alley and against all logic give the boy and I another chance.

All we had to do the first time was walk in the door.

The second time has not come without a price as I am no longer in possession of my nine, and to further foot the bill I had to yield to a thorough search of my person, which was not pleasant. If it had been Danica conducting the search it might have been pleasant, but the goons were doing the honors and, with all the attractiveness of Irish potato famine victims, conducted the search with nightsticks and penlights; if they left stones unturned, it was at the molecular level.

I protested to certain aspects, such as the numerous sharp jabs at my scrotal region, but Danica said, "You can leave anytime you want. You're the one who thought it was a good idea to bring a gun here in the first place."

I protested again, reminding her that Satanism's reputation precedes itself, only to have that painfully underscored when the second Epistemological Emendationist goon covered his nightstick with plastic wrap and barked at me to drop my pants and grab my ankles.

Naturally, I found such a demand hilarious and laughed accordingly (and fearfully): "Ha ha ha."

"Ooooooookay, weirdo." Danica said. "Careful, boys. He might actually have something up there."

After my rectal probe, which I took like a man, I was allowed to join Sparky on the nice comfy couch and was handed a stack of pamphlets.

I have been informed I will not be allowed to proceed any further in my quest until I digest them, and that could take some time. There's a lot of tiny print on these pamphlets.

I mentioned to Danica I was already familiar with most of Satanism's beliefs, even quoting the admittedly attractive one about the public obliteration of bothersome people, but I was ordered to read anyway.

"There's a lot more to it than that," Danica said.

So here I am: reading, reminding myself the important thing is that we got back inside, that getting back inside is quite the achievement.

I should be in cuffs in the back of a police cruiser. I should be pondering my impending arraignment, guessing as to the number of years it will be before I breathe free air again, and totting up all the great men who have overcome felony convictions. Needless to say, there aren't many.

I wouldn't dare say this out loud, but what the Church of E has done could be labeled an excellent example of Christian charity. I can tell you right now that if I'd pulled this stunt at Little Hat Pentecostal, I would have been hauled away and prosecuted to the limit of the law.


Not able to fully get around this irony, I asked Danica why she hadn't brought in the authorities. (Note: I did not frame things in terms of Christian forbearance.)

"If it were up to me, we'd have torn you limb from limb in accordance with our laws, but it wasn't my call," Danica said.

"Whose call was it?" I asked.

"The boss."

"Ah, right. Mephistopheles. Old Gooseberry. Mr. Scratch."

Danica snorted. "You're such a tool. I'm talking about the boss of the church. The *Reverend*."

"You guys really have reverends?"

"If we feel like it."

"So why did the Reverend let me back in?"

"Beats me. But if it makes you feel better, this is not the first time some whacko has come charging in here with a gun."

"Maybe if you called the cops every now and then to haul some of these gun-nuts away, they wouldn't keep showing up," I offered.

"Do you want me to call the cops, Mr. Horvath?"

"No, thanks. Just on the ones after me."

"It's a deal. Now shut the hell up and read."


# 2


ONCE MORE, AND NOT FOR THE LAST TIME, BACK TO THE PAST.

My wife was sort of screaming.

It looked like she really wanted to scream sans the sort of—her mouth was wide open and trembling, much like the Asian Toilet Princess had been at the sight of Sparky, Danica, and me—but the sound coming out was the same unnerving sound the old man makes when he's putting his thoughts together.

You know: *"Hee! Hee! Hee!"*

Considering how I can't stand that sound, I wasn't really attuned to what my wife was going through. Being her loving husband and all, I suppose I should have been in a state of mental and spiritual anguish commensurate with her physical pain. I should have been contemplating the Doctrine of Original Sin and the mystery of how, via the seemingly trifling whoopsie of the ill-advised consumption of a single piece of fruit, all women must now endure the cruel and unusual punishment of childbirth. I should have rushed to her side and clutched the bed sheets, yelled at the doctors to help—*Oh God, do something!*—torn my fingernails out, slit my own throat, whatever. Instead, I was watching the wife from the corner of the room with a numb, hollow dread. The nurses would mistake this for poise and courage and tell me multiple times throughout the birth how impressed they were with me.

To which I can only say I'm glad they were better at the baby delivery business than they were at divining the mood behind the blank expression of a deeply resentful father-to-be. One of the nurses was so blown away with my demeanor she had taken time out from tending to my wife to get me a cup of water. If she had known what was really going on inside my head, she probably wouldn't have gotten me something to drink. She probably would have stared daggers at me.

What was bringing on the numb, hollow dread was the series of memories my brain was disinterring, rotted cadavers long thought forgotten and gleefully marched through the thoroughfares of my soul, a procession of ridicule, a parade of disgust, created by me for me.

I was remembering my twelfth birthday with the old man and the human pyramid; I was remembering how he had damned me to a life of no consequence; I was remembering all the vows I had made to beat him, vows that I now saw as naïve and foolish. I was remembering everything that had happened since then, the monument to zilch my life had been, and how I had betrayed that proud, defiant boy who had dared to reject the meaningless life that had been thrust into his face as his inheritance—all while my father's greatest wish came true before my eyes, all while hearing his horrible wheezy-hees come out of my wife, as though his spirit had somehow possessed her to mock me with his victory, which at that moment felt to be complete, absolute, and unbreakable.

There I was, twenty-five years old, and like so many fathers before me, my life was over.

## 3

SO HOW DID THINGS CONTINUE TO GO SO WRONG FOR ME AFTER HIGH SCHOOL? How did I not find a way to overcome the trials before me and take my rightful place as the Great Horvath?

For starters—and raise your hand if this sounds familiar—I went to college.

And to no one's amazement I'm sure, not the sort of school one associates with the molding of great minds.

As middling grades tend to do, mine had garnered tepid interest at best from most of the universities across the fruited plain, while a proficiency in any sort of athletic or musical skill had eluded me. Thus, with the majority of my fellow Kokomo County comrades-in-blah narcotically preparing themselves for the Life Not-So Fantastic—everlasting minimum wage edition—and with my father nudging me toward an entry-level spot at the hardware store in the Hose and Tubing department, I unhappily realized that if I was going to wage successful war against all mortal and spiritual forces conspiring to keep me of low station, I would have to accept reality and attempt matriculation to a lesser school.

The good news is, once I lowered my standards to a notch below community colleges and a tick above ventriloquism seminaries and badminton academies, I discovered a school willing to give me a chance, a school I could practically see from my father's backyard, a school as undistinguished as myself (though no less ambitious); a school that was tickled to death I would want to join what they called, "Their little engine that did and was doing."

That school? The barely accredited Gremio of rural Midwestern colleges: The Southeastern Kokomo County Institute of Technology and Pickle Farm.


A little story about SKCITPF:

Like other universities, it interviews its prospective students. Unlike these other universities, it does not conduct these interviews on campus in the offices of undergraduate admissions, nor in the comfort of its more desirable recruits' living rooms.

Waffle House is the preferred location for the SKCITPF admissions team, though rumor has it, for the candidates they aren't too bullish about, the interviews are conducted in the parking lot.

For the record, I got to go inside. I even got to sit in a booth.

★

The admissions team was something of a motley crew. It consisted of Elden, a scabrous, wind-burned septuagenarian in overalls and wading boots; Clarell, a rotund, beehive-coiffed, bespectacled woman in a dress patterned after Andy Warhol's *Campbell's Soup Cans*; and two unidentified SKCITPF students, boy and girl, painfully constricted by matching school sweat suits that, in addition to being the color of canned spinach, appeared to be roughly toddler-sized.

The interview itself wasn't altogether grueling. I was asked almost nothing in the way of my personal history other than to confirm my name was indeed "Horvath" and not "Horsebath." My Strother Martin transcript, which I was surprised to see among us, was not pored over line by line but used by Clarell Campbell Soup to vigorously flag down our waitress for more toast. A speech I had prepared about my plans for greatness was interrupted by periodic winces and moans from Elden Overalls, who eventually cut me off by putting his greasy napkin over my mouth just as I was moving from my future distinguished tenure as a presidential cabinet appointee to my plan to spend my golden years touring with a Woody Herman-esque big band.

"Boy," Elden Overalls croaked, showing me his last remaining tooth. "We cud keer less 'bout all dat gunk. You git in-tu ar skule, and I gare-un-tee yule get yore edgy-kayshun. Wut we wunna nowe, wuts most impor-ent to us, iz how yew feel 'bout pikklez."

"To be honest, sir," I said in a small voice, astonished these were the people SKCITPF thought were its best hope to attract students. "I-I don't really know."

"Well dat, boy, iz sum'thin yu gone hav tu figger out," Elden said. "At 'dis skule, pipple nowe wut dey tink 'bout pikklez."

"As you're already aware, Mr. Horsebath," Clarell Campbell Soup interposed after swallowing her entire side of hash browns in one bite. "We're a developing university that has to keep tuitions low so as to compete with the big boys. Our innovative work with pickling is a primary source of funding. It's one of the main reasons why we've managed to keep accreditation."

"Bes got-dam pikklez in the hol' got-dam state of Indee-anna!"

"Hush, El, you're gonna scare the boy off," Clarell said, now pouring alarming amounts of strawberry syrup into her coffee.

"Who are you accredited by again?" I judiciously thought to ask.

"That's confidential, Mr. Horsebath. I could tell you but then I'd have to kill you. Ha Ha. Now, you were saying something about a clarinet?" Clarell said.

"Um, there's not much to say, ma'am," I replied, wondering if Elden Overalls might tackle me and sink his tooth into my neck if I tried to make a run for it. "I play the clarinet."

"Gosh, isn't that something?" Clarell said, nodding to the boy and girl students whose contributions to the proceedings had so far been to stare unblinkingly at the twin lakes of ketchup they had submerged their eggs in. "Isn't that something, kids?"

One of the kids, the girl, broke her scowl at an insolent yolk that had refused to yield to the moat of tomato goo around it, put her eyes on me, and sneezed.

"Maybe you could put a little band together, Mr. Horsebath," Clarell said, holding my transcript to the girl's nose as a tissue. "We like music."


Considering the school's name (and that interview), perhaps the oddest thing about SKCITPF was how ordinary it was. The hope that I would be a lone wolf of the mind with only my burgeoning wits to ward off legions of Elden Overalls' torch-bearing, pitchfork-wielding pickle hicks was dashed the first day of orientation. A quick look around the room revealed a bunch of eighteen-year-olds in circumstances identical to mine: students of unremarkable academic record and limited financial means, rejected by almost every other college of note. All of them, like me, looking to parlay strong starts here into transfers to better universities and, with a bit of luck, better lives.

Even the pickle part wasn't as bizarre as I expected. Every student had a partial scholarship that involved some kind of job with the enterprise. Some worked in the cucumber fields on the outskirts of campus, some in the pickling sheds nearby.

My job turned out to be the least interesting of all: I worked in the call center, taking pickle orders for five hours twice a month.

I wish I could say the experience taught me a practical thing or two about working in the real world, about how to interact with people on a professional level, or at least given me an amusing pickle story or two, but all it did was help me slowly, almost imperceptibly, lose heart.


Little by little, semester to semester, year to year, my resolve eroded.

My plans to earn top-notch grades and transfer to a better school never panned out. To my flourishing disenchantment, I found that even with a change of scenery, even with my mother dead and the old man out of sight, I could not reach a higher plane of accomplishment. Regardless of effort, attitude, or prayer, my place in this world simply would not budge, and over time, as mediocrity established itself in every facet of my collegiate career, the weight of it began to wear me down and I was forced to switch over to the miserable task of figuring out how to be okay with it all, how to forget the promises I had made to myself and silence the voice still alive in the core of my being, telling me without ceasing that I was meant to do something extraordinary in this world, that I was intended for more in this life than what all the evidence screamed to the contrary.

That I was still to be the Great Horvath.


Days of frustration, these were. Days of confusion. Days of stupor, insentience, and fog.

That said, there was one notable development during this period. Even though these were the days I first lost heart, I did somehow manage to replace it with someone else's.

Believe it or not: Penny Turney's.

She, too, had matriculated to SKCITPF and had, against all reason, decided I was the cream in her coffee, the salt in her stew.

Another surprise: she also decided the same thing about Jesus Christ. Starch in her collar, lace in her shoe, captain and crew. Sometime after that disastrous prayer session we'd had back in high school, Penny up and became a Christian, a Pentecostal just like me.

I wish I could say the seed for Penny's salvation had first been planted in that prayer session she had fled in terror from, that I had played an unheralded, but invaluable role in her eventual conversion, but one thing she remained adamant about to her dying day was that my actions did more to delay it than anything else.

So despite my lost heart, my lost way, my determination in shambles, staggering through what would be the first of many fogs in my life, Penny Turney unaccountably fell in love with me. And I was pretty okay with that. Wandering in fog isn't so bad if there's somebody there to wander with you.

Especially if that someone is known for putting penises in her mouth.

## 4

As I sit here, reading devilish brochures, Sparky is drawing with pens on some printer paper Danica has given him and, glancing over, I see he's sketched—abysmally, I might add—what appears to be a bright, sunny field, along with a man and a small boy holding hands and smiling wide.

How boring.

As for myself, I am about one third of the way through the pamphlet stack. Here's what I've learned so far:

First, there are the Six Emendationist Edicts.

1. The Church of E stands for the ENJOYMENT of the ENTIRETY of life, NOT the EVIL of self-EXPROPRIATON!

2. THE CHURCH OF E STANDS FOR ENERGETIC ESSENTIAL BEING, NOT ENERVATING, ENFEEBLING FANTASIZING!

3. THE CHURCH OF E STANDS FOR THE EMBRACE OF EXACT TRUTH, NOT THE ENTRAPMENT OF DELUSION!

4. The Church of E stands for **ESTEEM** FOR THOSE WHO PROVE THEIR WORTHINESS, **NOT EMOTION EXHAUSTED** ON WHINERS!

5. The Church of E stands for an **EYE** FOR AN **EYE, NOT** USELESS **EMPATHY**!

6. The Church of E stands for **ENDOWMENT** TO THE **EFFECTUAL, NOT ENSLAVEMENT** TO MENTAL PARASITES!

Next, there are the Eight Emendationist Laws of Existence.

1. **SHUT UP!** DO NOT OFFER THOUGHTS OR GUIDANCE TO OTHERS UNLESS THEY ASK!

2. **SHUT UP!** DO NOT COMPLAIN ABOUT YOUR LIFE TO OTHERS UNLESS THEY ASK YOU TO UNBURDEN YOURSELF!

3. WHEN ON ANOTHER'S PROPERTY, DISPLAY PROPER **ESTEEM** OR **ELSE** GET OUT!

4. IF A TRAVELER ON YOUR PROPERTY AGGRAVATES YOU, TEAR HIM LIMB FROM LIMB!

5. DO NOT ATTEMPT TO MATE WITH ANYTHING UNLESS YOU ARE CLEARLY GIVEN THE GO-AHEAD!

6. LEAVE LITTLE CHILDREN ALONE!

7. LEAVE ANIMALS ALONE UNLESS YOU ARE HUNGRY OR MUST DEFEND YOURSELF!

8. WHEN TRAVELING ON COMMON GROUND, KEEP TO YOURSELF. IF SOMEONE INFLICTS THEMSELVES UPON YOU, TELL HIM TO MIND HIS OWN BUSINESS. IF HE REFUSES, BASH HIS BRAINS IN!

Finally, we have the Seven Emendationist Evils.

1. Un-**ENLIGHTENMENT**!

2. Un-**EVENNESS**!

3. Un-**EXACTING**!

4. *In-EFFICACIOUSNESS!*

5. *In-EFFECTUAL EGOISM!*

6. *Anti-EMANCIPATION!*

7. *Anti-ESTHETIC!*


# 5

BACK TO THE BIRTH.

In addition to the awful pageant of depressing memories, I did have another reason to keep my composure as Penny pushed out what would end up being our one and only son: the gaggle of Strother Martin High School students watching us through an observation window.

Leaving aside other concerns and troubling thoughts, I did not want to lose my cool in front of them, as they were already making fun of the wife's wheezy-hees, and I just knew they were looking for any pretext to do the same to me. I'm not proud to admit it, but even with my teenage years well in the rearview, I was still scared to death of being mocked by high school students.

The reason the students were there to begin with was to fulfill the field trip requirement of their Sex Education class. The birth they were about to witness was the *coup de grâce*, the climax—if you'll pardon the pun—of the semester.

And the wife, as I've said, was having a rough go of it. This was why she had resorted to those wheezy-hees over what she had been doing prior: loud swearing punctuated with cries of woe. This was also why when the doctor pulled the sheet off her legs—so the students could see the crowning—she had pulled the sheet back, and, get this, emitted something like a giggle.

It seemed now that it was finally showtime, she didn't want these kids watching her anymore, and especially not the creepy doofus with the eyes as wide as sunny-side eggs and his nose mashed against the glass. Penny didn't want him to get one look at any part of her womanhood.

She even asked for him to be removed from the window.

To which one of the nurses said, "Hey, can we get rid of that kid?" One of the other nurses said, "I'm on it!" And nobody did anything.

That doofus so happened to be Fred Tecumseh Custer Hoover Jr., who, down the road, would end up with me in silverware design at Dagwood as a co-worker, a competitor.

Or, to be totally honest, my archenemy.

A couple of years ago, he came up with a fork with tines on both ends that was long in the middle like a spear.

He called it, "The Warrior."

It's not practical but it sells sells sells. Schoolboys love it.

Mothers love it too, because now they can get their schoolboys to eat almost anything they put on their plates.

The Warrior helped Fred win the Dagwood Corporation's Best Innovation in Design Award—the year I thought I had a good shot at winning it. It also helped Fred woo his wife, the runner-up to the Miss Indiana Pageant.

Odd what impresses girls sometimes.

On the other hand, The Warrior is an impressive piece of forkery.

I wish I'd thought of it.

As Fred would tell me during the Dagwood Christmas party that year, blitzed out of his mind on whiskey-fortified punch, still on cloud nine from receiving the Best Innovation in Design Award, he had never seen a vagina in real life until Sparky's birth.

For most of his teenage years he had been too shy to take his dates' pants off and had endured much derision and scorn for it, to the point where Fred had convinced himself that if something didn't change for him soon, sexual humiliation would ruin his life.

This was why he'd had his nose pressed against the window that day, waiting with bated breath to see my wife's vagina. He was hoping that by seeing it up close and personal in this unthreatening setting, his life would change. Like the rest of us, he was looking for a miracle.

"And bro, after seeing that shit with your kid coming out," Fred said. "I don't know, it just hit me! What the hell am I so scared of that thing for? That ain't no holy of holies! That thing is nasty!"

That was Fred's problem. He had been brought up to believe the vagina was divine and, like most gods, expected impossible things from him.

"That day changed my life, dudely," Fred said, bear-hugging me, lifting me off the ground. "Thank you."

To my own dying day I'll never understand it, but when the hospital offered Penny the chance to give birth in front of teenagers for educational purposes, she had fallen all over herself to sign up. She pooh-poohed my objections, even the ones made on what I'd thought had been pretty irrefutable grounds, such as the potential destruction of the sacredness of one of the most cherished moments in parenthood, as well as potentially bringing upon us the wrath of God, whom I felt was of the opinion kids didn't need to see this kind of stuff for educational purposes, but would, like everybody else in the thousands of years before the advent of Sex Ed, figure it out on their own.

"C'mon, hon," the wife had said. "These kids see sex only as something to satisfy lust and wield power over each other with. Together we can show them how beautiful and sanctified it is and how, through its proper use, life is brought into this world."

"Somehow I don't think they're going to get that message, babe," I'd said. "I think they're going to laugh, and I think we're risking God's disfavor by being indecent here."

"Oh, Frank. Don't be such a prude."

This from the girl who had steadfastly refused to put my penis in her mouth anymore once we'd gotten married.

"You know, sweetie," Penny had said the night of our honeymoon. "I think you were right after all. It is dirty."

"But sometimes it can be kind of fun, right?" I'd said. "Please?"

"No, not fun at all. I don't think God likes us doing it."

Therefore, it seems to me the blame for the events of that day, my wife's good intentions notwithstanding, fall squarely on her shoulders—by which I mean the giggling, swearing, and wheezy-heeing, but above all the tug of war between her and the nurses over the blanket covering her lower half that had prompted cascading waves of impudent laughter from the teenagers, something we'd both been desperate to avoid.

The view during the tug of war was as follows:

VAGINA! WOO!

No vagina...

VAGINA! WOO!

No vagina...

VAGINA! ACK! WITH PART OF A BABY'S GOOPY HEAD STICKING OUT!

The verbal exchange between the wife and the nurse during the struggle:

"Mrs. Horvath! Please!"

"*Hee!* No, stop, I don't—*hee!*—wanna!"

"You signed a form, Mrs. Horvath. You signed a form!"

"I—*hee!*—don't give a FUCKITY FUCK! *Hee!*"

"But you're cheating these kids!"

"Screw those little cockbags! OH GAWD! THIS HURTS SO BAAAAD!"

"Don't look now, ladies, but I think we've got a head!" the doctor interrupted.

At which point the wife relented, released her grip on the sheet, her vagina was revealed for all to see, and Fred T.C. Hoover Jr.'s life changed forever.

# 6

I'M DONE READING. THE SCARY FONT, THE E FETISH, EVERY ONE OF THE TOO many exclamation points, read and seen by me.

What a sad little religion.

They apparently don't even believe in an actual, honest-to-goodness entity called Satan. To the Epistemological Emendationists he is nothing more than a symbol, an idea, an excuse.

The rest?

GIMME! GIMME! GIMME! MINE! MINE! MINE! ME! ME! ME!

*That* is the best they could come up with?

It could be this pamphletry is nothing more than a front, a way to disarm the usual suspicions and allure all those enjoying the GIMME GIMME to keep going further.

Scientologists do this. They deny up and down all that stuff about space aliens and the billion-year contract, stressing nice, clean, confident living until you get past a certain point, and then they spring it on you. Mormons do this as well with their notion of becoming the god of your own planet (something that, in addition to being silly, also sounds like a pile of work).

I'm thinking it's gotta be the same thing here.

"No, there's no Satan," they say at the beginning. "It's all about being free to be what you want without the constraints of namby-pamby Judeo-Christian morality to bring you down with lame-o guilt!"

But later, when you've gone too far to turn back and have gotten used to doing whatever you want without the constraints of namby-pamby Judeo-Christian morality, they pull you aside.

"You know that business about there being no real Satan?" they say.

"Mmm-hmm," you respond. "No Satan."

"Well, we were kidding about that until we thought you were ready. There is a Satan."

"No kidding?"

"Yeah. AND HE'S RIGHT BEHIND YOU! "

"So what's your kid's name?" Danica says, looking up at us from her desk. To pass the time as she waits for me to finish the pamphlets and for her boss to get us out of her sight, she has been ferociously typing on her computer. About what I haven't the slightest clue. No blog post or email could require that much intensity. Whatever it is she's written, I want to read it. It must be hot stuff. Maybe about me. Or the boy.

"Uh, you gonna answer me there, Mr. Horvath? Or are you just gonna stare at me like my question blew your mind?"

"Er...Sparky...his name," I blurt, surprised and annoyed to be ripped out of my musing in such a discourteous fashion.

"The hell kind of a name is Sparky?" Danica asks.

"The hell kind of a name is any?" I say.

"Touché," Danica says. "Is Sparky the name on his birth certificate?"

"No, but it's what I've always called him," I say.

Danica chuckles. "I suppose it's cute."

"Cute?"

"Uh-huh. Cute cute cute."

Danica then regards the little old man. "How you doing there, Sparky?" she says. "What's your real name?"

Blushing, Sparky looks away, slumps his shoulders, and mumbles something inscrutable while poking holes in the paper he's been drawing on.

The drawing, by the way, has taken on morbid tones since last I checked. It still features the same father and son holding hands in a field, but what I had thought had been a friendly, warming sun was actually a destructive fireball that has set everything on the page ablaze. Additionally, the man's facial expression has taken on a different meaning. Upon further review, that wide-mouthed smile of his is much closer to a full-throated scream of agony. The only thing that has not changed is the child, who, even though the fire rages around him, is smiling wider than ever.

In contrast, Sparky does not resemble the happy boy in the drawing. He looks instead like he wants to crawl into the flames he drew and die.

For reasons I can't explain, I am seized by an urge to rip the paper out of Sparky's hand and yell at him: "Boy, stand up, look the lady in the eye, and answer her question!"

Sparky, at this command, would rise to his feet, look Danica in the eye without flinching, without fear, tell her his full name, that he was doing very well, and thank her for asking. He would then follow this with a slight bow before asking her politely but assertively how her day was going.

That's what I want him to do, but he's been too conditioned to do otherwise. No eye contact. Mumble. Slumped shoulders. The blush isn't something the wife or I ever demanded of him—as blushes either happen or they don't—but we've always been pleased to see them when they do. The anxious poking of the paper? A nice touch we never would have thought of.

It seems the kid's branching out on his own, expanding his repertoire, but I don't want that this time. What I want is for Sparky to surprise somebody. Danica, specifically, these goons standing beside us, me.

And so, unexpectedly overcome with the baffling desire to protect my son, I do something I've never done in the history of his life: I stand up and shield him. This one time I will defend him.

I puff up my chest as much as possible, put as much BOOM in my voice as I can manage, and roar the following, indignant and strong:

"MISS, HIS NAME IS MICHAEL JASPER HORVATH, AND HE IS THE ANTICHRIST!"

Danica arches her eyebrow again. "Good for him," she says and returns to her feral typing.

Maybe something about the boy. Maybe something about me.

8

AN HOUR AFTER SPARKY WAS BORN, THE WIFE WAS IN THE POSTPARTUM UNIT, laughing. She was no longer in pain; Fred T.C. Hoover Jr. was nowhere in sight; her vagina was hidden; and though her left breast was visible, it didn't seem to be that big of a deal because—*Oh, look at the baby!*

Maybe it was the endorphins coursing through her and being overwhelmed by feelings of pride, relief, and joy, but Penny seemed to think this was a great time to say some really dumb shit. Such as: "This was good. I'm glad those kids got to see this. I think they learned something about love and beauty today. Praise the Lord."

Some of the girls from the class were still in the room, having been given permission to ooh and goo over Sparky. Because of the inevitability of more nudity from my wife, none of the boys were.

Apparently, the Sex Ed ringleaders had decided that gazing at a goopy, baby-spitting vagina was one thing, seeing some bazoombas something else. So they had shoved all the boys back on the bus, where they remained with one of the male teachers, ready to go.

From what I overheard, they were playing a game most high school boys play when they are on a bus waiting to go someplace else: Grabass.

For my part, I was over in the corner, not playing Grabass (Grabassing yourself isn't much of a game). I had just gotten off the phone with the old man, who, after cursing the conjunctivitis that had kept him from being present for Sparky's birth, had wildly and stutteringly explained how proud he was of me; how absolutely thrilled he was that this, the moment he'd been waiting his whole life for—the only reason he could figure for my existence in the first place—had finally happened.

As you might imagine, I was still in a state of shock at finally being a recipient of my father's approval and was mulling the implications as I watched a televised college football halftime show featuring the Rock'em Sock'em Marchonaires. Looking back now, I would have to say they didn't really rock or sock much of anything—they sounded like all marching bands do (nerdy)—yet their music was still soothing to me somehow.

Nobody from the baby side of the room was paying me much mind. Between nurses coming and going and the wife's parents stopping by to ooh and goo along with the high school girls, I had been shunted to the side, and I was fine with that.

Until: "Frank, are you ever going to come over here and see your son?"

Pulling my attention away from a cathartic rendition of the Flintstones theme song, I saw that everybody had left the room but Penny, me, and the tiny human we'd made. The wife's eyes and smile were still fixed on Sparky, but her flat, cool voice was addressing me.

"If I didn't know any better I'd think you've been avoiding us," she said.

"Us" already? Taking sides against Daddy this soon?

I rose to my feet and reluctantly approached the bed.

"I guess I got lost in the shuffle. Your parents, the nurses, those girls—a lot of people, Pen."

"Uh-huh, huge crowd."

"Besides, honey," I said. "I didn't want to interfere with the vital mother-baby bonding window that experts say occurs during the first minutes after birth and is crucial to their emotional development."

"I know, and that was totally the right thing to do, Frank. I'm sure Reverend Phipps would approve of how you've handled everything so far."

Ho boy, and here we go.

Reverend Phipps had been holding a revival at Little Hat Pentecostal the past week, with the theme being the importance of a father's relationship to a son. This was something the wife had thought to be especially prophetic, seeing how we were about to have one, hence her mandate that I attend *every single goddamned meeting*.

"Michael? You want to see your daddy?" Penny said to the baby, kissing his forehead. "Now that he's decided to *grace* us with his presence? Now that I managed to *shame* him into doing it? Now that he *finally* wants to be a part of his son's life?"

"Pen, he's been alive for all of two hours—"

"Or would you like to make him wait like he's made us wait?"

To be clear, I never once hit my wife, despite there being a number of times I imagined doing extensive damage to her person. The method tantalizing to me at that moment involved gently removing the baby from her arms and then, while she lay there helplessly, tipping her bed out of the fourth story window and into oncoming traffic below.

I'm aware Christ speaks of murder done in fantasy as the same thing as committing the deed in reality, but that's easy for him to say, he never got married.

Rather than risk the judgment of God by reveling in images of my wife's defenestrated demise, I was, as usual, the bigger person. Mastering my pride, I bit my tongue, held out my arms, and behaved as though Penny had never stopped with the baby talk.

"Hand him over, love of my life," I said.

Penny smirked and held out my newborn son to me. Even then something didn't look quite right about him, but I chalked that up to the Ugly Baby Stage.

"Whatever, Frank," the wife said. "Try not to be a klutz—"

"WICKED! EVIL!"

I turned around.

Careening through the doorway, holding up a large wooden cross attached to a chain wrapped around his wrist was none other than Reverend Phipps.

"Uh, hey, Rev," I said, preparing myself for more stomach-churning fussery over Penny and the baby. But given the mad look in his eyes and the sweat pouring down his face, I got the distinct impression Phipps was not visiting to congratulate us on bringing forth another child of God into this world, nor did it seem he was about to remind me of my great responsibility as a father. Actually, he looked like an aquaphobe about to go down on the *Titanic*.

The wife, understandably, took the baby and covered herself up.

Still wobbling, trembling, Reverend Phipps staggered forward, cast googlie eyes at me, at Penny, and at our newborn son. Groaning, he then thrust out the cross and screamed, "T-THE S-SON OF PERDITION... RISES!"

# PART SEVEN

*Frankie, Frankie you need to call me back right away. The most wonderful, incredible thing has happened! Everything has changed! Everything! My life will never be the same and . . .*

# 1

OF THE TWO OF US, I WAS THE SKEPTICAL ONE. DESPITE MY LIFELONG ASSO-
ciation with Christianity in general and Pentecostalism in particular, I was
of the opinion the strange episode that had occurred in the postpartum
unit the day of my son's birth had been one of an exceptionally dubious
nature.

I was pretty sure Reverend Phipps had lost his mind or, at the very least,
gotten the wrong room.

The wife, as wives do, thought differently.

The following is the first talk we had about the incident, a month later,
as we washed dishes together after suffering through an inedible green
bean casserole (my unholy work) for dinner.

The wife was scrubbing the dishes, and I was in charge of taking the
scrubbed dishes and putting them in the dishwasher. Sparky—not yet
known as Sparky, but just as Michael, was in our room, asleep in his crib.

The stage set, off we go:

First, me, with a salad bowl in my hands: "Phipps was drunk, Penny.
Got into some expired communion grape juice or something. It's probably not the first time."

I bent over and nimbly put the salad bowl into the dishwasher.

"Reverend Phipps doesn't drink. He never drinks," the wife said, handing
me a scrubbed plate.

"Okay, he finally lost his marbles then." (Plate in the dishwasher.)

"He's not crazy, either."

"How do you know?"

"Frank. A woman knows when something is off about a man." (Scrub
scrub scrub.)

"Right, tell that to Eva Braun sometime."

"There are always idiotic exceptions, dear," the wife said. "Please don't
make me one of them."

"So you don't think Phipps is even a skosh out of his mind?" I countered.

"I didn't see any evidence to that effect."

"You mean to tell me that barging into a hospital room and waving a cross around, screaming like a maniac, and scaring the shit out of two new parents for no good reason doesn't qualify?"

Allow me to point out that as I said the above, I was using the scrubbed plate as a prop, poking it in the air to emphasize such words as "shit" and "for no good reason." In response, the wife took the plate away from me.

"Watch your mouth," she said. "We don't talk like that anymore." Penny now held the plate she had taken as far away from my hands as she could, regarding me—as she so often did—with disdain. This left me with no other choice but to disregard her—as I so often had to—yank the dish out of her hands and put it where it belonged in the dishwasher. I was done with that dish. I was not, however, done talking. Nor was I done poking the air, though I decided to use something she could not so easily take away: my finger.

"This (poke) coming from the reason the birth (poke) video (poke) can't be watched with the sound (poke) on."

The wife, incensed at this devastating truth, began scrubbing the casserole dish.

"That's (scrub) different. You try (scrub) passing something the size (scrub) of a watermelon through an opening the size (scrub) of a lime and see how clean (scrub) your language stays."

"Honey, I'm not saying what you did was wrong. I'm only saying it's not wrong for me either. It's my allowance, if you remember."

The casserole dish was ready to go in the dishwasher but the wife was too busy rolling her eyes to hand it to me.

"And all I'm saying is we need to pray about what Reverend Phipps told us, watch our baby closely, and not just dismiss this out of hand," she said.

*Hand me the casserole dish please*, I thought, getting antsy. There's a certain amount of fretfulness that develops if, when one is in charge of putting dishes in the dishwasher, there is too much delay in dishes being handed to them. I was not immune to this feeling and it found its way into my speech. Hence, what followed:

"Pray about what? There's nothing to pray about. Reverend Phipps went shitballs! It's been coming on for years! Believe me, I know!"

"I said watch your mouth!"

The wife thrust the casserole dish into my hands—hard—but I felt an immense amount of relief nonetheless. I even let out a small, satisfied sigh before turning back to lay further into her.

"You gotta give me a reason then, babe. A reason why I should take any of what he said seriously. Someone accusing a kid of being, you know, *that*, is precisely the sort of thing a person should dismiss out of hand."

I turned to put the casserole dish into the dishwasher, but get this, *didn't*. I instead placed it on the counter with the hope that not putting the dish in the dishwasher would have the same effect on Penny that not getting the dish after it had been scrubbed had had on me. I then followed this with a mutinous grin. *Give me a reason*, that grin said, *and I'll put your precious casserole dish in the dishwasher.*

"A reason?" she said. "You mean something other than the fact that Reverend Phipps has vanished?"

The wife had stopped washing dishes altogether and was letting the faucet run—something that, I should add, drives me up the wall.

"Like I said, he was drunk and wandered off. I'm sure he'll turn up here sooner or later."

"You are such a moron sometimes, Frank. He's been missing for over a month. Nobody can find him," the wife said, flapping her hands in my face, flouting what should have been my inviolate husbandly authority while, at the same time, emphasizing that Reverend Phipps was missing and nobody could find him. Meanwhile, the fucking faucet was still going.

"He's probably in rehab and the elders of the church are keeping it under wraps until he gets himself sorted out," I said, staring at the running water, oh so close to madness.

"While the police and the FBI are scouring the countryside for him? While Mrs. Phipps is ripping her hair out and eating the bedspreads all the ding-dong day?"

"Pride is a funny thing, Hen-Pen. And some people will go to any length to protect their institutions. Like I said, he'll be found."

"He's not going to be found, Frank. He's been silenced."

Right then, the wife turned the faucet off, as if to say, *Just like I silenced this faucet, so has Reverend Phipps been silenced.* Lame. And she was just going to have to turn it back on as there were more dishes to be scrubbed.

"Well, you could hardly blame them," I said. "But just who do you think this sinister silencing someone would be?"

I tried to get us back on track by putting the casserole dish that had been on the counter in the dishwasher, but the wife still didn't turn the faucet back on. I found the effect of this similar to when she wouldn't hand me dishes: agonizing.

"Who do you think would silence a pastor?" Penny said. "The Devil's minions."

"Minions? Oh, for crying out loud. There are no minions out there, Penny. Nobody has minions anymore."

"Satan has his followers just like Christ has his. It's no different. And in this situation, with what Reverend Phipps told us, they would want him rubbed out. So we must be vigilant."

On "vigilant" the wife turned the faucet back on. Again, lame.

"Penny, you can't honestly believe our son is the—"

"I'm not saying he is. I'm not saying anything one way or another. But I'm also not going to stupidly disregard the word of a man of God. A man of God who has healed people."

"*Allegedly* healed people."

The wife groaned and stopped her scrubbing again. It occurred to me I should consider giving in some here or we were never going to get this done.

"You are so cynical it makes me sick to my soul!" she said. "This is your pastor you're throwing under the bus! Your kidnapped and probably murdered pastor! You've known him your whole life! He baptized you; he taught you truths from the scripture since you were yea high! And this is how you talk about him?"

On the bright side we had gotten back on track, as Penny, finished screaming at me, handed me a plate. Maybe no compromise would be necessary.

"Pen, if he had predicted something else, or predicted nothing, just expressed concern over the welfare of our son and his future, then, yes, I wouldn't be throwing him under the bus. But this, sweetheart, this is nuts."

Turning this latest plate over in my hands, I realized the wife had not scrubbed it nearly as well as was needed and that if I put it in the dishwasher it would have to be rewashed after the cycle finished. I hate it when dishes have to be rewashed.

"It's not nuts, Frank. It was foretold eons ago in the Bible. The end will come and there will be an Antichrist. It has to happen at some point. Why not now?"

"Maybe, maybe not. But regardless, I'm not seeing how Reverend Phipps would be privy to the specifics of that prophecy, and I'm not seeing how we would be the ones to have that kind of kid. I mean, how could we? Did a bunch of naked old people roofie your chocolate pudding one night and toss you into the sack with Lucifer?"

"Oh, gimme a break, Frank. Satan is an evil spirit," the wife said, now waving a butter dish around, my clever *Rosemary's Baby* reference sailing comfortably over her head. "He has no body. He does not have the capacity to create. The Antichrist will come from human parents and Satan will corrupt his mind."

"And how do you know all that?" I said, deftly snatching the butter dish out of Penny's hand in mid-wave. Into the dishwasher it went. Take that, wife.

"Duh, Reverend Phipps! I pay attention in church, unlike some people."

"The same Reverend Phipps probably in a rubber room right now, anointing the doorframes with his urine?"

"Reverend Phipps was an underrated man of God. A healer who never got his due."

"Underrated, please. I've been going to his church for a lot longer than you and I never saw anything miraculous. Do I need to bring up my mother? Trust me, Phipps is no healer."

"Oh, is that so?" the wife said. "Did you just *block* Aaron Coker from your memory, then? Reverend Phipps healed him right in front of us."

"Aaron Coker had a sore big toe. That's hardly the lame to walk and the blind to see."

The wife passed me utensils crusted with vile casserole, but I choked down the rage their dirtiness filled me with and slid them into the dishwasher anyway, which was now almost full.

"All I know is he was limping before the service and he wasn't limping after," the wife said. "No task is too small for God."

"Well, praise the Lord then for one less ingrown toenail. I'm sure all the starving children with AIDS in Africa are rejoicing."

Off went the faucet. Dishes done. The wife dried her hands with a towel, her lips pursed in irritation.

"I don't know why this situation has brought out all your old bitterness. You promised me that was past."

I put the final salad bowl in the dishwasher and waited patiently for the wife to finish with the towel, as I, too, wanted to dry my hands.

"That was before Reverend Phipps went bonkers and raved a bunch of crazy crap about our kid," I said. "Crazy crap you're seriously considering all because of Aaron Coker and his big toe. Can I use the towel now, please?"

With a sneer, the wife whipped the towel across the kitchen where it landed on the stove. I, ever resourceful, dried my hands on my pants.

"You know," the wife said, lifting her eyes to the ceiling in exasperation, "it's like Jesus said—I find your lack of faith disturbing."

"What?" I said.

"You heard me."

"Hon, that wasn't Jesus."

"Oh. Well, who was it then mister smarty-pants Bible expert? Paul? Peter? Elijah? Moses?"

I turned on the dishwasher.

"Darth Vader."

# 2

IT WOULD SEEM I HAVE FINALLY COME ACROSS SOME CHURCH OF E WALL art—a mural, to be exact—in this room that I've been told is the Inner Sanctum.

Unlike the other unforgettable mural in my life—the one still violating the nursery walls of Little Hat Pentecostal—this one is excellent. In a background of almost blinding sunlight there is a young, muscular, blond-haired, thoroughly naked man with mischievous blue eyes, holding the Earth in his left hand and gazing at it thoughtfully. The Earth is in the shape of an apple with a large bite taken out of it. It even has a stem.

Evidently, this is a revisionist, Satanist rendering of Adam, though in this case Adam is a dead ringer for a young Robert Redford.

Because of my admiration for Robert Redford, I immediately like this Adam and am interested in what he plans on doing with the rest of the Earth-apple, despite the fact that if he finishes it—gulp, no more Earth.

On his left is a lady, same golden hair, same mischievous, mysterious eyes, same nakedness, with a snake wrapped around her shoulders like a shawl, which tastefully covers her breasts. She is regarding Robert Redford and the apple, waiting for him to share, or, if one is to assume quasi-Biblical accuracy here, waiting for him to take his bite.

She is a revisionist, Satanist adaptation of Eve, and in this version she looks a lot like Danica, who I might have mentioned looks a great deal like Jane Fonda.

At first glance, it is difficult for me to discern whether or not the mural Eve is meant to look like Jane Fonda or Danica. Not even the Robert Redford Adam can help me with this as, despite his being Fonda's co-star and love interest in *Barefoot in the Park*, he is also featured on Danica's desk in two picture frames.

So the question remains: Is it Danica or Jane Fonda?

Little mysteries everywhere.

# 3

SHORTLY AFTER I SPILLED THE BEANS ABOUT SPARKY, A MAN'S GRAVELLY VOICE
came through an intercom informing everyone that we were to be
escorted into the Inner Sanctum.

Finally, the moment we had all been waiting for had arrived. Danica told
the goons to escort Sparky and me, the goons obeyed, and Sparky and I
allowed ourselves to be escorted to the Inner Sanctum, where we are now.

I must say it is rather spacious and cozy in here. A lot of mahogany—
mahogany desk, mahogany bookshelves, though a tad too much red,
I'm afraid, and dark, sacrificial red at that. You know, like bloody walls.
Way to embrace those stereotypes, kids.

The couch in here is of the blackest black, like the skin of a panther,
and even more comfortable than the one in the foyer, so despite my
overall feeling that the design scheme is a tad on the derivative side, I
still can't help but like it in here.

The Jane Fonda/Danica portion of the mural probably has something
to do with it. I could sit on this couch and stare at it all day.

Sparky is not on the couch with me, but over in the corner near a glass
door that leads to an outside balcony, seated on a squashy crimson-col-
ored recliner. He is writing now instead of drawing.

When the goons brought us in, they motioned for Sparky to sit on the
squashy recliner and for me to sit on the panther couch. Handing Sparky
a clipboard, they twisted the dial on a mechanical timer in the shape of
a grinning Satan-head, and told him to begin.

"What the hell are you making him do?" it suddenly occurred to me
to ask. The mural had been too beguiling for me to pay close attention
to what was going on at first.

"He's taking the Black Catechism," one of goons rasped in a voice
thick with saliva (he's eating a piece of a candy). "So shut up. As you
can see, he is being timed."

"This is insane!" I spat, though I knew it probably wasn't. "You can't
make him take tests!"

"Sure we can," the other goon said.

"And how's that?"

The goon without candy pulled my 9mm pistol out from the back of his pants and winked as he showed it to me. I could tell he was feeling a fresh surge of confidence, and who could blame him for it?

"And no helping him there, bub," the goon with the gun said, closing the door behind him as he followed the candy goon out.

Clearly, he had no idea the sort of help this "bub" would have been good for.

With nothing else in the room to keep me occupied except the mural, I decide I can stare at that *and* check my voicemail. Whoever it was that called me in the alley has pretty much ruined everything so they'd better have left something good.

The first message up is a saved one from Little Nazi Eddie Reddingham, a message I had kept for his parents to listen to in the hopes of getting him into big trouble (but have so far not gotten around to doing). It's Eddie singing along with a recording, not from *The Producers,* but one dearly loved by actual Nazi people. It's the "Horst Wessel Song," one of the most notorious of the evil anthems of Nazi Germany, and maybe I'm too dumb to catch the irony or the satire here, but Eddie's singing along sure sounds like he means it.

Which means I was right when I warned the Reddinghams of where all of this supposed innocent singing could lead. I've since caught Sparky humming snatches of the tune here and there and, to date, he has not answered me when I ask him what it is.

The next message, the one that appeared after the ill-timed call in the alley, is from my father:

*Frankie, Frankie you need to call me back right away. The most wonder-ful, incredible thing has happened! Everything has changed! Everything! My life will never be the same and—*

Considering how things have been going for me the past, oh, thirty-eight years or so, you might think that's about all I can take.

And it is.


# 4


THE FIRST FEW MONTHS OF SPARKY'S LIFE WERE DIFFICULT, WHICH KIND OF goes without saying as newborn children are rarely the bundle of joy they're promised to be. Yet I don't think I'm wrong when I say there was, on top of the usual adjustments, an extra wrinkle added to our situation that the vast majority of new parents don't have to deal with.

(*Psst!* Antichrist.)

The wife was really having trouble—trouble processing Reverend Phipps's bizarre appearance, trouble with his subsequent disappearance; then there were the nightmares.

One in particular, the most influential:

A crib on a tiny island in the middle of a frothing lake. Add to this island a nightstand, dresser, and queen-sized bed—basically, the contents of the Horvath master bedroom.

In the crib was baby Michael, bawling his head off as hot, angry waves from the lake crashed around him. I was sitting on the bed by the crib, with what the wife insisted was a deranged look on my face, whereas she was traversing the boiling lake on a raft made from the closet door using a curtain hanger to pull herself along. From what she said, this traversing part took forever. The curtain hanger turned out to be a lousy paddle.

When she did at last arrive ashore, she said I greeted her with loud whooping while scrambling this way and that.

"He's hungry!" I said, jumping and howling. "He's thirsty!" I added. I then dove into the boiling lake.

The wife, unmoved by my suicide, proceeded to lift Sparky out of the crib. She cradled him with one arm as she lowered her nightgown with the other and attempted to feed him, only to stop in horror when she noticed she was lactating blood.

Sparky, at the sight of her bloody boob, began to squirm and fuss. The wife could not figure out whether it was to get away or because he wanted it. To add to the confusion, someone approached her from behind and placed a hand on her shoulder.

Reverend Phipps.

The wife said he looked at her, at Sparky, and then at her bloody boob. Somehow none of this was creepy to her.

The water frothed some more and something terrible seemed about to rise from under the surface. Maybe me. I, every now and then, like the idea of being something terrible about to rise from under the surface.

But Penny said she never saw what came out of the water, as Reverend Phipps suddenly clutched her bloody boob in what she swore was a completely non-sexual way, and said, "You don't have to."

"Yes, I do," the wife replied. "He's hungry. He'll starve."

Smiling, Reverend Phipps squeezed her boob, spraying blood everywhere. Why he did this never made sense to me. Same with what he said next: "No, he won't."


The immediate fallout from all of this?

The wife decided not to breastfeed Sparky anymore. A too-literal interpretation of the nightmare, I suppose, but not without cause. I mean, if you had the same dream, wouldn't you at least consider doing the same thing?


Even with that decision made, the nightmare continued to haunt her steps through the following weeks, to where the wife decided to get a bit more up to speed on Christian eschatology—specifically the doctrine of the Antichrist.

Within a matter of months our home became something of a warehouse for every book, magazine article, recorded sermon, and third-rate horror flick even remotely related to the subject, and Penny consumed them all. From sober-minded, deliberately vague books by respected theologians—books that treated the end times with the utmost caution, refusing to guess when the Antichrist would come and who he would be—to shockingly exact, hysterical tomes that, depending on the year published, breathlessly pointed to whatever Hollywood star was at the peak of their popularity, or to whatever Kennedy was mulling a presidential run as the Beast prophesied so long ago.

In the end, faced with so many crackpot theories and contradictory viewpoints, Penny decided to limit her scope and put all her eggs into the basket of one book. Gathering all Antichrist materials into a big pile in the living room floor, she stood in front of what I liked to call "Book Mountain," closed her eyes, prayed God would guide her hand, and then plunged it into the middle.

Here is the title of the book she pulled out (with or without God's assistance):

## HE'S HERE!

Its subtitle:

## 666

And that was that. The one for her. Penny reasoned that if she reached out in faith, God would not lead her to the wrong sort of information.

Besides, she liked the name of the author, Dr. Demetrius Thesseloniki, and figured if Dr. Demetrius Thesseloniki didn't know what was what with the Apocalypse, who did?

"You can always trust the Greeks," she said.


A quick summary of Dr. Thesseloniki's book:
He's here.
As in the Antichrist. As in 666. As in alive and well.
Watch your step.

More from Thesseloniki's book:

Who is the Antichrist?

Ultimate evil personified.

But he pretends to be a real swell guy for a bit. Then, right about the time you start feeling comfortable with him...KABLOOIE!


According to Dr. Thesseloniki, the Antichrist, who will come to power, rule the nations, and destroy the lives of billions before suffering defeat at the hands of a very angry Jesus Christ, will be a charming, brilliant man.

He will fix a lot of things that have gone wrong with the world. He will come from Russia or Eastern Europe. He will be born into wealth and position. He will be a homosexual. He will engineer a seven-year pact that will deliver world peace, economic stability, and religious freedom. Three and a half years into this pact, he will break it and start killing lots of people. He will then impose a new credit system, make everybody wear a mark in order to buy goods and services, outlaw all religions, and force everybody to worship him.

Lots of people will. Lots of people won't. He'll kill the lots of people who won't—and some of the others who will too, because, hey, he's the Antichrist.

Then, after another three and a half years of mayhem, murder, and destruction, God, who after thousands and thousands of years has finally had it up to here with all this nonsense, will send his Son down to destroy the Antichrist and his cronies and set up a new kingdom where He will rule mankind in Person forever and ever. Those who endure will be saved. Those who perish, refusing to bow before the Antichrist, will be brought back.

And then, let the good times roll.

No more pain, no more death, no more Democrats. Hallelujah, praise God, amen. Everything will be perfect and wonderful all the time and forever.

Unless you're the Antichrist. Unless you're all of the people who threw their lot in with him. Then things won't be wonderful or perfect all the time and forever.

No, things will kinda suck.


So do I think the above is true? Do I believe that Dr. Thesseloniki got it right on how to interpret all those foggy passages at the end of the Bible about how everything will shake out?

Sometimes.

In my younger years, I thought it true a lot more than sometimes; since then, I go back and forth. Sometimes it still sounds ridiculous, while other times, like today, it not only seems possible, but inevitable.

Either way, one thing never changes: I really *want* it to be true. Don't you?

Somebody's coming to save you! You're going to live forever! Everybody bad will get their ass kicked! You're going to be happy all the time!

How could you not want that?


Okay, but how could the wife believe, when Dr. Thesseloniki stated in his book that the Bible pointed to the Antichrist as being of Eastern European origin, born into an aristocratic family, gay, and all the rest, that Michael could possibly be a fulfillment of those prophecies?

Easy: Ask and you shall receive. She wrote a letter to Dr. Thesseloniki asking if it was possible the Antichrist could be an American of humble birth who could rise to power from lowliness and do all that KABLOOIE stuff from America; and after a month, she received an answer from Thesseloniki that said while most reputable Christian eschatologists were in the same camp as he was and were following the traditional idea of the Antichrist being from Europe, there were some scholars, "cranks mostly," who felt the Antichrist could come from America.

*So it is possible, Mrs. Horvath, though, in my opinion it wouldn't make a whole lot of sense and it doesn't seem to fit with the scriptures very well. But perhaps God intends to surprise us.*

And that was all the wife needed. She loved surprises; so she ran with it. Better Safe Than Sorry.


So after reading Dr. Thesseloniki's book and spending copious amounts of time ruminating over what it all meant, the wife was able to come up with a final interpretation of her bloody boob nightmare, that being we could stop Sparky from becoming the Antichrist.

For justification, she referred to a section in Dr. Thesseloniki's book that compared and contrasted Jesus Christ, the true Messiah, from the coming false one, which led her to rediscover that part in the Book of Matthew where Jesus in the Garden of Gethsemane asks God to let him off the hook with the whole torture/crucifixion/die thing.

The wife deduced that Christ would not have asked this of God if it had not been possible. The wife further deduced that if Christ could get out of his calling, then Sparky could get out of his. Perhaps Mommy and Daddy could even lend him a helping hand.

After all, wasn't that why we had both been warned by Reverend Phipps and the dream? Why tell us if we weren't supposed to do something about it? Perhaps we were the main line of defense here and perhaps it was all up to us if mankind would get a chance to delay the end of the world one more time.

Her heart and mind exploding over finally having a decent reason to get up in the morning, the wife dashed off another letter to Dr. Thesseloniki, asking about the possibility of staving off the ascendancy of the Antichrist. To which the good Greek doctor responded that, although he agreed God would warn his people of the coming of the Beast, he was convinced nothing could be done to stop it.

*It all has to happen, Mrs. Horvath. Sooner or later. And it will be the worst thing that has ever happened. Hardly anyone will survive. That being said, it can't hurt to do all one can to be a gadfly to the Antichrist wherever possible.*

And that was all the wife needed. She loved being a gadfly, so she ran with it.

Thanks to Dr. Thesseloniki's letters and book, the bloody boob dream, and scads of how-to parenting guides, the wife, with a little help from little ol' me, began to develop what she thought would be as close as one could get to a foolproof plan that would ensure Sparky would never get the opportunity to have his Garden of Gethsemane Moment.

Her plan can be summed up as follows:

That our son would become, through our strenuous efforts and a big assist from Upstairs, a socially inept, overweight, intelligence-deficient bumblefuck of virtually no trade, skill, or use. Eminently forgettable, extraordinarily dull, but, let's hope, nice; and maybe, in his own unsophisticated, dimwitted way, happy about his lot in life.

At worst, our son would bottom out as a small-time criminal, in and out of prison here and there for small-time crimes. Nothing too evil, murderous, or destructive. At best, he would become a custodian somewhere. A bartender. A dull—but friendly—convenience store checkout clerk, or an agreeable, feckless postman.

The wife said she could live with Sparky becoming any of the former, and with the latter, maybe even find it in her heart to be proud of him a little.

Either way, she needed my help.

Help me, she said. Help me make him the construction worker who sleeps on the job, cat-calls at women, and drinks a twelve-pack of beer every night. Help me make him the guy who can't assist the customer when asked a question, but cheerfully takes them to the person who can.

In other words, help me make him into someone just like his father.

## 5

THE GOONS HAVE COME AND GONE AGAIN, HAVING TAKEN SPARKY'S COMPLETED catechism out of the room to grade it.

A few minutes ago, the Devil timer went off with the sort of baleful laugh one would expect from a Devil timer, and Sparky, not finished with the exam, continued to write as fast as he could as the Devil laughed at him until the goons reappeared and ripped the clipboard out of his hands.

My eyes might have been deceiving me, but it sure looked like Sparky was trying to do his best. This trait, the trying thing, the wife and I could never completely stamp out of him.

He's like his daddy that way.

Speaking of me, I'm no longer goggling the Eve portion of the mural, nor torturing myself with voicemails. No, I'm regrouping and reassessing and recalculating just how I am going to fulfill my life's purpose and save everybody from certain doom today.

Everything seemed so much easier when I was beaten and desperate in Old Tuna with a 9mm stuffed down the front of my jeans. I mean, how am I going to get a definitive answer as to the truth about Sparky without a gun? What Satanist worth his brimstone tells the truth in that kind of situation without a gun in his face?

Just how am I going to fight them off when they realize why I wanted the answer, and what it means for Sparky?

Just how am I going to shoot Sparky without a goddamned gun?

## 6

THE ORIGINAL PLAN TO DISPATCH SPARKY, AFTER HIS AWFUL DESTINY IS confirmed by the Church of E:

Still in possession of my nine, I grab the boy and run back to Old Tuna. Hordes of Satanist goons (called from hither and yon) come after us; gunfire is traded before I, through skillful driving and misdirection, manage to put enough distance between us and the goons to take Sparky to a deserted church fifteen miles outside of Berry to finish it. Like

Gregory Peck in *The Omen*, except I win. Though like him, I'll be gunned down. Martyred, as they say.

The Satanists will likely cover it up and the bodies of my son and I will be done away with. Or, if the local authorities catch wind of what's going on, everything will be blamed on the Church of E despite their protests that all they were trying to do was save a boy from his filicidal father.

Who would believe Satanists?

But as things stand, the chances of me getting the boy out of here and to the church are getting close to nil, and I'm not sure what I can do to get things back on track. As far as I can tell, the only weapon available with which to dispatch both myself and the Antichrist is the letter opener on the mahogany desk in front of me.

The letter opener is shaped like a miniature broadsword, sharp in a vicious way, with a hilt shaped like a smiling goat. What the goat has to smile about I have no idea.

Hay, perhaps.

Of course, the question begs, why must I die?

If I'm so certain of the terrible righteousness of my actions, so sure in my convictions, why do I not wish to live and take the consequences that will come?

Because Sparky's not the Antichrist if I kill him—acts of prevention usually create such dilemmas—and once apprehended, a lot of well-meaning people will tell me I was wrong. Given enough time, I might start thinking they're right, and then what? I'll be left with nothing but the worst thing a person can ever think:

*My God, what have I done?*

But man, I don't know about this. The smiling goat letter opener. Stabbing the boy then myself. Dying.

183

It's not an appealing way to go. A lot could go wrong. A lot always does.

There's also nothing aesthetically pleasing about it. This new plan reeks of beaten and desperate and that's *not* how I want to finish—even if, in this scenario, if I manage to stagger back to my seat in time I would get to die on a comfy couch. Not to mention the confirmation thing. You know, the entire reason I'm here. Don't I still need that?

Don't I also need some more time to think over my life and what might have been? Contemplate one final time all the promise I once had, all I could have been and done?

I don't even have any decent last words.

Like Oscar Wilde: *Either these curtains go, or I do.*

Humphrey Bogart: *I should have never switched from Scotch to martinis.*

Marx: *Last words are for fools who haven't said enough.*

Beethoven: *Applaud friends, the comedy is finished.*

Joseph Addison, Theodore Dreiser, Giles Corey, Henry Ward Beecher: *See in what peace a Christian can die. Shakespeare, I come. Curse you, Corwin and all of Salem. Now comes the mystery.*

Assuming after I stab Sparky and myself that my last breaths will be gasps, gurgles, and spits, I'm not so sure I'll be able to get anything out anyway.

Not that it matters much. Who would I be saying any of it to? The boy? I doubt he'll be in the mood to listen.

## 7

So here I am. Still on the couch. Mighty comfortable but, as usual, disgusted with myself. I probably should have erred on the side of caution and stabbed the boy, but the moment has passed. It's now too late.

That said, there has been a startling development, which, coupled with the luxuriousness of the panther couch, is helping take some of the edge off my self-loathing.

The development has just entered the room and seated himself across from me at the mahogany desk, picking up the smiling goat letter opener along the way and twirling it with his fingers. The development looks like a grizzly old man with long gray hair, and a full, equally long and gray grizzly beard.

The development is missing an eye. I think, anyway. The reason I've backed up to that is because he is wearing an eye patch. I figure, in this life, it's about as safe a bet as you're gonna make, even though you can never know for sure until you lift the patch up (something I have no plans of doing, by the way—ick).

The development has just spoken. Here's what the development has said: "Well, well. I'll be goddamned. Franklin Bartholomew Horvath."

The development is Reverend Phipps.

# PART EIGHT

*"Has he ever done anything unusual? Something not easily explained?"*
*"There's been some weird stuff."*
*"Tell me about the weird stuff."*

# 1

I AM THUNDERSTRUCK, I AM SPEECHLESS, AND YET, SOMEHOW, I SPEAK.

"You're dead," I say to Phipps.

"Declared as such, yes, after being missing for—oh, god—how long have I been away now?" Phipps says.

I am astonished; I am astounded.

"They ripped up the world looking for you," I say. "The police, the FBI. The church even put together a search party. They made t-shirts."

"I know. I have one," Phipps says, beaming.

I look to Sparky. Is he seeing what I'm seeing? The impossible in the flesh? The man who's had, next to his mother and me, the most influence on his life?

Nope, he's drawing and humming what I'm pretty sure is "Horst Wessel," in his own little world.

I look back to Phipps, who is as confident and happy as I've ever seen him—well, as happy and confident as someone who has lost an eye can be. I, meanwhile, with two eyes, am dumbfounded. I am staggered.

"What are you doing here?" I say.

"This is my church," Phipps says.

"You're one of *them*? A Satanist?"

"And a Pisces. I also recycle."

Phipps points to the back of the room, where two trash cans sit side by side. One says, in a font that looks like gnarled tree branches, "Cans and bottles only." The other: "Paper, please."

"I suppose, Frankie, you would like to know how I came to be here, and to number myself with the enemy of everything I used to stand for," Phipps says.

"I'd also like to know how you lost that eye," I say.

"I know, me too."

"You mean you don't know?"

"No, I don't," Phipps says, shrugging. "Oops."

188

★

The door opens and Danica strides to the former head of Little Hat Pentecostal Church, the man who baptized me, mentored me, practically taught
me everything I know about God and life. She hands Phipps a manila
folder then nods curtly to Sparky and me before letting her eyes rest on
the mural likeness of her (or Jane Fonda). It could be my imagination, but
I can almost swear she's trying to stifle a laugh.

"Thank you, Danica," Phipps says. "You may go now."

I try to fight the urge to stare at Danica's hindquarters as she leaves, but,
in the grand Horvath tradition, fail.

"Perhaps we can delve into our personal mysteries later, Frankie...among
other things," Phipps says, snapping his fingers, bringing my attention back.
"In the meantime, let's get down to business, shall we?"

He holds up the folder. I'm gonna take a wild guess here and say it
contains Sparky's graded Satan quiz.

"Remarkable score for a boy his age," Phipps says. "His mind is quite
advanced, as is his temperament."

I am flabbergasted; I am gobsmacked.

"You are surprised by this news?" Phipps says.

"He's had to be held back a grade twice," I say, my jaw bouncing around
my ankles. "His teachers have threatened to put him in with the develop-
mentally challenged. He's not even fully housebroken."

"Maybe he was saving his best for the right time then. Maybe, if you
will allow me to extrapolate a theory, he did not wish to give himself away
too soon," Phipps says.

"But you already gave him away," I say. "When you blew into our hospital
room and waved that cross around right before you disappeared."

At this, Phipps looks, for the splittiest of seconds, pretty surprised himself,
but he recovers quickly with a sweep of his right hand and a chuckle.

"Of course, of course," he says.

"Come on, don't you remember?" I say.

"How could I forget, Frankie," Phipps says, "the day my entire world
was shaken? The day I met Lord Lucifer and He revealed to me the true
order of things."

Big breath and on he goes:

"In a vision, on the way to the hospital to congratulate all the new parents that day, He showed me beyond all doubt the fallacy of Christianity and the true nature of man. Not as a simpering, weak, sycophantic peon, meant for enslavement to a god not even willing to show himself to his own people, but as a ruler himself, as a king. Man was meant to govern the Earth, to subdue the universe. That nature has been stolen, corrupted. Lord Lucifer aims to give it back."

"I thought you people didn't believe in a real Satan," I say, proud at my ability to recall this piece of information and with it box Phipps into a corner. "I thought he was just a symbol for the baser impulses in human nature."

"Not even Christianity reveals all of its secrets at the beginning," Phipps says. "And it's even more so with us. Our converts are but mere infants when they join and must be trained and prepared before they are introduced to their master. He does not pander to the weak the way God does. He does not have the patience to bear the timid first steps, the growing pains, of neophytes. Our people earn our Lord's favor by learning to harness their own dark strength and thereby prove themselves worthy."

"Seems to me you didn't have to earn it," I say. "You got a visit from the big cheese himself the first day."

"Trust me, Frankie," Phipps says, lifting the patch so as to expose the disgusting glob of flesh where his eye used to be, clearing that mystery up. "I have earned it every day since."

"I thought you said you didn't remember how you lost that?"

"I did and I don't. I was trying to make my point with a visual flourish."

"If your point is you're an idiot who can't keep track of his body parts, then consider the point taken," I say.

I know. I'm holding my own here—well enough to at least warrant a thump on the skull, if not an outright beatdown from the goons, but they aren't here right now, and all Phipps does is laugh.

"That's good, Frankie, very good. I can't fathom how you must feel seeing me, of all people, on the other side of this desk. Just remember it is not I who has betrayed you, but God."

"Go to Hell, Phipps."

"With pleasure."

I lean back and regard Phipps with hatred as he leans forward and plucks a candy from a dish near the edge of the desk. I must say, some of his rhetoric about man being king of the universe and harnessing his dark strength doesn't sound half bad, but I know from my Pentecostal teachings these are but tempting words meant to mislead and destroy me. At the same time, the irony is not lost on me that the one who taught me the most about the deception of Satan is now one of his lieutenants, peddling the same sort of doctrine he would have vehemently fought against more than a decade ago—an incomprehensible reversal that very much pisses me off. Is no human being capable of sticking with anything?

Furious, I lean forward, and Phipps leans back, popping the candy into his mouth.

"Let's cut the crap here," I say. "Why did you barge into our hospital room and wave that cross around?"

Phipps jerks forward to answer, and I, frightened by his suddenness, lean back. If anyone is watching us it must look like we're sawing the same invisible tree together.

"I was in a frenzy, Frankie," Phipps says. "Everything I'd ever known was a lie, and I could not come to terms with what I believed then to be the most awful of revelations."

"Which was?"

Phipps looks to Sparky, who is still humming, still drawing, then back to me.

"That Lucifer's champion has finally come."

## 2

"I never saw you or your wife," Phipps continues. "All I saw when I entered the room was the boy.

"I saw, in that moment, that I had been on the wrong side all along. In a vision, I saw that child, with but a glance, shatter the cross in my hands. I ran out of the room, out of the hospital; I ran and ran until I collapsed in a cornfield. There I slept a day and a night."

"Was that where you lost your eye?"

"No, Frankie, it wasn't, but it was where I lost my faith in God. How vivid my dreams were! Horrible, terrifying, but true. The next morning, Lucifer appeared to me. He asked me if I was ready to serve Him. I said I was—and I have, since then, with distinction. I have done His grim but necessary work and I have done it with a certainty and gratification I never knew before."

With a sigh meant to convey the extent of how certain and gratified he was and is, Phipps leans back again.

"And now, here we are," he says. "Our paths have crossed once more, just as it was foretold. Hail Satan!"

Needing a break from this garbage, I sneak another peek at Sparky who continues to scribble like mad on the paper. It occurs to me that since neither of us have had a bathroom break since early this morning, it's almost certain he's putting the finishing touches on a nice big dump.

A nice big dump I will have to remove from pants I will have to clean.

Not able to square this with everything I've just heard, I can't help but shake my head.

"What is the Black Catechism anyway?" I say.

"It's an exam we give to all young children brought to us," Phipps says. "It assesses cognitive abilities and personality."

"Like an Iowa Test for Satanist kids?"

"Something like that."

"And he did okay?"

"Like I said, remarkable."

"How remarkable?"

"One of the best scores we've ever seen."

I am stupefied. I am flummoxed. I am defeated. I am also, maybe, a little bit proud. That's *my* kid who got one of those best scores ever. Señor Poopy Pants. Just imagine how he might have done had I not been screwing him up all these years!

"So as you said Frankie, let's cut the crap," Phipps says. "Tell me about him."

"What do you want to know?"

"Has he ever done anything unusual? Something not easily explained?"

"There's been some weird stuff."

"Tell me about the weird stuff."

# 3

Let me preface this by saying the lion's share of the weird stuff is hearsay from the wife, with much of it occurring, oddly enough, during her more severe menstrual fits.

I, ever the dutiful husband, listened to her outlandish interpretations of mostly common events, expressed my doubts, and kept her crammed to the gills with Midol. I said her mind was playing tricks on her. I said she was getting carried away with those Antichrist books and should get rid of them. But other than harsh, stinging words, I did nothing further to stop her. Despite the bickering and constant ridiculing of her point of view, I always went along with her decisions in the end, up to and including when she came up with the plan to turn our son into a socially inept, overweight, intelligence-deficient bumblefuck of virtually no trade, skill, or purpose.

I even stopped most of the bickering and belittling after a while.

Why?

I don't know, probably because I thought the wife would come around to the improbability of the whole thing at some point and that marginal damage could be done to the child in his early years so long as he was fed and watered.

Or maybe it's because I loved Penny in weakness, and like Antony with Cleopatra, I would always follow her ships wherever they sailed.

It also could have been because I was still more or less a Christian, and this meant I had to grant the possibility she might be right about everything and if there was a chance, who was I not to take what she was saying seriously?

I'll also admit I was pretty wrapped up in myself back then and at the beginning of a long series of fogs that would leave me scattershot, depressed, and resentful, incapable of much concern as to what was going on with my son.

But if I'm going to hold nothing back and be completely honest here, it's mostly because I had, over the years, become something of a monster.

Here's what I'm saying: I wanted revenge against my old man.

During the first year or so of Sparky's life, he was over to the house almost every night to tut and dote and drool over his brand new grandson. I could see it in the way his eyes brightened. I could tell in the way his voice became solemn and still: he believed Sparky was Him, the Great Horvath. My father had convinced himself the only reason God had told him about it at all was because he was destined to bear witness. Which would explain why, to Penny's and my severe annoyance, he started showing up to the house just about every day, shit-slobbering grin on his face, Camcorder in hand. He wanted every moment, he said, from first teeth to first steps to first words, recorded for posterity.

"Hundreds of years from now, our descendants will still be watching these videos!" he said many times, always breathlessly.

Also: "Frankie, get out of the way, I only want Michael in these shots. Seriously, son. Out!"

As you might expect, the old man's behavior drove me to explore the more malevolent aspects of my fallen nature.

Hence, revenge.

Combining these reasons together, despite my doubts that our son could ever truly become the Antichrist, I played along with the wife and watched with a hidden, though no less wicked glee, as my father's pride in Sparky faded, his smile dimmed, and his visits became increasingly sporadic, sans camera.

How I loved the sound of his voice in those days, the familiar, strained, panic-stricken sound of a Charles Bronson whose beloved watermelons are withering, one at a time, before his eyes.

"Shouldn't he be potty-trained by now?"

"Don't you think he's getting heavy for his age?"

"Why doesn't he say anything? He just sits there and stares out into space."

"Why is his hair falling out?"

"Will he ever stop scratching his crotch?"

"What do you mean they want to give him a do-over for Head Start?"

In less than five years, I had the old man on the ropes. At his breaking point. Beaten and desperate.

I, on the other hand, was in the sort of boundless ecstasy only arch villains can appreciate. I felt like Baby Jane Hudson singing to piano accompaniment and staring at herself in the mirror. You know: *I've writ-ten a lett-er to Dadeee*. Like Alex DeLarge in the throes of his first successful sex fantasy after overcoming the Ludovico Technique. You know: *Oh, I was cured all right*. Like Jabba the Hutt gazing upon Han Solo in carbon freeze. You know: *Ho ho ho*.

Thanks to my machinations, Sparky was well on his way to becoming every bit as unimpressive as anyone in our family had ever been. It took long enough, but finally here was an unqualified success I could claim for my own.

Excuse me for a moment, as I savor the peak of this delectable victory. On the phone with my father, while inwardly twirling around like Hannibal Lecter to the *Goldberg Variations*, I was reassuring him he need not worry about the future, as I was convinced God had told me Sparky would one day sire a male heir and keep the Old Horvath Machine up and chugging.

"But I don't think I'll be making such a big deal out of it with him as you did with me," I said.

To my everlasting delight, the old man let out a dejected moan and hung up on me.

Apparently, Sparky extending the Royal Horvath Bloodline wasn't good enough for him anymore. Now that he was closer to the end of his life, the old man didn't consider it such a good thing to see the Great Horvath from the view of Eternity. Clearly, he wanted to say he'd had a hand in the Great Horvath's development—more than just DNA—a place of honor in the whole process, something to make himself feel better about the jack squat his life had amounted to.

Normally, I would have sympathized with this yearning for purpose and meaning. Not this time.

Of course, that triumph, as all of mine have been to date, was short-lived, and it was followed by a rout more humiliating than anything that win could have accounted for.

My father, though old, paunchy, sad, wrinkled, and hobo-faced, miraculously managed to woo a waitress more than twenty years his junior, wed her, and, through her, beget another son.

A son who appears to be, at age eight, a genuine fucking genius.

So much for revenge.

## 4

On to the weird stuff.

For the first eight months or so of Sparky's life: nothing. Unless you find the little processes all babies do to be weird, like Penny did; and those first months, she could be found spending most of her waking hours analyzing baby Sparky's every movement, be they of the motor or bowel variety. She also liked to pester me for my point of view.

"He's smiling. Why do you think he's smiling? What do you think he's thinking about that's making him smile?"

"Is that a snarl?"

"Did you hear that grunt?"

"Why does he never laugh?"

"Why does he never cry?"

I suppose she might have been right to ask some of these questions, as it is worth noting that Sparky rarely, if ever, cried—though I hardly thought it confirmation of anything. I had heard of lots of babies that had never cried. As it so happens, I was one of those babies, something I pointed out to the wife once as we were sorting laundry together.

"He's like me that way," I said, putting all the socks in a pile. Mine and hers. Some of them, probably mine, were smelly. "I never cried."

"Well, he doesn't laugh either," the wife said. She was gathering underwear, but only hers. She refused to touch mine.

"He smiles, that's enough for right now," I said, gathering up the socks and putting them into the machine. I noticed one of the wife's had a gaping hole in it. I left it in the wash.

"Disturbing smiles, Frank," the wife said. She had moved on to her bras. "Disturbing serial-killer smiles that keep me from sleeping at night."

"Penny, no baby smiles like a serial killer," I said, picking out my own underwear, boxer briefs, and throwing them into the wash. A top pair, a white one, had multiple skid marks in the seat, indicating it needed to be put out to pasture; but, like the holey sock, I left it in, a decision that did not go unnoticed. The wife was now looking into the washer with Gross Face. She had seen the skid marks.

Stronger of mind than ever, I pushed on. "Let's not project our worries here and turn a bunch of reasonably normal baby stuff into some kind of omen."

The wife said nothing to this pearl of wisdom and just stood there, transfixed by the agitating load in the machine and the thought of how much havoc my shit-stained boxer briefs might be wreaking upon her defenseless panties. It took a moment or two longer for her to recover, but she did. *C'est la vie.*

"Explain to me why won't he laugh, then?" she said. "When I make goofy faces and dance around, sing songs and oochie-coochie?"

"I don't know, maybe you're not all that funny," I replied. I was still a bit miffed at the extended repugnance directed at my boxer briefs.

"I'm plenty funny, Mr. Man," she said, closing the lid to the washer, now full of smelly socks, sweaty bras, and skiddy underwear. "Funnier than you'll ever be."

"Show me what you do then," I said.

She did.

"I'm afraid I'm with the boy on this one," I said.

The wife became suspicious of strangers, many of whom she thought might be the aforementioned Satan's minions stopping by under various guises to check on the welfare of their infant savior.

She bought a handgun: the precious 9mm now lost to the goons of E.

During small breaks from baby scrutiny, she would glare out the window at the postman, cable man, and utility man as they performed their various jobs. By her side was the pistol, just out of sight.

I can only imagine how confident she felt then, how sure of herself. If only one of them had actually been a Satanist. Man, he never would've known what hit him!

Anyway you slice it though, the wife's over-sensitive Antichrist detector aside, nothing really happened that first year. Nothing obviously evil from the baby, no minions or toadies attempted to take him away or perform satanic maintenance on him. No Rottweilers passed by to communicate with him via tongue-lolling telepathy. All quiet on the western front. Except for us.

During that time, I was in the midst of a fog, handling the situation with our son with equal parts apathy, skepticism, and vodka, whereas the wife was going nuts over anything and everything and feeling a lot of anger toward me for my lack of faith, support, and sobriety.

It's possible we would never have made it as husband and wife if things had gone on like that; it's possible, if we had stopped being husband and wife, I would now have no input, say-so, or control whatsoever concerning my son and, therefore, the fate of mankind; it's possible I wouldn't even be in his life at all right now if things had kept on like they had started, that's how close I was to failing the world and not knowing it.

So what was it that turned this thing around? Grab your hanky and snuggle up with the one you love.

Sparky's first Christmas.

## 5

To help you appreciate the magnitude of what happened, let me first temper your expectations by taking off the board some of the things that didn't.

For instance:

Sparky's skin did not sizzle, nor did he prophesy in a deep, demonish voice the coming destruction of the Kingdom of Heaven and the end of all celebrations of Christ's birthday. The corkscrew pasta nativity scene in our living room window didn't explode or melt. The wife wasn't impaled by the Christmas tree or electrocuted by the lights. Eggnog was not turned into bloodnog. The living room stereo didn't magically change from Bing Crosby to "Tubular Bells."

The only thing that did happen was that Sparky came down with a wicked case of colic.

That's right, he cried. All goddamned day and all goddamned night. Making up for lost time you could say.

What statisticians would call "regression to the mean."

Not a thing we did could make him stop. Not patting. Not burping. Not changing. Not even a special holiday appearance of the wife's left breast for Christmas dinner.

It was incredible. Nothing seemed to be wrong with him and yet, there he was, bawling his head off.

Finally, at my suggestion, we took him to the hospital in Indianapolis, and there, in keeping with the sterling reputation of their profession, the doctors couldn't find anything wrong with him either. They didn't even bother with a decent guess this time. They took his tiny temperature. They took his tiny blood pressure. They poked and prodded him a little here and a little there.

No clue.

"Aaaaand we're out of here," they said. "Happy holidays."


We drove Sparky back to Little Hat, back to the Christmas prayer vigil being held at Little Hat Pentecostal, where he was prayed and gibbered over and sang to until Reverend Worley, Phipps's replacement, kindly asked us to remove him from the service.

"Try reading Galatians to him," one of the church ladies suggested to us on our way out.

"Jangle some wind chimes," Ken Huckaby said.

"Coochie-coo him," Mrs. Worley said.

Back home we tried gibbering and singing and dancing churchily around Sparky in his crib, in the hopes that doing these things in a more intimate setting would prove more effective, and when that failed, we went back to the traditional stuff and goo-goo'd extra hard and rocked him.

At some point, you gotta figure the baby would get tired, right? Fall asleep? Suck his toes? Didn't happen. Not until the clock struck twelve and rang in December the 26th. At that moment, with the clock in the midst of its chimes, with Penny and me at the absolute end of our sanity, Sparky blew out his diaper and barfed all over his crib.

And that was that.


And nothing was said.

We never did discuss what shrieking for the entirety of Christ's birthday followed by an expulsion of stomach and intestinal contents might portend for the future of a child whom a missing and presumed dead minister had said would be the Antichrist. The wife didn't send any letters to Dr. Thessaloniki, and there was no way we would tell our parents about it other than to assure them everything was peachy now and that their ideas had been a big help. ("Did you rub castor oil on his chest?" Penny's mother had asked. "How about a pillow over his face?" her father had joked. Meanwhile, the old man, hysterical from taking care of my flu-ridden Aunt at Sioux Falls: "DO YOU NEED ME TO COME HOME?") The only result from Sparky's first Christmas, besides the purchase of a new crib, was that my skepticism and doubt could now be shouted down.

I have to admit I even found myself wondering if Penny might have been right after all. I know it was only crying, but then, context is everything.

So, unless seen from our unique perspective, most of the oddball happenings during the opening years of Sparky's life weren't much to be concerned about. Take that away and what we had on the whole was, admittedly, dismissible: the occasional unhinged look on his face when regarding something alive, an early obsession with fire, dismembering teddies with relish, and so forth. But as time went on, we began to notice that a number of strategies we had employed to hinder his growth had not worked as well as we'd hoped, as by age three, Sparky was able to walk, talk, and do most things most normal three-year-olds can do (though it should be said he couldn't do them very well).

The wife, as she was wont to do, was going shitballs over it. She wondered how he had picked up so many things without being taught. She then, as she was also wont to do, blamed me.

And into a fog I would go.

Things went on pretty much like this until the next major occurrence: the Saturday after Sparky's fifth birthday. That afternoon the wife raced into our bedroom in a full-on sprint, flapping her hands and hyperventilating.

I was already there, in bed, comfortably ensconced in malaise, a state of mind for which I had cleared my schedule for the rest of the day to properly enjoy. I also might have snuck in a few drinks.

"Oh Jesus, oh Lord," the wife said, dramatically pulling the bedspread up to cover her mouth. "It's happening. It's starting to happen."

She raved about the starting and the happening for a few minutes while I made multiple attempts to sit up and figure out what was starting and happening. Sad to say, because my stomach was well past "bit of" stage and my brain was addled by a tad more booze than any rational human being would have consumed by 1:30 in the afternoon, these two tasks took much longer than they should have. It eventually took calling up previously untapped reserves of concentration and strength before I was able to prop myself up on an elbow and get the gist of what had thrown the wife into such a panic. The What being two things, the worst being something Sparky had said, which had come right on the heels of his having done Something.

Something horrible. Something Antichristy.

What did he say? Allegedly, the following: "Grandma sucks pee-pees in Heck!"

The wife understood that to mean her mother was performing fellatio on unnamed persons in Hell. Penny was petrified as to how Sparky would have any clue what her mother, dead for eight months, would be doing with her time in the Big Adios. Unfortunately, the wife had failed to recognize the line for what it was: a quote from a movie.

Which movie? *The Exorcist*. Which quote? From the demon Pazuzu, spoken through Linda Blair: *YOUR MOTHER SUCKS COCKS IN HELL!*

The original quote is obviously a bit more randy than the more sanitized one Sparky used, which I believe was his way of conforming to his mother's law that no profanity was to be used in the house by anyone for any reason at any time (a law I frequently, shamelessly broke).

This led me to wonder how Sparky, at age five, knew the bad words well enough to supply cleaner substitutions for them. This also led me to wonder why he would say such a thing—sanitized or not—in the first place. What I did not have to wonder about was how he came across *The Exorcist*. That one's on me.

Earlier that day, in the midst of fog, I had turned the TV on for Sparky without first checking what was on it and told him to have a good time before stumbling off to descend into my whiskey-fueled gloom. So there was a logical explanation for why Sparky had said what he had, and once explained, the wife calmed down a little, though she was not all that happy with me.

Which brought her to the thing Sparky had supposedly done.

"He made the fan spin," she said.

The ceiling fan in his bedroom, she meant. The ceiling fan that hadn't worked since we'd moved into the house. The ceiling fan I had been promising to fix for years now.

Penny said she walked into Sparky's room where he was sitting on the floor, staring at the wall—in her words—"like a psycho." Above him, the ceiling fan was spinning.

The wife, thinking I had finally fixed the fan went to turn it off. She flicked the switch. The fan didn't stop. She flicked it again. The fan didn't stop.

Sparky then purportedly giggled and said, "Grandma sucks pee-pees in Heck!"

Hearing this, the wife ran out of his room and into ours, lost her shit, and I, now fully apprised of the situation, lurched out of bed and lumbered off to the boy's lair.

When I got there, I found him not sitting on the floor but by the window. He was staring out of it, but not in a way I thought "psycho" at all. He looked kinda sad to be honest.

Above him, the fan wasn't moving.

"I swear to God it was moving before, Frank," the wife said, trailing in behind me. "I swear it."

I flicked the switch. The fan didn't move. I flicked it again. The fan didn't move. The wife started crying. I left her to her pathetic tears and approached Sparky.

"Hey, buddy," I said. "Did you make the fan spin earlier?"

Without ever looking at me, Sparky considered this question and clicked his tongue. He then pushed his nose against the window and, glum as can be, said, "Who cares?"

# 6

THE INNER SANCTUM IS FILLING UP—AT LEAST IF ONE WANTS TO SIT ON A chair or the sofa. We could fit another twenty people or so in here as long as they didn't insist on being seated.

Roll call: Danica, the goons, Reverend Phipps, Sparky, and myself. All present and accounted for.

After hearing the spinning fan story, Phipps had called Danica and the goons in to join us as I repeated it, and they all exchanged looks, scratched their heads, and hemmed and hawed.

Perhaps the most perplexing aspect to the scene is Sparky. I'm talking about him—the peculiar things he's done, and the peculiar things that have happened around him—but he continues to appear oblivious. He has not looked up once from his drawing and made a single nod or facial tic that would signify awareness that he is the center of the discussion, nor has he attempted to correct any part of my narrative.

He is behaving like there's nobody in the room but him, and man, is he ever going to town on that paper and smiling smiling smiling.

I have to admit this is the happiest I've ever seen him.

# 7

THE HAPPIEST ANYBODY'S EVER SEEN ME: SATURDAY, NOVEMBER 6TH, 2004 at 11:07 a.m.

That's right. I know the date and time to the minute. Don't ever say we manic depressives can't appreciate happiness. We can. A little too well.

I had been out of my latest fog for a long time now, a year and a half plus, and though the next fog wasn't too far down the road, there was no way I could have known that then.

Times were good. The best they'd ever be. The wife and I were fresh off another massive win over Sparky and the Chicago Cubs, who, after collapsing in such legendary fashion in the playoffs the previous season, had decided to fold the last week of the regular season this year, losing five of their last seven games, thus eliminating themselves from postseason contention and saving the wife and me a ton of worry and prayer and God knows what else.

Penny was training for a half marathon and was looking as svelte and sexy as ever. I had been half hoping for another stressful Cubs postseason, entirely for the chance to see her dancing around in the buff again. I was even joining her on some of her runs as well as eating the healthy meals she was preparing and as a result I had gotten rid of a great deal of my blubberish belly.

Sparky, on the other hand, was ballooning splendidly from all the burgers and pizza and French fries and milkshakes we kept plying him with and, perhaps brought on by the frustration of the latest Cub meltdown, was sporting a fresh bald patch on the back of his head, making him look more aged and wretched than ever. Furthermore, his grades were still wonderfully below average, and better yet, we weren't doing his homework just well enough for him to get a by-the-skin-of-his-teeth passing grade anymore—he was doing this on his own.

He was involved in no activities and sports. He had no friends to speak of.

As I said, times were good. Strike that. *Great.* The best they'd ever be.


More great stuff:

The old man was out of the picture for once, utterly caught up with his new life, wife, and son, who at the time was two years old and had yet to demonstrate any hints of being a genuine fucking genius.

At work the previous week, I had gotten my idea approved for a springy, pliant spoon that would help people better scrape food from the bottom of bowls.

You know: Bendy Spoon.

In contrast, my archenemy, Fred T.C. Hoover Jr., was suffering from creative block due to his recent separation from his wife, the previously mentioned Miss Indiana runner-up. The split had come after her recent explicit turn in *Hustler*, an issue every male at work had tormented Fred with whenever he would chance by their desks.

Oh, what happy days.

But even all that could not make me the happiest I'd ever been. There needed to be a little more for me to go from happy to happier to happiest. And as the Lord would have it (He and I were getting along famously then) I got that final boost on Saturday, November the 6th, 2004 at 11:07 in the morning.

I know, I know. The madness. Just say it already. All right, all right: I published a poem.


# 8

THE ANTICHRIST OF KOKOMO COUNTY
*The beast in first form*
*As fat child, burps burger, toots*
*Does mankind tremble?*


To be fair, it was the most modest of modest successes, as even the best haikus tend to be. The magazine that accepted "The Antichrist of Kokomo County," *The Vincennes Quarterly Review,* had a circulation of about four and didn't pay anything. But hey, it was my first stab as a writer and I had managed to get something published right out of the gate. And the *VQR* people loved "my little whimsy," as I called it. They thought it was funny. They even published it in the Giggle Issue because they thought so highly of it, a fact that sent my soul a-soarin'. And just how many competitors had I dusted along the way, eh? How many verses and stories and vignettes had been rejected to make room for mine?

At last, others had been denied because of me, and standing there with the acceptance letter in my hot little hands, it began to occur to me that being funny might be my path to greatness, that abandoning that quality in myself in school had been a terrible mistake.

And the best part of being great for being funny?

Everybody likes you.

★

So there I was: the happiest I've ever been. My mind was racing with all the endless possibilities now in front of me. I am embarrassed to say I was so over the moon at that moment that I raised my arms in celebration. I am just as abashed to say I shouted out in joy and laughed in bliss before strutting back into the house, a changed man.

I got as far as the threshold of the living room before my celebration ended, before joy and bliss departed from me, perhaps never to return. Once more, alarm and dread became my companions. Doom and calamity my cohorts.

The wife was seated on the couch, shuddering. She was mumbling to herself. She was covered in bird shit.

She had gashes and cuts all over her face and neck, and I, ever the devoted husband, tended to her wounds. I used a soapy washcloth to clean off the bird shit and blood. I applied bacterial ointment to the cuts and gashes to speed healing and prevent infection. I served her a couple of shots of whiskey (typically reserved for sore throats and a certain somebody's fogs) to help even out the trembles and the mumbles. I then put on the best look of concern I could muster and asked her what happened.

To which, with more shudder and mumble, the wife lifted a blood-stained hand and crooked a finger out of the living room window at our son in the front yard, seated on a tire swing.

"H-he did," she murmured.

When I reached him at the tire swing, Sparky was staring off into the distance again—which is to say, into nothing. Before I could get a word out, he started swinging.

"Is Mom all right?"

"Yeah, she'll be fine."

"Oh." I couldn't tell if he was pleased by this news or disappointed. When someone is swinging on a swing, it's tough to get a read on their facial expression unless it's an extreme smile or frown. Whatever look was on Sparky's face, I couldn't glean it. His swinging back and forth made him a blur to me.

"Is it true what happened to her, son?" I said. "Did you tell a bird to attack her?"

Back and forth Sparky went, quiet as can be.

Not in the mood to wait around for him to take his sweet time in answering me, I stepped behind the swing to stop it, and it was here that Sparky did the unthinkable—at least, the unthinkable as far as I was concerned, as I didn't think of it.

He jumped off the swing and ran.


Now, you wouldn't think that a fat child—even if he is the Antichrist—running at top speed would be able to put much distance between himself and a grown man who has been doing quite a bit of jogging of late.

And you would be right not to think that. I caught Sparky after about five steps.

Sparky was squealing with laughter when I grabbed him by the collar and dragged him to the ground. "Tickles?" he said.

"Give me an answer first," I said, not tickling Sparky, but not ruling it out. I knew I had to dangle the potential for tickling in trade or else he wouldn't feel obliged to answer me.

"What?" Sparky said. "What did I do?"

"I don't know," I said. "You tell me."

"Tickles!"

"Answer my question first. Did you tell a bird to attack your mother?"

"Oochie-coochie!"

"Answer me!"

"Ha haaaaa!"

I grabbed Sparky by the shirt again, pulled him up to my face, and boomed another "ANSWER ME!"

Much like he had every other time I had employed some BOOM in his direction, I expected the boy to cry, but this time he seemed unfazed by

Angry Daddy's Boomy Voice. He screwed up his face in contemplation, perhaps mock, perhaps not, and said, "Uh, I don't *think* I did."


# 9

"OH, HORSERABBIT!" THE WIFE SAID, DIPPING A SCRUBBY SPONGE INTO A bucket. "Oh, bullsocks!"

"I'm only telling you what he said," I replied.

"And you believe him?" she said, flicking water from the scrubby sponge in my direction. "Over me?"

I had come back into the house to find the whiskey bottle empty and the wife furiously cleaning the master bathroom tub.

"No, I'm not saying you're wrong, honey—"

"Not wrong. *Lying!*"

"I'm not saying you're lying." I opened the bottom cabinet and took the second scrubby sponge that had come with its brother in the package of two and, with it, started in on the sink. "All I'm saying is this might not have been what it appeared to be."

"What part of a bird flying from Sparky's hand and pecking my face off is not what it appears to be?" the wife said as angrily as she was scrubbing.

Nonplussed, I stopped my own scrubbing. Soap and dirt were now commingling in the sink. I would need to rinse them down the drain soon or they'd dry that way. Together. The good and the bad.

"The bird flew off his hand?" I said in disbelief.

"And pecked my face off," the wife said, turning on the shower to wash away the orgy of soap, dirt, pubes, and mildew that were romping together in the tub. She had done that for the same reason I needed to rinse my orgy in the sink, and soon.

"What was Sparky doing with the bird on his hand?"

"Whispering to it!"

The wife climbed out of the tub and started washing the outside of it.

"Creepy whispers?" I asked. I had resumed scrubbing and the orgy of bubbles and scum in the sink had gotten impressively large. Not one part of it was untouched by the debauchery.

"What do you think? Yeah, creepy whispers!" the wife said.

"And so you—where were you?" My orgy had now spread to the countertop.

"I was by the back door, watering the dogdang flowers."

"And so you looked up, saw Sparky whispering to a bird on his hand, and then it up and flew after you?" (I was trying to avoid the part where she'd gotten pooped on.)

"That's right."

With about fifteen hundred paper towels, the wife wiped away the orgy on the outside of the tub and started on the floor.

"What kind of a bird was it?" I said, finally rinsing clean the sink and countertop.

"I don't know, a brown bird," the wife said. "A little brown bird came at me."

"A little bird made all those marks on your face?" I said, spraying the bathroom mirror with Windex.

"Most of them, yeah."

"What do you mean 'most of them'? Where did the rest come from?"

The wife paused to make a face at the overwhelming Windex smell. "Some of the marks might have come from my fingernails, okay? But I was scared out of my mind, trying to get the bird off my face!"

The wife was now using another too-many-paper-towels wad to wipe the linoleum clean. Somewhere, trees wept.

"So some of those scratches are from you?" I said, using a single sheet to clean the Windex off the mirror, demonstrating how little paper towel was necessary in order to get the same result.

"What difference does it make if some of the scratches came from me?" the wife said.

"Seems like you or the bird would have really had to go to town in order to get some of those marks. Just strange is all," I said, trying to get too much out of my single sheet of paper towel and smearing Windex all over the mirror.

"Are you saying I did this to myself?"

"No, I'm getting all the relevant information."

"Oh, is that so?" the wife said, shaking her enormous paper towel wad in my face. "Well, here's some more relevant information for you, Mr. Man. The reason my fingernails were able to scratch my face up so well is because *you* asked me to keep them long and sharp so I can scratch *your* back up during dirty stuff!"

"Are you saying this is my fault?"

The mirror was almost done. I was thinking it was time to get out of the bathroom before I got saddled with toilet duty.

"As much as it is mine. You think I did this to myself for some reason, which is ridiculous, so I'm doing the same thing by saying you made me keep my fingernails long because you *knew* this would all happen."

"So you think Sparky and I are plotting with birds to hurt you?" I said.

"Why not? It's just as plausible as me doing this to myself for whatever whacked-out reason you've come up with."

The wife tossed her massive paper towel wad into the trash and her face changed.

"Toilet time," she said.

We took a break from our discussion to play Rock, Paper, Scissors for the pleasure of not being the one to scrub the toilet.

I picked scissors. The wife picked rock.

I said, "Best two out of three."

The wife left the bathroom.


# 10


"LET ME GET THIS STRAIGHT. YOUR WIFE SAID A BIRD ATTACKED HER?" DANICA says, her eyes narrowed skeptically, her arms folded doubtfully.

"That's correct," I say, my arms unfolded, my eyes doing nothing.

"You didn't see the bird attack her?"

"No, I didn't."

"Then how do you know for sure it happened?"

"I don't know for sure. But I believe it did."

Danica scoffs. "Have you ever seen your son do any of these *strange* things?" she says. "Has it ever occurred to you your wife is off her rocker and is making this stuff up?"

"Why would she make up something like that?" I say.

If I tell Danica the truth, that I, too, have wondered from time to time whether the wife was making up stories about Sparky in order to justify what was being done to him, then I might also be forced to speak about our design to thwart the Antichrist from the beginning of his life, not to mention my recent decision to maybe kill him. I don't think that would be such a good idea to bring up, so I pretend such a notion is outrageous.

"That's crazy," I say. "Do you think she *wanted* her son to be the Antichrist?"


"Michael?" Phipps says. "Did you send a bird after your mother?"

It finally seems to have dawned on somebody in this room to go to the one other person who has been involved in all of these events. Why it didn't dawn on me, I couldn't tell you.

Oh, wait, yes I could. Here's why:

Sparky looks up from his drawing and says, "I like birds." Then he adds, "They fly around, and I wish I could fly with them."

Phipps's face falls. Danica snorts. "No disrespect here, but this kid's mentally defective or something," she says. "Not to mention a pervert."

"My dear, feel free to adjourn back to your desk and finish your secretarial duties for the day," Phipps says.

"You got it, *Reverend*," Danica says, getting up. As she leaves, I can't help but imagine a very spirited game of Grabass.

"Why are we even listening to any of this?" Danica says, whirling around. "When it's clear this doofus is the father of that kid? Lord Lucifer couldn't have possibly made such an ugly little troll."

"That is an outdated interpretation of prophecy, Danica. As you know, the consensus in the church is that the idea of our Lord's son is metaphorical concerning conception. We are not cockeyed fundamentalists clinging foolishly to myths like our God-fearing adversaries," Phipps says. "And you will not insult children in my presence."

"Whatever," Danica says, turning her blazing eyes on me. "You're nothing but a liar. You've never seen anything this kid's supposedly done!" she yells, slamming the door behind her.

"Oh yeah?" I fire back into the door. "I saw him bite that bird's head off!"

The goons and Phipps seem more than a little taken aback. "Uh, he bit the bird's *head* off?" candy goon says.

"Yeah. I went into the backyard the day after he sent the bird to attack his mother, and I found him standing there with a headless brown bird in his hand."

"Where was the head? How do you know he bit it off?" Phipps says.

"Because it was in his mouth."

Understandably, a silence follows. The goons blink in unison. Phipps strokes his beard.

"Is there anything else, strange or weird, that you yourself have seen the boy do other than bite a bird's head off?" Phipps says.

"As a matter of fact there is," I say, pausing for dramatic effect. Phipps smiles, appreciating it, but, at the same time, not taking the bait. The goons, though, can't handle it. In tandem, they lean forward, licking their lips and rubbing their hands together and I lean forward as well, beckon them to come closer so I can whisper it, so Sparky won't hear.

"What did he do?" gun goon says, on the verge of losing his mind, it seems.

"He killed his mother," I say.

# PART NINE

*"Well, I'll be. That looks like quite a squall."*

# 1

REMEMBER THAT "HAPPIEST I'D EVER BEEN" GARBAGE? THIS IS THE FLIPSIDE, brace yourself.

Rewind from today, a year or so. I was in my living room, spread out on the couch, watching television.

No, no bear cartoons. A sitcom this time, featuring a naughty though ultimately good-hearted orphan doing various naughty-funny, ultimately good-hearted things that exasperate his foster family while bringing them all together in love and understanding.

I would have changed the channel but I was too anesthetized by a belly full of sweets and booze. I was also lost in a head full of fog.

The old man was there too. He had stopped by with some of Joyce's excellent homemade macaroons, and in a tick under five minutes I had taken down a baker's dozen along with a pint glass of half-and-half.

"The holy heck's the matter with you?" my father had said.


As was par for the course, the old man had an ulterior motive for coming over, other than to provide the materials for my astonishing cookie blitz. He wanted to show me a photo album of the little brother (note: my father never brought the little brother over) and brag about him.

Even though I had garnered some pretty thick skin when it came to the incredible feats of my precocious younger sibling, I had no defense for what my father had decided to unburden himself of that afternoon.

"This is it, son," he'd said. "*He* is Him."

The old man was in the midst of showing me an earlier incarnation of the little brother: as a three-year-old in the bathtub wearing the biggest goddamned smile nobody has any right to.

"He's barely seven years old, Dad," I said. "How do you figure?"

"I just do," the old man said. "Call it a father's intuition."

To this, I crammed a fourteenth macaroon into my rapacious maw, and washed it down with bitterness (and more half-and-half).

"I was getting worried, you know," the old man continued. "Was beginning to think I'd heard the Lord wrong and I wasn't going to live to see it."

"So what decided it?" I said, my voice heavy with milk fat and long-term paternal resentment. "Was there some sort of angelic visitation or did little bro just react better to that human pyramid crap?"

My father answered this with the loudest goddamned laugh nobody has any right to.

"What a funny day that was, Frankie. We were both fumbling around trying to find our way, weren't we?"

Down the hatch went cookie number fifteen. "Yep. Good times."

"I know, they really were when you think about it, and at the end of the day all water under the bridge," my father said, tapping another photo, this one of the little brother in full t-ball gear and wearing the same unjustly rapturous look. "And now we are both going to witness something special, something great."

"You can witness it all you want," I said, "I have my own family to take care of."

"I know you do, son, and I'm proud of you for the most part."

*Shut!* went the photo album.

"You know, for a little while there, I really thought it might be Michael," the old man said.

"Sorry to let you down," I said.

"Oh—*hee*—son, you didn't let me down."

I turned my head to look at him. After all that had happened between us, I didn't think he could do anything to surprise me anymore, but he managed to here. With a loud "Oof!" he got up from the couch, wheezy-hee'd exactly twice, and then proceeded to genuflect in front of me. As one might expect, such a humiliating, painful-looking posture was accompanied by tear-filled eyes (and a fart).

"You've never let me down, Frankie. And neither did—*hee*—Michael."

I'm ashamed to say that seeing my father on bended knee, looking at me with such billowing love, couldn't help but make my eyes well up too, even though I knew this was a sham. My father's affection was borne of the kind of squishy altruism you feel toward another person only when everything is going right for you.

"You've done the best with what the good Lord gave you, son, and I have no doubt—*hee*—Michael will also do his best with whatever measure he's been given," the old man said, rising to his feet. "And—*hee*—while there can only be one Great Horvath, that doesn't mean there can't be some pretty durn good ones too."

I, quite emotional in the midst of this fog, let tears dribble down my face, and when the old man pulled me in for a hug, I may have even let out a sob.

I was heartbroken, angry, insulted, but somehow comforted by what he had told me. It was soothing to know I could still be a Pretty Durn Good Horvath. Yet, I was still pissed and miserable.

What a mélange of emotions the heart can hold at the same time!

Why was I so pissed? So miserable? At no point had my father said he'd ever believed the Great Horvath might be me.


The hug now over, I was back on the couch. The old man had decided to stick around for a bit and was fast asleep on the recliner.

I was alone again in my fog, full of cookies and a few handfuls of jalapeno-cheese crackers. My brain was soupy with television.

Moments ago, I had gotten off the phone with the wife, who was now on her way home from a parent-teacher conference.

"How'd it go?" I had asked her sleepily, junk-food drunkily.

"Not good," she'd said. "Not good at all."

Did I detect a note of dread in her voice? An entire symphony, actually. But my numbed, sedated state assured me that she was overreacting as always and that the brisk, friendly colors of a laundry detergent commercial were more important things to consider.

"I'll be home soon," the wife continued. "We'll talk about it then."

"Sure thing," I mumbled.

"Make sure you save me a couple of cookies, okay?" she said.

"Wuh?" I asked, but she had already hung up.

That would be the last thing I would ever say to my beloved wife. *Wuh?*

Not knowing this, I burped.

In less than ten minutes, I would be a widower.

Not knowing this, I scratched myself.

One week from this day, I would be standing in a graveyard in front of her closed casket, suffering through torrents of inane vapidities from other mourners and trying not to run myself through on a miniature obelisk stationed a few feet away.

Not knowing this, I picked cookie crumbs out of the creases of my shirt and sprinkled them into my mouth.

What a slob.

2

IN ALL FAIRNESS TO MY SLOVENLINESS, EVEN BEFORE THE OLD MAN HAD stopped by with the photo album, it had been a rough day, week, month, two years.

I had once again lost heart, lost my way. The wife had also, to some extent, lost it for a period of time, meaning she too had become something of a slob.

This is what consistent disappointment and failure does: it makes you slobby.

We were losing the war with Sparky. Even with our prayers and schemes, the boy was improving at everything, and we had noticed, perhaps too late, that we were losing control.

The boy had begun to figure out how to circumvent his parents and take certain aspects of his future into his own hands. Hence, the whispers of a friendship with some kid from school. Hence, some significant weight loss over the past year or so, as Sparky, to our amazement, began eating smaller portions of his typical atrocious diet, even asking from time to time for fruit, vegetables, and lean protein, citing information *learned* from a sit-down with the school nurse. Hence, and worst of all, two B's on his last report card.

Alarmed by Sparky's progress, the wife had begun discussing more drastic measures. Pulling him out of Elmo Lincoln and homeschooling him was one option. Pulling up stakes and striking out for a new district was another.

"Maybe a fresh start is what he needs," she said. "Everybody here knows him too well now. Everybody here is trying so stinking hard to *help* him."

Another possible solution was to figure out some way to get Sparky on antipsychotics or sedatives. Dope the kid up, for real this time—not with high fructose corn syrup, caffeine, and Benadryl, but the hard stuff. No more messing around.

Also of concern in those foggy times: the Cubs. They were good again, fresh off a division title after finishing in the cellar the previous year; and although they were promptly swept in the first round of the playoffs, they appeared to be on the brink of a long run of sustained success that I feared would give the wife and me innumerable fits, and could very well pay off a virtue I was not happy to see Sparky still possessed: hope.

Added to this, no more weirdness. Sparky was as behaved and normal as he'd ever been. No more Kamikaze crapping birds. No more mysteriously spinning ceiling fans. No more twenty-four hour crying jags on Christian holidays.

Sparky had even started showing interest in church and had quickly become known in the congregation for singing loudly (and badly) at worship services, attentively listening—or doing a damn good job of faking it—through Reverend Worley's meandering, point-free sermons, and going to the front for altar calls every Sunday to confess and wash away his sins.

"Don't be fooled," the wife had said to me on more than one occasion. "He only wants us to think he's like us.

"He's learning to become the Great Deceiver."

★

What did I think of all this?

Not much.

I was utterly immersed in fog.

3

I WAS NO LONGER A WRITER. A POET NO MORE. MY DREAMS OF BEING FUNNY and becoming great for being funny had been dashed.

All funny poems after my first credit had been rejected. Same with all my funny fiction. The most depressing setback was a story I had been convinced was something exceptional—the one I had taken to the mailbox to submit while practically dancing, so sure was I that it would be published and I again seen as great and funny for writing it.

That story?

"The Can."

It was about this uppity Manhattan billionaire who, with a rumbling tummy and every toilet in a dystopian New York City occupied, has no choice but to take a dump in a trash can.

To this day I don't get why, but nobody picked it up. Not *The New Yorker*, not *The Paris Review*, not even the *Vincennes Quarterly,* who responded to the story as follows:

*"Um, no."*

Silverware design was in the toilet as well. My attempt to piggyback on the success of Fred T.C. Hoover Jr.'s Warrior fork with a Saracen Sword-looking kitchen knife (you know: Sheiky Knife) flopped.

As luck would have it, Fred T.C. Hoover Jr. was still rolling in the bonus money for the Warrior, which had just become the company's all-time bestseller. He was also still hitched to the Miss Indiana runner-up.

Completely reversing course from his earlier revulsion to her sluttish behavior, Fred T.C. Hoover Jr. made peace with his wife's turn in *Hustler,* so well that, in addition to salvaging their marriage, they started their own pornographic website together. For twenty bucks a month anyone with an internet connection could (and can) view photosets and videos featuring Fred T.C. Hoover Jr. having sex with the Miss Indiana runner-up in a variety of exotic positions in a variety of not-so-exotic Kokomo County / southern Indiana locations (such as the Little Hat town dump, a filthy Ponderosa restaurant bathroom, an abandoned Bookmobile, or in the front yard of the Quilters Hall of Fame). As always, classy.

Because of his website, Fred T.C. Hoover Jr. was raking in an extra four grand per month.

"And it helps keep the little lady and I in great shape!" he said.

Even worse, this licentiousness made him more of a hero than ever around the Dagwood offices. Everybody—from the interns to the sales staff to even the big dogs upstairs—thought Fred T.C. Hoover Jr. to be the bee's knees. Progressive, modern, innovative, notorious, shameless, successful, husband to a drop-dead gorgeous, promiscuous wife. Nobody in the entire state of Indiana was like Fred T.C. Hoover Jr.—much less in Kokomo County.

I hated him more than ever. Not just because of his success at work and certainly not because of his stupid porno site. No, what bothered me was not how he lived his life, nor how he was celebrated throughout the town for it (though these things did irritate), but how he used it all to mock me.

It would seem that somewhere along the line Fred T.C. Hoover Jr. began viewing me as I did him. That is, as an adversary. That is, as someone whose soul he must devour.

This might have stemmed from the low point he experienced back when he had suffered from his own creative block and was oh so close to being divorced from his drop-dead gorgeous, promiscuous wife. It was around that time that he had seen me at my high-water mark, when I had, like Napoleon from Elba, triumphantly returned to Silverware Design with the idea for Bendy Spoon after a temporary banishment to Napkin Patterning. How he must have blistered with envy when my published haiku, "The Antichrist of Kokomo County," was mentioned at the Dagwood Awards that year, the same ceremony where I received Best Innovation in Silverware Design, the one and only time I've won in the fourteen years.

How he must have fumed when he had seen the award-winning Franklin and Mrs. Horvath arm in arm at the company picnic that year while simultaneously imagining his wife mingling other, more private human equipment with those *Hustler* photographers.

I can't say that I blame him much for begrudging me my success. Neither he nor I could have known how brief it would end up being. If we had, then perhaps I wouldn't have been so cavalier in the way I carried myself in those days. Perhaps I would not have sauntered up to Fred's desk, held up a picture of his wife demonstrating, via engorged cucumber, a remarkable vaginal capacity, and said, "I guess this makes us even there, buddy. I know my life has changed."

Perhaps he wouldn't have determined himself to beat me, to humiliate me, at any cost.

As it stands, I did what I did and said what I said. And so did he.


A sampling of the lengths that Fred T.C. Hoover Jr. went to:

After winning the Best Innovation in Silverware Design Award two years in a row, he put the plaques on both ends of his cubicle wall, so that no matter which way I was walking down the aisle, I would come face to face with an award that went to him instead of me.

He also took to decorating his Employee of the Year award—posted by the vending machines—with twinkling Christmas lights, so that when I got a hankering for some Fritos, my attention would be drawn to his name on the award as I am powerless to avert my gaze from things that twinkle.

Additionally, Fred T.C. Hoover Jr. had gotten a bunch of erotic fiction published through his wife's contacts in the smut biz, and from what I heard (I've not read them) they all featured the sexual mishaps and misadventures of a time-traveling putz named Hankie Vorfath, who, in his voyage through the centuries, is ridiculed for his diminutive penis and rejected by every famous woman in history.

Lastly, from what I've been told, in those web videos where Fred T.C. Hoover Jr. has sex with his wife (at the Piper Flight Museum, at Schimpff's Candy Kitchen), after finishing he turns to the camera, wiggles his eyebrows, and says the following:

"Eat your heart out, Horvath."

The camera then zooms in on the face of his breathtaking wife, and she moans the exact same thing:

"Yeah, eat your heart out, Horvath. Mmmm..."

Somehow, I don't think Aaron Burr would have had Mrs. Burr do that to Alexander Hamilton. Same with Tommy Edison, his wife, and Tesla. Never would have happened.


# 4

BUT BACK TO THE COUCH. THERE I WAS, THE PRETTY DURN GOOD HORVATH, in a fog, staring at a photo of my younger brother.

Was I at bottom? Was this as low as I could go? Not quite. I was in a fog and bummed out, to be sure, but I still felt I had options. I had not given up. I still believed my father was wrong. I still believed I had time to prove him wrong. I was not finished. I was just having a tough go of it. Down deep, I still believed change was right around the corner, right around the bend.

And I was right. Change *was* coming.


As I attempted to rally my spirits with these upbeat thoughts, the orphan sitcom was interrupted by a weather alert.

A bleached-blond nineteen-year-old weatherman, Joey Frasca, part of the Kokomo County Fox affiliate's recent decision to gear the local news to the age fifteen to twenty-four demographic, came on the tube jolting his arms this way and that at a map of Indiana nearly crowded out by an advertisement for a new energy drink called Yakk.

"Killer storm coming, yo," he said, making horns with his hand and pointing at a sea of red covering the lower half of Indiana. "The most killer storm of all time."

Curious to catch a glimpse of this most killer storm and thinking, as was customary, I wouldn't be in agreement with the designation, I stepped out onto the back porch to take a gander.

For once, Joey Frasca was right on the money. The angry red on the TV screen had translated into commensurately angry black clouds advancing across the sky. I saw flashes of lightning in the distance. I heard grumbles of thunder from a storm only beginning to vent its fury. I felt the ominous chill from a gust sent ahead of the storm.

"Well, I'll be. That looks like quite a squall," my father said. He'd also gotten out of his chair to get a look, though, due to his aversion to raindrops, he did not venture beyond the screen door.

Since I'm not all that into getting rained on either, I turned my back on the storm to reenter the house, only to be halted in my tracks by my father's raised, pointing finger, which turned me around.

There, in the middle of the field beyond our backyard fence, arms outstretched like a wizard mustering the winds, was Sparky.

He was yelling into the storm—yelling *at* it maybe. When he wasn't yelling, he was cackling. When he wasn't yelling or cackling, he was thrashing his arms like an unhinged orchestra conductor who believes his baton is what makes the music. All the while, the storm closed in on him.

"What is that dipstick doing?" my father said.

Despite being full of cookies, half-and-half, crackers, booze, and the not-so-proud owner of quite a lot of stomach, I was still able to haul ass into the field, grab Sparky, and drag him to the house in a surprisingly short amount of time.

I, gasping, was about to vomit, about to have a stroke. My father, about to do neither of those things and breathing normally, wrapped the boy in a towel and sat him on a chair in the kitchen.

The boy was breathing almost as hard as I was, but unlike me, it did not appear to be because he desperately needed the oxygen in order to live. It looked instead that he was thrilled about something. His eyes were huge, shining.

It was a look I had seen in my own eyes many times. Exhilaration. Illumination. Euphoria. Like Archimedes about to run naked through the streets of Syracuse.

You know: *Eureka!*


Disconcerted by those shining eyes of his and furious with him for being outside in the most killer storm of all time, my father and I attacked Sparky with a barrage of questions and rebukes.

"What were you doing out there?"

"Do you know how dangerous that was?"

"Who were you talking to?"

"Why were you laughing?"

And on and on.

Sparky, as usual, wouldn't answer us. He just kept his shining eyes on the storm outside and his breathing labored and hoarse.

Given the look on my father's face at that moment, I got the impression that I might be able to finally let him in on Sparky's little secret, that it was possible he might join forces with Penny and me—even more so when Sparky looked up with those same glistening eyes and, with a voice deeper than it had ever been before, said this:

"I'm kinda worried about Mom."


## 5

THE GOONS ARE BACK AND IN MOTION, HAULING THE MAHOGANY DESK TO THE far corner of the room, next to the open balcony door. Reverend Phipps is hunched over what looks to be an open guitar case, and from it he produces a piece of thick, purple chalk and a black mat. The goons remove the rug that was underneath the desk, and with the hardwood floor exposed, Phipps rolls out the mat, kneels, and draws with the chalk what I understand is called the Sigil of Baphomet or, as I know it, a pentagram.

Which disappoints me.

Just once I'd like to hear of a satanic ritual with some other logo. Like General Motors or the US Postal Service. But then, I guess others would say the same thing about us Christians and our crosses and stick-on bumper fish.

"Michael," Phipps says, "I would like you to come here and sit down in the middle of this circle."

"Gentlemen," he says to the goons, "you are not worthy of this moment. You will go."

"What about me?" I ask as the goons unworthily trudge out.

"You are the father of the boy, correct?" Phipps says.

"Absolutely."

"Then you are worthy. You may stay."

"Great," I say, and feeling just that, especially since I can stay on this couch.

I am comfy. I am worthy.


What I am about to observe is what the Church of E calls a Summoning. What's going to be summoned is a demon of some sort, who will give various commands and guidance to Phipps, perhaps even deliver a message from his satanic majesty himself.

The Church of E, Phipps tells me, is only allowed so many Summonings per year, and as this is October, they are near the bottom of the barrel in how many Summonings they have left. Which means either Halloween, the Yule / Winter Solstice, or Casino Night will be Summoning-free this year, and entirely because of me and the fruit of my loins.

"But I wouldn't be burning one of our last Summonings unless I felt the situation to be so special as to warrant it," Phipps said. "I would burn one hundred years' worth for this moment."

Now how do you like that?

I wish I could call up my father right now. I wish I could tell him all about this and then ask him to put my younger brother on the line.

What would I say?

"Eat your heart out, Horvath."


What the demon is being summoned for is to tell Reverend Phipps and me, once and for all, whether or not Michael Jasper Horvath is the Antichrist.

Sparky's Black Catechism score and my stories, as good as they were, weren't enough to convince Phipps into going all in. They were, however, enough to summon a demon to settle the issue.

That's nothing to sneeze at.

The tough part is, once the answer is given—and in the affirmative, I'm sure—I will still have to figure out a way to take care of Sparky before Phipps and his goons can whisk him away, and preferably without having to go toe to toe with that demon. Call me unsure of myself, but I just don't like my chances in such a fight.

Then again, I don't like anybody's chances in such a fight—except Jesus, who has yet to show up. And if I'm up to speed on how this end-of-the-world stuff goes, he's not going to get here for a long time still.


Speaking of Jesus, as I watch Phipps make final preparations (a small black altar has been brought in and there are various, standard satanic artifacts being placed on it, such as bone of some sort, a tattered black book—*Necronomicon* probably—and a vial of what I'm thinking must be baby's blood), one question troubles me.

"Why would you guys want the Antichrist to be alive if he's just going to get his ass kicked by Jesus in the end?"

"Our prophecy ends a little differently than the one in your Bible," Phipps says.

"Oh, like you guys win or something?"

"Something like that."

I sneer. I laugh. I may doubt the existence of God and my religion from time to time, but one thing is certain: if it is true, if God is there, then He certainly isn't going to lose.

"You sound skeptical about our prospects," Phipps says. "Too indoctrinated with Christian propaganda to fathom the possibility of defeat?"

"What's my alternative? That some ego-maniac ex-angel can beat the One who created him?" I say.

Phipps smiles. "I guess we'll just have to see what happens, but until that day—if we survive the war long enough to see it—let me give you this to think about: If the Biblical account of the fall of Lord Lucifer is to be believed, why did God, after the rebellion, not destroy Him outright? Why did he allow Him to continue to exist when there is no hope of forgiveness?"

"To prove a point," I say. "To teach us all a lesson about God's nature."

"Spoken like a true sheep, Frankie," Phipps says. "But even you have to know that isn't much of an answer."

"Fine. Why didn't God destroy Satan then?"

"Because he can't, Frankie. Because he's not strong enough."

At this complete and utter rubbish, I sneer a second time but do not laugh. (Why? Eh, don't feel like it this time.)

"Okay, Phipps. If He's not strong enough to destroy Satan, why wasn't Satan strong enough to stay in Heaven?"

"*That* is nothing but a spin-job courtesy of God, the true loser of the so-called Celestial Rebellion. You see, Lucifer and His followers, dissatisfied with the weak, unstable rule of Jehovah, left Heaven of their own accord and came to Earth to establish a new kingdom. God fought to keep Lucifer, his brightest star, from leaving, and was soundly defeated. Lucifer, out of respect for His old commander, allowed God to keep Heaven, while He took control of Earth. For ages an uneasy truce was had, with God still nursing his wounds and lusting after the Earth; whereas Lord Lucifer, not the crazed, megalomaniac depicted in scripture, but a strong, wise, and just entity, was content with His lot and kept little interest in the goings on in Heaven. Knowing full well he could not defeat Lucifer in another war, God approached Him with a wager."

"Mankind," I say.

"Very good, Frankie," Phipps says. "The idea was God and Lucifer would wage war in a different sense. A battle of wits over the hearts and minds of these newly created beings. During the long timeline of humanity's existence, each would have the opportunity for one champion, one member of the human race who would be given the power to drive God or Lucifer into banishment in the far recesses of existence, a gruesome, teeth-gnashing place referred to in the Christian Bible as the Outer Darkness, but which we Epistemological Emendationists call... Tijuana."

"Mexico?"

"Yes, but don't interrupt again. Now, God—out of the graciousness in Lucifer's heart—was allowed the first turn and brought forth Jesus Christ two thousand years ago."

"And Jesus Christ won," I say. "He died for our sins and went down to Hell and broke the chains of death, liberating souls before resurrecting himself and ascending to his glorious throne in Heaven."

"That, my friend, is pure fiction."

"How do you figure?"

"Oh, Christ died all right, in brutal fashion. Lucifer made sure of it. God's champion was a poor realization indeed. Christ, who thought he was to lead a successful *coup d'état* in Jerusalem, subdue the Roman Empire, and rule a thousand years, didn't even get much more than a handful of followers who promptly deserted him when the proverbial going got proverbially chewy, right before Lucifer snuffed him out.

"God did not take too well to this latest debacle. For all the puerile accusations in the Bible calling Lucifer the father of lies, God himself is the true master. His champion destroyed, God deviously invented a ridiculous fairy tale to keep mankind under bondage to weakness and make the way as difficult as possible for Lucifer's champion. But the best he has managed has been to temporarily stave off the inevitable, and Lucifer, who has been patiently biding His time, using God's plan against him, is now poised to end this little game that was begun so many ages ago. His champion is at hand, and so is His ultimate victory."

"Hm. That's quite the imagination you got there," I say. "Gonna be a pretty bad day when you realize none of it's going to happen."

"Like I said, we'll see, won't we?" Phipps says, going back to his altar business.

"There's no way you can win, Phipps," I say. "It's impossible."

"Look around you, Frankie. What in this world tells you we are losing?"


# 6


A DAY AFTER THE WIFE DIED IN JOEY FRASCA'S MOST KILLER RAINSTORM, hydroplaning the Horvath family station wagon into a telephone pole, the old man invited Sparky to come live with him, Joyce, and the Great Horvath for a while.

This invitation was not extended to me—not that I would have accepted it anyway—and that Friday, after Penny's funeral, Sparky got into the old man's Datsun instead of into Old Tuna with me and we went our separate ways: Sparky to his grandpa's, me to that now haunted house of mine.

Where, liquored up, I communed with ghosts.

Where, stoned on some Xanax Joyce had slipped me, I slurred and groaned at God.

Where I punched walls, kicked doors, fell down, ate too much, slept too much, cried too much.

Oh, Penny! Oh, my love! *How this pillar of the world has been transformed into a strumpet's fool!*


Throughout these mournful weeks, I bore constant visits from the old man, who, in spite of my objections, came over every day and attempted to pick me up with more pictures and stories of the little bro.

I withstood obligatory condolences from work, from everybody, including Fred T.C. Hoover Jr., who declared our feud dead. In the lunchroom the day of my return, he approached me, and we tearfully hugged like two mafia dons at the truce of a mob war.

Fred said he wanted to be friends from now on.

I, sick with grief and tired of ugly feelings, said, "That would be fine by me."

As a show of good faith, he took down his award plaques and the Christmas lights by the vending machines. He promised not to mention me in any new videos he made with his wife, and the next chance he got, he would have Hankie Vorfath get, in his words, "a hummer from Helen of Troy right after beating the shit out of Achilles."

To which I said, "I appreciate that."


The big dogs at Dagwood, pitying me as well, gave me an Honorable Mention in Best Innovation in Silverware Design at that year's Dagwood Awards for my admittedly uninspiring, yet functional, knife and fork combination.

You know: Knifey Fork.

I was even commended for my equally uninspired slogan: "For when a spork won't cut the mustard anymore, Knifey Fork will."

Yeah, they gave me an award for that, an award I littered a section of highway in the greater Asshat, Indiana area with after chucking it out the driver's side window on my way home from the ceremony.

Where, liquored up once more, I communed with ghosts.

Where, stoned out of my mind again, I ranted and raved at God.

Where I cried, ate, fell down, slept.

Don't ever say we Horvaths don't know how to party.


# 7


More about the demon as we wait:

Tituba is her name. She's an authentic, bona fide devil-whore, an honest-to-goodness, genuine bitch-demon.

Either she's taken her name from the seventeenth century slave accused of witchcraft during a rather embarrassing chapter in Puritan history, or we're talking quite the coincidence here.

Her territory is the northernmost tip of the Bible Belt, which includes the northern tip of Kentucky, a sliver of southwestern Ohio, and, unfortunately for her, all of Kokomo County.

I wonder how she feels about this dreary charge, this lackluster lot in her infernal existence. I also can't help but wonder what she did to piss off Lucifer.

As part of the ritual, Reverend Phipps is chanting to Tituba, presumably to let her know her presence is requested, and maybe my memory's off here, but it sounds pretty much identical to what I remember his Tongues being.

You know: *"Yee-ya-yee!"*

Then, switching to English: "She is coming. She is coming,"

"Glad to hear it," I say.

Phipps kneels before the black altar, his eyes closed, his arms outstretched, and I am, once again, reminded of his efforts at my dying mother's bedside.

"Did she happen to mention her approximate ETA?" I say, looking at my arm like I have a watch there.

"She will get here when she gets here," Phipps says.

"So what do we do until then?"

"WE WAIT!" Phipps booms.

"Super-duper," I say. "I love waiting."

## 8

BACK TO THE PAST. BACK TO MY KICKASS ONE-MAN DAGWOOD AWARDS AFTER-party. Back to being asleep.

I was in the midst of the most vivid dream of my life. It was similar in setting to the wife's nightmare where her left boob bled.

You remember. Lake, island, crib.

Except in my dream, the lake was not just boiling, it was on fire. My dream was nice enough, though, to put me on the island at the start—no closet door boats or curtain hanger paddles for me; and I was checking the crib for Sparky and the queen bed for Penny—all over the place, really—until I realized my dream wasn't being so kind to me after all, as the only jackass on this island in the middle of fire was me.

And to my shrieking surprise, I discovered I was as flammable in the world of dreams as I was in real life and just as incapable of remembering to do what had been drummed into my brain during my six years of fire safety instruction in elementary school: stop, drop, and roll.

Instead, I did as most people do who forget the Big Three of fire safety: I screamed and ran around. When I could take the pain no longer, I jumped into the fiery water. I think the plan was to drown.

Through the flames of the fire, I looked up.

Floating through the smoke in the sky were balloon heads of my mother and wife, attached to strings. It would seem whomever had been in charge of holding on to those strings had let go.

I paused from my dream-immolation for a second in order to take some time to uncover the meaning behind the balloon heads of the two most important women in my life, but I quickly discerned that, whatever that meaning was, it wasn't likely to be of practical use in the predicament I was in, and so I resumed dream-screaming in unimaginable dream-pain, and it was right around this time that the balloon heads began to talk.

"Don't—fizzwaawaawwerrrrrnt—" the balloon head of my mother said as I screamed.

"Flurntiwizzzilyspek—with you!" the balloon head of the wife said.

There was more at the beginning and the end of what they said, but I was screaming too loud to hear everything clearly, so those parts were unintelligible.

This went on for some time—me screaming and the balloon heads talking—until I looked to the island again and saw Sparky.

He was a full-grown version of his little old man self, but red-faced, yellow-eyed, like an extra from Michael Jackson's *Thriller*. He was jumping on the queen bed—my bed—laughing like a loon. Pissed at his brazen insolence, but helpless to do anything to stop him, my eyes went back to the balloon heads and it was then I finally dug deep enough to find the requisite dream-strength to keep my dream-wits about me long enough to pick out the entirety of what they were saying.

Here it is:

"DON'T…FORGET…TO…TAKE…HIM…WITH…YOU!"

## 9

UPDATE FROM THE SUMMONING. NO DEMON YET, BUT I HAVE MANAGED TO get myself bound and gagged. A moment ago, I'm proud to say, while Phipps was jabbering to Tituba, imploring her to make haste, I had yelled the following:

"GORZY-MORZY-WORZY-GORZY-WORZY!"

That's right. Suck on that, Phipps. The language of the angels. Where's your "baby babbling" now, eh?

Why would I do such a thing?

To slow down the demon.

And why would I want to slow it down?

Um. Not sure. If I want a definitive answer as to Sparky's identity, then slowing the demon down would qualify as a shitbrain idea, but I guess I just felt like putting up a fight. It seems like this is the kind of situation where a Christian should.

So I fought. *Gorzy-morzy*. Take that, Phipps. Take that, Tituba.

At which point the goons reappeared and bound and gagged me.

## 10

THE MORNING AFTER THE BALLOON-HEAD DREAM, I LEAPT OUT OF BED WITH an excitement I hadn't felt since the days of my pursuit of the Perfect Attendance Award, and in my eagerness, I ran to the bathroom and whizzed all over the toilet seat before racing to the phone to call my father.

My fog had lifted. Everything was as clear as it had ever been.

My purpose. My calling.

I knew—I just *knew*—that the wife had been right all along. That these weird happenings and occurrences were pointing to one thing and one thing only: unchecked, my son would become the Antichrist, but I, God willing, was to be the one to stop him.

Everything else had been a trick, a trap. All my other yens, my lusts, my need for achieving greatness in other facets of life: deception by the Devil.

I was still right—I was still going to be great—but it was to be according to God's Purpose, God's Will, not my own. I would have the kind of Greatness known only to me and the Almighty, the kind that comes with acts of prevention. Small consolation considering my big plans maybe, but then again, if the Bible is correct with how the Lord rewards the faithful, maybe not.

After ordering my father to send my son home, I fell to my knees and begged God's forgiveness. I rededicated my life to Him—to His Intentions, His Objectives. I swore to hinder and hamper this son of mine, this soon-to-be man of mischief and mayhem, with all my strength.

*I,* God willing, would keep the boy dumb.

*I,* God willing, would keep the boy fat.

Friendless. Insignificant.

All by myself.

True, I had been sort of helping with these things already, but I hadn't ever put forth the world-famous one-hundred-and-ten-percent Horvath effort. I had been in and out of fogs for far too much of it, couldn't really say my heart had ever been in it, and to top it all off, my motives were terrible.

I had been too wrapped up in myself, in revenge, and that was why we were losing, and perhaps that was even why my wife had died. It was like the Old Testament here. Such a thing as this had to be done in a holy way or somebody was getting squished.

But no more mistakes, I vowed. No more distractions. No more screwing around. This was my charge, and I would not fail again. I would save mankind. I would stop the end of the world, and if worst comes to worst and I was to die in the process, well, I'd do exactly as the balloon heads of my wife and mother had instructed:

I'd make sure to take him with me.


Not that I should have to point this out anymore, but obviously my attempts to please God and save the world through the stultification of my son's growth didn't work out as I'd hoped—surprise, surprise—but not all of the blame can land on me this time. I too was fought against. Hindered at my hindering. Dark forces, which I can only assume had been taking more of an active interest in the matter, decided to turn up the heat.

In short, Sparky saw even more growth.

His grades came back with B's again—three this time—and even worse, no D's, no F's.

His friendship with Little Eddie Reddingham blossomed.

With my father around more than ever and Joyce in charge of the cooking, Sparky began to eat better than at any point in his life and dropped some serious poundage. Moreover, my father also signed Sparky up for pee-wee football, and Sparky managed to stay on the team all year as a sub on the offensive line.

I know, nothing too incredible here, but still, this was not good. Territory long thought safe was now in jeopardy.

How long before B's became A's? How long before fat became fit? How long before friend became friends?

And in the maelstrom of compassion and charity that had invaded my world, with Sparky's grandparents and teachers and other parents and coaches fussing over him due to the untimely death of his mother, I soon realized that I, now alone, was powerless to stop them all.

This, my only trust, my only purpose, and I was going to fail yet again—miserably as always.

## 11

ALTHOUGH I HAD TOYED WITH THE IDEA OF OFFING SPARKY SINCE THE REDED-
ication of my life to God, I don't think I ever would have considered
putting any kind of plan in motion had he not tried to off me first.

Fair's fair after all.

Sparky had come home from school one afternoon with Little Eddie
Reddingham. They were singing the official song of the Hitler Youth—
"The Rotten Bones Are Trembling"—and goose-stepping around the
living room.

The songs and marching were punctuated with laughter (and the occasional *Heil!*)—the laughter of boys at play, and with this latest instance
of my failure paraded in front of me, I exploded. With my voice at its
boomiest best, I sent Little Eddie Reddingham racing out of the house
cursing at me in German, and Sparky to his room with a spanked bottom.

Through the wall I yelled that he was grounded, that he would never
see Little Eddie Reddingham again nor sing Nazi songs, satirical or otherwise. At the very least, I said, not for one month.

It was sad. Feeble. A hollow victory. Penny was long gone and virtually
the entire town was now of the opinion it should meddle in Sparky's
life; it would be impossible to enforce this.

Still, it was satisfying. Best of all, it made Sparky cry.

It also made him come flying out of his room a few minutes later
wielding a Swiss Army knife.

"No more! No more!" he yelled, trying to stick the knife into my right
quad. "No more! No more! No more!"

I easily dodged his clumsy thrusts, grabbed his arm, and lugged him
back to his room.

"What the hell, kid?" I hissed in his ear. "Am I not worthy of one of
your crazy storms? Not good enough for one of your birdy pals to come
and crap me to death?"

I threw him back on his bed and slammed the door.

"Two months!" I yelled.

To which the Antichrist responded by kicking the wall and screaming all night.

By three a.m. my mind was as set as his was. My son and I were in total agreement.

No more! No more! No more!

## 12

YOU JUST MISSED IT. AFTER JUMPING IN FRONT OF THE PENTAGRAM AND SPIN-ning around exactly six times, Reverend Phipps is now on the floor face down. Sleeping, dead, or just dizzy, I know not.

Me? I'm still bound and gagged, and Sparky is still seated in the penta-gram, tracing a finger over the purple chalk and smearing the residue on his face.

He's looked over at me once or twice, and I have made noises and motions consistent with the kind one would make if one wanted to be untied and un-gagged, but so far Sparky has shown zero interest in doing either of these things for me.

I'd make him promises, promises to be nicer to him and let him see Little Nazi Eddie Reddingham from time to time, but I can't make them verbally, nor do I know how to make my constricted motions propose them. My only hope is that he can see it in my eyes, but then he would have to look at me again.

And how does one make someone look at them? I mean, other than by looking at *them* and hoping for the best?

It is then I hear a voice.

A crackling, popcorny, cellophane-ish, ancient-sounding woman's voice, whispering.

Craning my head, I see no woman at the door behind me, which means there are no women in the room, which means I am—as one should be upon hearing a bodiless ancient woman's voice within the context of waiting for a female demon—sick with fright.

Unless something shows up to prove otherwise, it would seem I am face to face, or ears to voice, with pure evil.

The voice continues whispering words I can't make out, then this: *"I...am...TITOOOOOBAAAAAA!"*

Reverend Phipps, alive after all, rises to his knees. He does not speak, but takes a vial of what looks to be dust, empties its contents onto Sparky's head, and waits as Tituba goes *"Ahhhhhhhh..."*

The wind blasts through the open balcony door, tosses papers off the desk, and blows through what's left of my son's hair. His reaction to this is to raise his arms in a worshipful pose and, catching a glimpse of his face, I can see his eyes are closed and he is smiling.

Well, shit. I probably should have just strangled him in his sleep. Or poisoned the Grape-Nuts Joyce gives him. Or shot him in the car; stabbed him with the goat opener; beat him to death with Phipps's recycling bins.

The demon will only confirm what I have known all along: I, bound and gagged, will be dispatched of with ease. My son, protected and prepared, will emerge, years from now, brilliant, cruel, and all-powerful; he will unleash devastation across the globe, command nations, and maybe, if Phipps is right, deport the Creator of the Universe Himself.

All because of me. Because I'm a doubting schnook.

Why did I need this confirmation again? Why do I always falter when Greatness is in my grasp?

Tituba is still whispering in demon-ese, praising the incipience of the Dark Messiah, but it's not as scary as it was a few seconds ago.

I've kinda gotten over it.

Maybe because I have just discovered a slim possibility of victory, what in naval warfare parlance is called a long shot.

Take heart, oh mankind. Rejoice, rejoice, my fellow Christians. We're not completely screwed yet.

And how's that, you wonder?

Because I, Franklin Bartholomew, the Great Horvath, have just undone my knots.


# 13


BEFORE I CAN EVEN THINK, I'M UP OFF THE COUCH.

To do what, I don't know, but here I am. Still with no memorable last words, but in my head is music.

What's playing?

Nothing good, nothing fitting or appropriate for the occasion. If I had my druthers, I'd prefer something sublime, something ethereal, heavenly. An old hymn like "Jesus, I Come to Thee" or "It Is Well With My Soul." Something to prepare this spirit of mine for evacuation, ascension, and acceptance into Heaven. I'll take "Great Is Thy Faithfulness," "A Mighty Fortress Is Our God," and, if that's too much to ask, I'll even take one of those candy-ass contemporary Christian pop songs.

Anything but "Joy to the World" again.

Ah, but hey, that's still not so bad, you say. It still works, as, whatever it is you're planning to do here to stop the Antichrist once and for all, from a Christian point of view, the celebration of the birth of Christ ultimately results in the redemption of humanity which—

Just knock it off, already, okay? It's not the hymn, it's still the pop song, and to make matters worse, it's Sparky's version.

Something I suppose I wholly deserve.


Assuming the sneakiest sneaky crouch I can, I creep toward Phipps and Sparky, "Joy to the World" slow and swelling in my head, a la Frank Sinatra at the end of "New York, New York."

*Joyyyyyyyy to the worrrrrrld…*

Nobody is paying me any mind as I inch my way closer. Phipps is swaying back and forth, eyes closed, in telepathic conference with Satan himself at this point; Sparky is smitten with whatever the lint from his navel smells like, and Tituba is still flapping her jaws about how super-definitely certain she is my son is, like, *totally* the Antichrist.

*Allll the boyyyyys and girlllllls...*

Nobody notices me cross the threshold of the pentagram. Nobody (other than Sparky), notices me take him up into my arms.

*Joyyyyyy to the fishes...*

Everybody though, and especially Tituba, notices when, clutching the boy, I go full tilt in the direction of the open balcony at the far end of the Inner Sanctum.

*In the deeeeep...*

How do I know she has especially taken notice?

*...bluuuuue seeeeea...*

For one, she's screeching. It's high-pitched, metallic, and—this is weird—familiar: "RHEEEEEEEEEEEEEEEE!"

And for two, well, there is no two, but I don't need a two. Tituba's too late. So is Phipps.

*IIIIII LIIIIIIIKE...*

"Frankie, stop!"

*...TO POOOOOOOOOOP ...AAAAAANNNND...*

Hello, balcony. Goodbye, all.

*PE—*

# PART TEN

*Even if he tops out as the Antichrist of Kokomo County and nothing more, that will be enough.*

# 1

I'M AWAKE. THE BRIGHTEST, MOST BLINDING LIGHT I HAVE EVER SEEN IS IN my eyes.

Is this it? Heaven? The Promised Land? Paradise? Did I make it? Is this Greatness?

I think it just might be. Stand by; let me get my bearings...

Okay. I hear voices, which is good, though whether they are angelic or the recently arrived dead like myself will take a minute or two for me to figure out.

Another good sign: I think, even though I'm probably nothing more than spirit at this point, I'm lying down somehow, and whatever it is I'm lying down on is mighty comfortable.

I'm thinking a nice, comfy cloud.


Of course, as I have always feared, there are reasons to be disappointed in Life Everlasting right out of the gate, starting with the fact I am in quite a lot of pain, most notably in my upper spirit-head area.

Second, something here smells rotten. Like shit-sandwich breath.

But wait. I'm starting to pick out the voices better; maybe they will help clear things up.

"Shhh...He's awake," one of the voices says. "Turn that off."

And poof, the brightest, most blinding, most heavenly light I have ever seen is snatched away and my sight is restored.

Do I see cherubim soaring through the skies with their golden trumpets? The gates to New Jerusalem? A lion canoodling with a lamb?

No, dammit, I don't.

What I see is a grizzly-haired, one-eyed old man with cabbage in his teeth holding a penlight, with a young Jane Fonda doppelganger behind him chewing on her fingernails.

"Say something, Frankie," Reverend Phipps says, and lo and behold I do.

"Boy, does my head hurt."

I am groggy. I am hurting. I am not happy.

I am in the Inner Sanctum, in the offices of the Church of Epistemological Emendation, on the sixth floor of the Lawrence P. Fenwick Building.

I'm still in Berry. Kokomo County. Indiana. America. Earth. The Milky Way. Whatever's after.

I am still totally and undeniably Franklin Bartholomew Horvath, hopelessly mortal edition.

Sparky, still alive and himself as well, is back on the squashy recliner, icepack on his shoulder, and I'm once more on the panther couch, wondering where the hell my icepack is.

Everybody is laughing. Except us Horvaths. We still don't get whatever it is that's going on, or I don't get it, Sparky does, and doesn't find it to be all that funny.

Either way, we're not laughing.

"*That* was awesome," Danica says.

"What was?" I say.

"You picked up your mutant kid and tried to jump off the balcony," Danica says. "But just before you got there I managed to close the door, so all you did was bounce off and knock yourself out."

"Oh, I guess that *was* awesome," I say, and with a hatred so powerful it would take more than a thousand years of perpetual sex with her to mollify it.

"What were you trying to do anyway, Frankie?" Phipps says, having adorned himself with a more compassionate tone than his bitch of a secretary.

"Escape," I lie. As mortifying as this all is, I see no need to betray my intentions toward self-martyrdom. While I am powerless to stop the Satanists from keeping the Antichrist, I still might be allowed to leave, and if so, then I can regroup. Running into a door and concussing myself doesn't have to be the finale here. As long as I draw breath, there's still hope.

"You're aware that if you had made it off the balcony, you both would have fallen to your deaths?" Phipps says.

"Maybe, maybe not," I say. "All I knew was I had to get him away from that demon."

The laughter returns. The goons are howling. Danica is bent over, covering her face, trembling from beautiful head to pulchritudinous toe. Phipps attempts to shush them to no avail.

"Frankie, there's no demon," he says. "There's never been any demon. She—"

Phipps points to Danica but can't continue, in stitches now himself.

"Look, I know what I heard," I say. "Don't try to trick me into thinking none of this happened. Tituba was here. I felt her evil breath, I heard her whispers and her awful demon-shriek when we tried to escape!"

More howling, more stitches, and then me, *en fuego*:

"WILL YOU KNOCK IT OFF AND JUST TELL ME THE TRUTH?"

"Truth about what?" Phipps says.

I point at Sparky. "Is he or isn't he?"

"The Antichrist?"

"No, the second coming of Wilford Brimley," I say.

"Frankie," Phipps says, pity in his eyes, "Look at him. He looks like—he's—I mean, good grief, isn't it obvious?"

"That he's him?"

"Oh God, what a lunatic," Danica says. Then: "Of course he's not."

# 2

OLD TUNA IS SHAKING. BECAUSE MY HANDS ARE ATTACHED TO THE BILE-GREEN colored steering wheel at ten and two, I'm shaking. Sparky, in the passenger seat, is a little shaky too, but he doesn't seem to care. He's asleep.

It's been a long day.

For those wondering why I would be driving my car fast enough to make it shake, don't get excited. Nobody is chasing after us. No Satanist goons, no police. At least not yet.

I guess it's worth mentioning that the Asian Toilet Princess did see us as we exited the Lawrence P. Fenwick Building and immediately began yelling for everyone to take note of "those peeper who watch me winky!", but nobody in the vicinity was roused into action by her accusation (they may not have been all that sure what "winky" meant). And considering how Sparky and I managed to get in Old Tuna, down Main Street, and out of Berry without anybody accosting us, I'm thinking the chances of public outrage over "winky" building to lynch mob / state-wide manhunt levels are slim.

For those concerned about the welfare of Sparky, you may rest easy. I'm not going to shoot him anymore, and not just because I never got my gun back. The plan to kill him is done. Over with. It's not going to happen. So why do I make Old Tuna shake with over-exerted speed?

One, because I can, because it's my Old Tuna and I'll do what I damn well please with it.

Two, because my heart is on fire: with purpose, with promise, with change.

## 3

So, it was a joke. The altar, the pentagram, the demon.

In case you've forgotten, there is an intercom in the Church of E's offices. Due to budgetary constraints, they can't afford anything even remotely modern, so they modestly make do with a series of speakers linked to microphones, similar to the antiquated PA systems in all the schools throughout Kokomo County.

Instead of going back to her desk as per Phipps's earlier order, Danica—or should I say, *Tituba*—doubled back into the adjacent room. Then, according to the plan hatched by her, Phipps, and the goons while Sparky took the Black Catechism, she whispered the hair-raising demon stuff into the intercom system as Phipps did the fake Summoning.

What gave the whole ruse away, besides my attempted geronimo with Sparky, was when Danica, in order to sneak a better look at what was going on, got too close to the speaker with the microphone, thus causing that ear-splitting shriek, known as the Larsen Effect, or as more commonly understood, audio feedback.

How could I have fallen for all of that?

Easy. I wanted to.

You would have too.


I did not give it up without a fight either.

"What about the bird Sparky sent at my wife?" I asked Phipps.

"I don't know, Frankie. Even if it did happen, which I doubt, what does that have to do with him being the Antichrist?" he said.

"Why does he look like an old man?" I shot back.

"Where in the Bible does it say the Antichrist will look like Gene Hackman?"

"Okay, how about his Nazi best friend then, hm? Crying on Christmas? The ceiling fan? 'Your mother sucks pee-pees in Heck'?"

Phipps just stared at me.

"Fine. Explain to me the storm," I said. "What he did during the storm."

"What about it?" Phipps replied, packing the various demonic paraphernalia into the guitar case. He would tell me later these trinkets were just that: knick-knacks he had bought here and there to freak out townspeople who got on his nerves (the bone was plastic, the vial of baby's blood was Kool-Aid, and the black book was a dog-eared *The Omnivore's Dilemma*).

"Sparky stood right at the front of the storm, thrashed and yelled at it, and then it went berserk and killed my wife," I said. "He even predicted it before it happened."

Phipps took a wet rag and began scrubbing the pentagram off the floor. "You said he expressed concern over her safety, which is not the same thing as a prediction."

"But the look on his face! He was glowing—*Eureka!* Remember?"

Chuckling, Phipps kept on scrubbing. My prognostic abilities being what they were, underdeveloped, I did not know it but it was story time.

"When I was fourteen, my father took me camping." Phipps said. "The idea was we'd explore, catch fish, sing songs, cook marshmallows. The standard kind of trip a man takes his son on so he can cover over a thousand other instances of neglect and still get credit for being a good father. Anyway, the first night there he came down with food poisoning after disregarding my warnings about eating from a bloated can of beans, and I ended up spending the majority of the trip listening to him groan through the outhouse door and spoon-feeding him chicken soup."

Phipps squeezed the rag into a bucket. It dripped purple.

"The next-to-last day, cabin crazy and more than fed up with my father's refusal to convalesce in a timely fashion, I decided to go for a walk in the snow. The minute I hit open air, the minute I felt the cold touch my skin, for reasons I couldn't explain, I became overwhelmed with a sudden feeling of...something. Everything became magical, and that feeling pushed me to go deep into the woods, deeper than I had ever gone on my own before. After many miles, I came to a clearing, and you want to know what I did next?"

Another squeeze of the sponge, more dripping purple.

"I stripped naked, opened my arms wide, and screamed my goddamned head off."

"Gee," I said. "That does sound magical."

"It was one of those moments that changed my life, and when I returned that night to my father, I was no longer a boy, but a man."

Having finished with this useless anecdote, Phipps looked at me expectantly.

"Sparky wasn't naked." I said.

"Fair enough," Phipps said. "But let me ask you one more thing, something you failed to mention: How did your son respond to the death of his mother? Was he happy?"

"Uh, he wasn't doing cartwheels over it or anything—"

"Or did he mourn her?"


As it turns out, the Church of E honestly and truly does not believe in a real Satan. They faked that too for the sake of the prank.

"Too bad you went off your nut and I made all that feedback," Danica said. "The fun was just getting started."

Because the Church of E does not believe in a living being called Satan, they also don't believe in the Antichrist, which differentiates them from Theistic Satanists, a group I had not heard of. According to Phipps, he had ripped off their version of the end of the world when he was weaving his web of gag around me.

"They're out of their minds, but I can give you their number if you want," he said. "Maybe you'll have better luck with them."


Even after these depressing revelations, I still did not want to believe any of this.

"All right," I said. "If this was all a trick, what's the business with the Black Catechism?"

"It's an examination we give to all children who are a part of the congregation." Phipps said, pulling one out from inside his desk. "Like you guessed, it's an IQ test of sorts. We have them for adults, too."

"Why would you care what the IQ of your congregation is?"

"We don't. But like any other religion you've got to find ways of excluding people, otherwise what's the point? You should see the obstacle course."

"So how did Sparky do?" I asked. "Honestly."

"Based on his score, we would not have been able to accept him," Phipps said.

"Wait," I said. "That's my fault. I, we—my wife and me, I mean—for years, his whole life practically, we were trying to make him..."

"Yes?"

"...er, as dumb as possible."

"Why would you do something like that?"

"To stop him from becoming the Antichrist, obviously."

"Congratulations. You did a magnificent job, then."

"Was he at least close? I mean, theoretically, if he put in some extra work, he could come back next year and take the test and get in, right?"

"I wouldn't count on it, Frankie."

Beside myself, I lurched from the couch and thrust a finger in Phipps's face.

"This is bullshit!" I said. "I know what he is and you know what he is. You even saw it yourself, at his birth, when you barged in and waved that cross around like a maniac. You were flipping out.

"That was real," I continued, taking some of Phipps's candy from his desk and popping it in my mouth. "And everything since then has been nothing but confirmation of it."

"Oh, Frankie," Phipps said. "How sad your life has been because of that, and I am sorry."

"For becoming a willing pawn of the Devil? You should be."

"No, not for that," Phipps said as he rose from his chair and turned to face naked Robert Redford and Jane Fonda?/Danica? on the wall. "You know that day? The day your son was born and I came in waving a cross around like, in your accurate description, a maniac? Calling your newborn son the Antichrist?"

"Yeah?"

"I was drunk as a skunk that day."

"I KNEW IT!"

# 4

As Old Tuna shakes, the boy sleeps, and my heart burns, I pull the phone out of my pocket and dial my father.

It's time one of us acknowledges the unspoken rivalry between him and me and his son and mine. A rivalry that has, until now, not been much of one, due to my obstruction of Sparky and my penchant for fogs.

No more.

Four rings go by and the machine picks up, the soft, unfairly wise-be-yond-its-years voice of my younger brother offers the greeting:

*God Bless, you have reached the Horvaths: Robert, Joyce, and I'm Christopher. Please leave your name, telephone number, reason for calling, and we will be sure to get back in touch with you at our earliest convenience. In the meantime, did you know that it rains diamonds on Neptune? Or that twenty-five percent of all your bones are in your feet? Or that pearls dissolve in vinegar? BEEP!*

In addition to our unit, Phipps visited all the new mothers in the post-partum ward the morning of Sparky's birth and went through the same song and dance.

Cross waving! Googlie eyes! Son of Perdition!

Even if it was a girl.

This being done, exhausted and hungover, he wandered out to his truck, and, in his words, "drove from sign to sign."

Using money he had embezzled from the church, Phipps was able to get all the way to Nevada before running out of fuel and funds. He removed the license plate, the insurance, and registration from the truck, abandoned it, and hitched to New Mexico from there, getting rid of his own identification along the way.

Then, without money, without ID, Phipps became a bum. And, as a bum he grew his hair out. And, as a bum, he achieved a beard. And, somewhere along the way, he lost an eye.

One question remains: Why?

Why turn in a life of respect, as a pillar of a community, as a man of God, for the impoverished, itinerant existence of a vagabond and, eventually, a Satanist? Why toss aside a wife of sixteen years? Why risk criminal charges for destroying your identity?

And why New Mexico?

"I don't know. I guess I always wanted to go to Albuquerque," Phipps said.

Wading through Phipps's nonsense, I finally got him to admit that somewhere along the line he suffered what religious people refer to as a crisis of faith; something that, regardless of other reasons given, can most of the time be boiled down to one, disheartening, belief-crushing question:

*Why doesn't my religion work the way I was promised?*

The event that led to Phipps's crisis:

A prophecy that was said over him when he was fourteen years old, the same year he went out into the woods and shook his pecker at the sky.

At a Christian youth camp in South Carolina, one of the most anticipated events of the week was the final day, where the camp faculty would get all the kids in a large group and, one by one, forecast their lives for them.

These prophecies were many times pleasant, fuzzy, overwhelmingly optimistic predictions for lives of success and fulfillment, provided the subject in question not stray from the Church and start committing a bunch of sins.

Phipps, though, got a little more than the other kids when it was his turn.

It was prophesied he would be famous. That he would counsel kings. That he would move nations. That he would heal terminal diseases. That, provided he stay holy and faithful to God and the Church, he would be celebrated and cherished all the days of his life.

Basically, he would be, you know, *great*.

"And you know what happened after that?" he said. "I went on to pastor some rinky-dink church in Asshat, Indiana and heal one goddamned sore toe."

An appreciation for irony and the satisfaction of a quiet revenge are the reasons that Phipps, after years of drifting and slumming, came to be a leader in a satanic church.

"But all this stuff is baloney, too," he said. "There's a reason why it's never caught on, despite pandering to everybody's favorite vices."

So why would Phipps be a part of it?

"Well, they know people who make fake IDs," Phipps said. "And I figured if God truly gives a rip about me, then this is the one thing I could do that would really burn his bacon."

"If scripture is to be trusted," I said, "then burning God's bacon is a pretty stupid thing to do."

"A deal's a deal, Frankie," Phipps said. "He promised me a life less ordinary and then welshed. This is payback."

"Maybe those prophecy guys were making it up."

"That's impossible, don't ever say that to me again."

"Maybe your life turned out the way God wanted it."

"IT'S NOT THE WAY I WANTED IT!"

## 5

SPARKY IS AWAKE NOW AND GAZING OUT OF THE PASSENGER SIDE WINDOW AT all the delightful amounts of nothing-to-see. Old Tuna is no longer shaking as I have slowed things down a tad. No sense in getting a ticket. I'm not made of money here.

The boy, who has not said five words since we left Berry over an hour ago, appears to have found something worth saying. Here it is:

"Are we going home?"

"As a matter of fact," I say, "we are."

"Considering how everything turned out, I'm surprised you can't see what's going on here," I said to Phipps. "God, no matter what you might think, did use you to warn me and my wife about what this boy would be on the day he was born."

"And I can assure you, Frankie, beyond all doubt, that was not God, merely a lot of bitterness mixed with a very affordable house red."

"As the Bible says, Phipps, God uses the foolish things of the world to confound the wise, and He has used you, a clear fool, twice now to prove this truth—and from both sides of the aisle."

"That's quite the unique application of that scripture, Frankie. If nothing else, you do posit an interesting theory."

"It's no theory. My son is the Beast," I said. The Beast, having lost control of his ice pack, was now regarding the ice pieces on the floor with interest. If I'd had to guess, I would have said he was deciding whether or not it would be okay to pick up dirty floor cubes and put them in his mouth.

"Out of curiosity, what was the plan if we had agreed he was the Antichrist?" Phipps said. "I can deduce from the gun that violence had to be on the table."

"That was only if you had tried to nab him."

"Ah, we would do that, wouldn't we? If we believed he was *him*. Nice thinking."

"He is *him*."

"Okay. And assuming he is who you say he is—"

"And who you said he is—"

"Under the influence, let's not forget. What was your plot going forward? What did you intend to do about it?"

"Exactly as I had done before," I said, resorting to more falsehoods. Everything in my head had gotten a little foggy post-bouncing off that balcony door, but I was still planning on doing away with the boy. I mean, what else was left? I hadn't allowed myself to imagine an alternative. "Continue to do whatever it took to make it not happen," I said. "To make that cup pass from him."

"By keeping him a dunce?" Phipps said.

"By keeping him ordinary enough, insignificant enough not to matter too much to anyone ever."

"You mean, keep him like us?"


I stood up to leave.

"Speak for yourself," I said, then nudged Sparky. "C'mon, let's go."

Sparky stood, angrily kicked the ice, and stomped out of the Inner Sanctum with me. Phipps walked us out the rest of the way.

"It was good to see you again, Frankie. And if nothing else, thank you for a wildly entertaining afternoon."

"You know I should call the police and tell them who you really are."

"I should call the police and tell them what you do to your son."

"Like they'll believe Satanists."

"But we're not Satanists, Frankie, we're Epistemological Emendationists."

"Whatever."

"Indeed."

We passed Danica's desk on our way to the front door and Sparky presented her with the final version of his drawing of the field with the grinning boy and the man burning up. The end product included a girl who looked about as close to a Jane Fonda lookalike as Sparky is capable of drawing, holding hands with the drawn boy and leading him away from the fire and the man being consumed by it. And in case there's any question as to how the relationship between the boy and the girl was to be interpreted by the viewer, Sparky had drawn a heart around the two of them. A heart that, given the boy's artistic shortcomings, looked more like a butt.

Danica, deeply touched, dropped Sparky's masterpiece in the wastebasket the second he looked away.

If I was going to follow the original plan, then this would have been one of his last interactions in life, but for some reason killing him no longer seemed necessary or desirable. More than anything, I wanted some of Joyce's macaroons.

"Before we part ways, Frankie," Phipps said, "never to meet again, I hope, let me ask you one more thing."

"Fire away," I said.

"According to the Bible, what happens after the Antichrist does his thing?"

"You mean after he takes control of the world and kills millions of people?"

"Correct."

"Christ returns to obliterate him, Satan, and his followers. You know this."

"Yes, but then what? The end of all evil? Heaven on Earth?"

"Basically, yeah."

"So a little bit of bad, followed by a whole lot of good?"

"Pretty much."

"Then riddle me this, Frankie, if all that is true, and your son is what you say he is...*why in the world would you want to stop him?*"

## 6

NEVER IN MY LIFE HAS THE ROAD AHEAD LOOKED AS CLEAR TO ME AS IT DOES now. Figuratively, that is. In reality, as I drive Sparky back to Little Hat, back to home, a thick fog is rolling in, but in my head and heart the road is clear, extending to the horizon, where the sun, the future, is blazing.

We'll show you, you goddamned Satanist bastards.

My son *will* be the end of all things.

The first thing I'm going to teach him is how to study. Flash cards, study guides. I'll grill him like no father has grilled a son. I will require excellence. I will demand perfection.

Commence your trembling, oh Humankind, there will be an A, or three, on the Antichrist's next report card. And just you wait until I get him on word power exercises. Memory-builders. The human calculator.

On top of this there will be music to beguile and seduce you—piano, trumpet, guitar. Sparky will learn Hendrix. Miles. Beethoven. He will knock your socks off.

I will get him in shape; the best shape a kid can be in. Running, lifting, calisthenics, Pilates, yoga, karate. He will be the best goddamned athlete in the state.

He will have the highest goddamned SAT score in the country. He will go to Yale, Harvard. He will be picked for the Skull and Bones.

He will be a lawyer. He will work for oil corporations (or solar power). He will go into politics. Democrat, Republican: pick one.

He will consolidate his power from behind the scenes; he will grow in reputation, wealth, and influence; he will become the toast of Washington; he will answer the cries of a desperate citizenry yearning for a savior who will sweep him into the White House. There will be peace and calm and happiness for a short time, until:

KABLOOIE!


Crackling with an excitement I'm certain I've never known before, I take the hat off of Sparky's head and throw it out of the passenger side window.

"And to hell with the Chicago Cubs!" I say.

"NOOO!" Sparky cries.

"Screw those losers," I say. "When we get home we're going to get you a Yankees hat, and the jersey of that pretty-boy shortstop of theirs."

"Yankees suck," Sparky says. "The Cubs can win it next year if they just—"

"Even if they do somehow figure it out—which they won't—it's still not going to change anything. No matter how many times the Cubs win, they're still going to be losers. It's their identity and it'll never go away. What you need is a total sports reboot, son. What you need, only the Yankees can provide."

"The Yankees are queers," Sparky says savagely.

"Well, that's fine son, and so are you. Or at least you'll need to be. I think."

"But I don't wanna!"

"Too bad, it's in the Bible. And if you don't like it, take it up with the Almighty."

"How do I do that?" the boy says.

I can see now where I had it wrong, where I had messed it up—out of pride, out of fear, out of just not thinking it through. The suffering, the starvation, the wars, and the death that will come with the rule of the acme of human evil—it all has to happen.

God mapped it out that way. It is His Will. Who am I to try to stop it?

I mean, it's not as though we've been trying all that hard, anyway. One could even make a compelling argument that all we've been up to the last two thousand years has been trying to produce a human being so terrible he could single-handedly bring back Jesus Christ.

Jubilant, euphoric, but also hungry, I park Old Tuna at a hamburger stand in Punchy Hills for an economical, though no less celebratory, junk food dinner.

The boy, to my wonder, orders what the menu calls a "salad cone" along with a small skim milk.

"That's good, son," I say, finishing off the first of a trilogy of foot-long chili dogs. "Hitler was a vegetarian too, you know. Maybe you and Eddie can sing about that sometime."

As Sparky ponders his connection to the Führer, "Eye of the Tiger" starts blasting away from my phone on the dash.

I choose to ignore it for a second so I can radiate with pride at my son—a new experience—and imagine the mushroom clouds and rivers of blood that will herald the arrival of the Four Horsemen of the Apocalypse. I imagine myself walking through all the destruction and misery, arms raised in triumph. I imagine myself stopping various refugees as they cry out in terror, as they run for their lives.

I'd like to think I'd say this to them:

"Isn't this incredible? *My* kid did this."


"Frankie!" the old man says after I answer the phone. "So glad you picked up. I've been dying to talk to you all day."

"I know, Dad," I reply good-naturedly. "So what totally awesome, totally tubular thing did he do this time?"

"What do you mean?"

"Come on now, don't be coy with me," I say. "Did Christopher become the first eight-year-old in sports history to sign with a professional soccer team, or did he work out perpetual motion right after getting a Pulitzer for his 'My Summer Vacation' essay?"

Sparky, his salad cone finished (not counting what's all over his front and the floor), is now squirting ketchup packets into his mouth, a fitting symbol for the amount of work I have in front of me. I motion for him to take one of my chilidogs, but he doesn't acknowledge me.

Meanwhile, my father is laughing way too hard at my sarcasm, defeating it.

"That's funny, Frankie," he says. "But actually, I wasn't calling to tell you about him, I was calling to tell you about me."

"You?" I say, diverting my attention to the fog outside the car window in an effort to keep the agreeable tone in my voice. "That's a change."

"It is, and I am changed. A life-altering experience. A real one this time."

"Isn't that something?" I say, starting to finger the grooves of the steering wheel. "Believe it or not, I just had a real life-altering experience, too. You remember Reverend Phipps, right? Well—"

"Frankie, just be quiet and listen to me. I met him."

"Met who?" I say, wiping gunk from the steering wheel grooves on my napkin.

"Jesus," the old man says.

Suddenly inspired to turn over a new leaf in the cleanliness department,

I begin to pick at crusty, old boogers—the Ghosts of Road Trips Past—from the underside of my seat.

"*The* Jesus?" I say. "Or *a* Jesus? Like the guy who runs that taco truck next to the Mini Mart?"

"Ha ha, *the* Jesus, son. Jesus Christ."

"Really? The Son of Man Himself. What did he look like?"

"Frankie—"

"Was he like Ted Neeley or like Mom always pictured him? You know, Telly Savalas?"

"It wasn't a face-to-face encounter, Frankie. It was in prayer."

With great concentration of effort, I pry a booger loose. Rolling it around in my fingers, I realize it has tenaciously taken some of the upholstery with it and that can't help but earn my respect. This one is a fighter.

"How do you know you met him then?" I say, flicking the boog out of the window, where it will, I assume, doggedly attach itself to the pavement.

"Trust me son, when you meet him, you know."

"Kind of like all the other times you said you met him and knew?"

"No, not like those other—well, yes in a way, but—"

"Allow me to get right to it then. Is this the part where you tell me for the billionth time that God told you little bro is going to be the Great Horvath? Because I already saw that billboard."

"That's not what I was going to say at all. Actually, Christopher isn't going to be the Great Horvath."

"Yeah, right. Who then? Did you get Joyce knocked up again or something?"

"No, son. There is no Great Horvath."

All attempted booger removal ceases. I'm so surprised it takes a second for me to register that Sparky is holding up one of his fingers to me and that finger is covered with a freshly picked specimen, ostensibly an offering to replace the one I had tossed out the window.

My father continues. "There is no Great anybody. None of that means anything. Not like we think. We were wrong, son, from the beginning. None of what we've been driving ourselves crazy over is important. Your wonderful wife, about a week before she got smushed in that car crash, we were talking—and this is so perfect. She quoted me that passage in Ecclesiasticks, the one that says we're just running against the wind. And—"

"Dad?"

"Yes, Frankie?"

"I have to go."

"No—listen, a quiet life son—*hee!* To be humble and work with your hands and—wait, let me—*hee!*—back up here and—"

Leaving the old man to his stammers, I grab Sparky's finger and smear the booger on his pants while mouthing a soundless *No!* Sparky's face darkens, and I see him struggle to fight back fury.

"No, Dad. You listen to me," I say. "I've got some change to tell *you* about. This son of mine, Michael, the boy you so thoughtlessly disregarded, the entire reason you remarried and had another kid? Well, he's about to hand to you the mother of all comeuppances."

"Hold on a sec—"

"He's gonna wipe the floor with your precious Christopher. In every category. Stomp his ass flat. Just wait until you see what we've got up our sleeves. Just wait until this whole thing plays out. It's gonna blow your mind."

"Frankie. Is this how you think of your brother?"

"Yeah, it's how I think of Christopher. The little fucking twerp!"

I stop to allow my father a moment to deal with the shock of learning something he should have figured out long ago (also so I don't choke on my own slobber).

"Let me give this another go here," he says. "Ecclesiasticees. We're all running on empty. So we must be quiet and humble and help people and—"

"Chrissy is going down, Daaaaad," I say.

"No—*hee!*—he's not, don't—*hee!*—talk about your brother like that. Don't call—*hee!*—him 'Chrissy.' Think about what you're saying, Frankie."

"Chrissy gonna get his aaaasssss kiiiiicked."

"CHRIST CHRIST JE—*HEE!*—SUS CHRIST!"

"What?"

"That's all that matters—*hee!*—son! That's all that's ever mattered! CHRIST CHRIST JESUS CHRIST!"

"HORVATH HORVATH FRANKIE HORVATH!" I yell.

And that's that.


With the gauntlet officially thrown down to my father, I turn back to Sparky. "Michael," I say, addressing him by his real name for the first time since maybe ever. "Things are going to be different from now on, I promise."

"You and me," I tell him, "we're going to be great."

"I hate you," Sparky says.

"That works," I say. "As a wise man once said, hate makes you powerful. So you keep that close to your evil, little heart and don't let it go, okay?"

Clearly not listening to a word I'm saying, Sparky lifts cupped hands to my face to show me the ketchup packet nestled inside. He is smiling wickedly. It's not bad as that brand of smile goes, but that's not what I should be encouraging from him. What I need are smiles that beguile, seduce, and attract, and by attract, I don't mean restraining orders. But before I can offer my critique of his smile, before I can proffer a question about his intentions, before I realize what his malignant smile means for me, my clothes, the upholstery, the windshield, he claps the ketchup packet in his hands and screams,

"GIMME BACK MY CUBS HAT!"


Whether the boy likes it or not, things will be different, and we will be great.

Sparky, for being what he must so that the good times can roll for the rest of us, and me, for helping him be what he must so that these said good times can one day roll.

I expect I will be infamous for a time as the enthusiastic father of the Antichrist. As God cleans up the world and straightens everything out after destroying Sparky and his legions, there might be some backlash for me to endure, some vitriol. But at some point, if the Lord is as good as He is portrayed, He will, at whatever Awards Show in the Sky there is, declare my work, my sacrifice, as perhaps the greatest of all since His own, when He sent His Son and then manipulated everything so He would have to die.

I imagine He will gush on and on and on about what I did in helping to usher in the new Heaven and the new Earth. I imagine at some point all this fuss over me will get a little embarrassing—though I'll find some way to manage.

Finally, after hours of introduction, hours of praise, days of exalting me (it's Eternity after all, so there's plenty of time), an endless succession of fêtes and toasts and dinners in my honor, God will finish with the following:

"This is My beloved son," He will say, about me, "in whom I am well pleased."

Then: "Ladies and Gentlemen, I present to you, the Great Horvath."


And what will you say then, Dad? From the back row of the ceremony, Christopher seated beside you, green with envy, holding his gold-foil, God-stamped Participation Certificate with shame? Will you gloat about me then like you do with him now? Will you turn to Mom and lie, "I always kind of had a feeling it was going to be Frankie"?

Will you admit you had nothing to do with it?


And yet, it would be remiss of me if I didn't grant the possibility that I might be wrong about all of this. That my efforts here, as in everything else, will come up woefully short. That Sparky will be as much a schlep as he was ever going to be. That I will one day die as underwhelming as ever. That all of it—God, the Antichrist, eternal life, and joy—are lies. That there's no afterlife, good or bad. Or that it's there, but Sparky isn't the Antichrist, and I'm a total ass.

Or other fun variations.

Even still, if I'm wrong, if it's a lie, it's worth it. Even if Sparky doesn't become anything more than a villainous checkout clerk, a ruthless UPS man, a cold-blooded lettuce washer, it's worth it. He may not rape the nations, ravage populations, and gather an army of demons to fight a last stand against God. Maybe the only thing he'll do is build another Wal-Mart or fuck up some mailboxes. No matter, it's worth it.

Even if he tops out as the Antichrist of Kokomo County, and nothing more, that will be enough. For him. For me.

At least we tried, right?

7

THE FOG HAS ENGULFED THE CAR AS I FINISH THE LAST OF MY CHILIDOGS, MY face, hair—everything, really—covered in ketchup (the hamburger stand refused me extra napkins). Sparky is fiddling with the radio. He's skipping a bunch of songs I wouldn't have minded listening to in order to find one whose lyrics can be changed to his favorite words, eventually stopping on the Turtles' "Happy Together," which he sings along to like this:

> *Imagine PEE and POOP, and POOP and PEE*
> *No matter how dey—la la la, I POOP and PEE*
> *I really like to PEE and POOP, and POOP and PEE*
> *So HAPPEEEEEE TOGETH—*

"Stop that, Michael," I say, turning off the radio. "You don't sing like that anymore."

"Why not?"

"Because it's stupid."

"I dunno. Sometimes it can be kinda fun."

"No, it's not. It's not fun. It's silly and gross and you're better than that, okay?"

"Okay."

I realize the more important thing for him to learn is to not poop his pants, but, gotta start somewhere.

"So, rule number one," I say. "No more poop and pee songs. Got it?"

"I guess," Sparky says.

"What, you don't think you're a little old to be singing about going to the bathroom?"

"It's not that it's—oh, nothing."

"No, tell me. Conversation is a two-way street. And I promise you, son, the suggestion box is open for business from here on out."

"It's just," he says, looking out into the fog, smearing the window with ketchup and residual salad cone goo, "what do I sing then?"

# END